PRA ... ⌐ ⌐ ⌐ ⌐ **OF**
KATIE MacALISTER

Steamed
Starred Review There's danger, adventure, romance, and lots of
humorous moments as Jack and Octavia discover that the laws of
love always trump the laws of physics. —*Booklist*

Memoirs of a Dragon Hunter
"Bursting with the author's trademark zany humor and spicy ro-
mance ... this quick tale will delight paranormal romance fans."—
Publishers Weekly

Sparks Fly
"Balanced by a well-organized plot and MacAlister's trademark
humor."—*Publishers Weekly*

It's All Greek to Me
"A fun and sexy read."—The Season for Romance
"A wonderful lighthearted romantic romp as a kick-butt American
Amazon and a hunky Greek find love. Filled with humor, fans will
laugh with the zaniness of Harry meets Yacky."—*Midwest Book
Review*

Much Ado About Vampires
"A humorous take on the dark and demonic."—*USA Today*
"Once again this author has done a wonderful job. I was sucked
into the world of Dark Ones right from the start and was taken
on a fantastic ride. This book is full of witty dialogue and great romance, making it one that should not be missed."—Fresh Fiction

The Unbearable Lightness of Dragons
"Had me laughing out loud. . . . This book is full of humor and
romance, keeping the reader entertained all the way through . . . a
wondrous story full of magic. . . . I cannot wait to see what happens
next in the lives of the dragons."—Fresh Fiction

ALSO BY KATIE MACALISTER

COMPANY OF THIEVES

A STEAMPUNK ROMANCE

KATIE MACALISTER

FAT CAT BOOKS

Cover by Fay Lane
Formatting by Racing Pigeon Productions

Katiemacalister.com

This book is dedicated to you. Yup, go ahead and write your name in below to make it official.

Dedicated, with oodles of warm fuzzies, to:

Smooches!
Katie Mac

ONE

"Cap'n Pye! Cap'n Pye!"

"No, I'm Hallie." I gave the teenage boy who burst into the navigation room a quelling look. Dooley had what I thought of as an alternate-world form of ADD, and could hardly stand still let alone focus on anything for longer than a few minutes. He was forever flitting around the airship like a deranged, but friendly, puppy. "You know this. I've been on the *Enterprise* for a year now. Even if you suffer from the same facial blindness that affects me—and I fervently pray you don't, because it takes me years to recognize people, and then, I rely heavily on cues like hair or clothing—then surely you must still know who I am."

Dooley bobbed a little bow, his freckled face flushed with excitement. As a fellow heavily freckled person who also blushed easily, he had my sympathy, but I wasn't going to let that emotion keep me from putting the kid right. "Aye, I do know you, Miss Norris, but I thought it must be the captain making some sort of repairs to the autonavigator to make the ship go so badly awry."

I squared my shoulders and gave him another stifling look. "We are not going badly awry. Awry implies off course, and according to this—" I pointed to the machinery that sat on a wooden desk. It was clockwork, like so much of this new world into which Jack and I had been dumped a year before, and contained lots of whirring gears, dials, and leather belts that constantly seemed to need adjusting. "—according to this, we are perfectly on course."

Dooley had the nerve to raise his eyebrows. I looked at the three rows of dials, and sighed. "Dammit, we *were*! I just set it! Where is this taking us—really, airship? To Spain? Oh, I don't think so." I recalculated the dials, spinning the disks that adjusted the settings until they matched the numbers I'd written down from Octavia's map. "Blasted thing has a mind of its own, I swear. Did you want something in particular, Dooley?"

He bobbed another little bow. "No'm. You wouldn't happen to know where the cap'n is? It's just that Mr. Piper, he wants to know what she intends to do with the cargo that we liberated this morning."

I watched the autonavigator closely for a minute, just in case it decided to reset the numbers I'd input into it, but this time they seemed to stick. "Hmm? Oh, she's probably in her cabin with Jack having a quickie."

"A what, now?"

I was about to answer when I remembered his age. Even in this world, I deemed him too young for such things. "They have a quick … er … conversation with each other. Privately."

"Oh, aye," the lad said, nodding, the confusion on his face clearing. "Without Mr. Francisco bothering the captain, you mean."

"Is the Lothario of the skies back with us?" I gathered up my notes, and left the small navigation room to stroll down the metal gangway running the length of the topmost of three decks that made up the gondola. A slight wind ruffled my hair, the faint but persistent rush of air that skimmed the airship an ever present reminder of just how different this world was from the one in which Jack and I had lived. "I thought he was in Spain visiting family?"

"He was, but we picked him up when we liberated the emperor's supplies at Annaba."

I made a rude face. "Oh, great. Now we'll have him stomping around being a drama queen and making risqué comments about Octavia's hair."

Dooley flitted ahead of me, the walkway vibrating with not just the thrum of the boilers but also his footsteps. I took secret delight in the click of footsteps along the metal walkways, even though looking down through the struts and beams made me a bit dizzy. "I'll tell Mr. Ho that the *Enterprise* isn't about to crash, as she thought."

"Yeah, well, you can also tell her that I'm just pinch-hitting with that damned autonavigator, and the sooner that Mr. Christian gets back from his holidays, the better I'll like ... oh, hell. He's gone." I stood in the middle of the empty walkway and slapped my hands on my legs, feeling more than a little adrift.

I'd been that way for a year, and dammit, it was time that changed.

With a muttered curse to myself, I spun around and marched to the other end of the walkway, taking a right turn at an intersection, and climbing down a spiral staircase until I came to the crew quarters. I tapped on the door that bore a brass sign indicating it was the captain's quarters. "You guys decent in there?"

Muffled voices exclaiming in surprise could be heard in response, along with a couple of thumps, and what sounded like a chair being hurriedly pushed back.

"Hallie?"

"Yes, it's me. Come on, you guys, it's not even noon. You can't possibly be doing it again. Not after going at it all last night."

The door opened to show Jack buttoning his shirt, his mismatched eyes narrowed on me, his hair tousled as if someone had just run her hands through it. Behind him, I could see Octavia hurriedly pulling on a white lacy blouse. "We are newlyweds. Thus, if we choose to engage in connubial acts all night, with a few additional midday reminders of just how happy the wedded state has made us, that is no one's business but our own."

"You were married ten months ago. At some point, the honeymoon phase has to end." Since they were both mostly decent, I pushed past Jack and went into their cabin to plop down in a blue upholstered armchair that sat in front of a desk bolted to the floor. "And it's my business when you keep me awake all night with thumps, giggles, and assorted cries of sexual ecstasy."

Octavia, who was pulling on her boots, cast me a horrified glance, which she almost immediately turned onto Jack. "You heard us? Blast it, Jack, I told you that the leather cuffs were going too far. Now your sister heard you making me … making me say …" She stopped, a faint color lighting her cheeks.

Jack grinned at her, slipping on the black wool jacket that was part of the crew uniform Octavia and he had devised. The silver compass embossed on the jacket over the word ENTERPRISE glinted in the sunlight that streamed through the porthole. "Ignore her, Tavy. She's just jealous because I found a fabulously sexy airship pirate captain, and she's still looking for Mr. Right."

I made a face. "I couldn't care less about having a man. I had one, divorced him, and was happier for it. Until …" I bit off the words, having promised myself almost a year ago to the day that I was going to stop whining about what had happened. What was done was done, and I needed to move past being torn out of my reality and put down in this one.

Jack's grin faded as he and Octavia exchanged glances.

"I'm sorry," I said before either one of them could express sympathy. I slumped down with my elbows resting on my knees, my hands over my face. "I didn't come here to snivel."

"I'm sure you didn't. But do tell us what it was that has you so distressed that you would disturb our … er … quality time together?" Octavia's words were spoken with her usual crisp British delivery, but there was real warmth behind the words that did much to take the sting out of them.

"I want something to do." I let my hands drop and pinned them both back with a look that should have curled their respective hair. "I *need* something to do. Back in our old world, I was a champion fund-raiser. I volunteered at three different animal shelters, a woman's shelter, and a memory care facility filled with former biker chicks who are hair-raising even in their declining years. Jack will tell you that our parents raised us to devote our lives to others."

Octavia looked a question at him. He nodded. "She's right. The folks were very big on giving back to the community, and Hallie took that to heart."

"That's why I'm going crazy just wandering around the ship being a glorified gopher."

"A gopher?" Octavia glanced again at Jack.

"It's someone who does a variety of menial tasks," he explained, then knelt next to me, his hands on my knees. "I'm sorry you're feeling out of sorts, Hal, but you are doing important work with the autonavigator."

"Temporarily. Until Mr. Christian gets back, and even then, Mr. Mowen could do the job ten times easier than me. He's just letting me do it because I begged him. What will I do when Mr. Christian gets back, and there's not even a pretense of a reason to have me doing that job?" I looked into his eyes, but found no answer there.

"There are lots of things you can do around the ship," he said slowly.

"Oh? Such as?"

"Well … Tavy must have tasks you could help with. …"

Octavia made a frustrated gesture, and sat on the edge of the big bed that dominated the cabin. "I wish I did, but the crew is so efficient … and you do everything else that's complicated, Jack. … Hallie, you know the crew are happy to have you train on any or all of their jobs—"

"But they don't really *need* me to be their backup," I interrupted, having heard this explanation all too often in the last few months. "Other than Mr. Francisco, Mr. Christian is the only one who's chosen to take a vacation in the whole year we've been sailing around being thieves."

"Pirates," Jack and Octavia said at the same time, then sent each other adoring looks.

"If you name your organization *Company of Thieves*, then you have to suck up being called a thief," I said grumpily, then immediately felt ashamed. "I'm sorry, that was rude."

"I thought you liked the name," Jack said, looking mildly offended.

"I do. I like what you guys stand for. I like that we're basically three airships full of Robin Hoods helping people who need it, but that doesn't mean I enjoy having no part in that do-gooding. I need a cause, Jack, something I can sink my teeth in. You and Octavia are always so busy, what with planning where we're going to raid next, and delivering the supplies, and picking up gossip about whose ships are where, but I don't have anything to do."

"What is it you want to do?" Octavia asked, her brown eyes serious.

"Well …" I gnawed on my lower lip for a few seconds. "I've been thinking about it. I don't have the mechanical wherewithal to help Mr. Mowen with the machinery. Besides, that's kind of Jack's forte."

"I do have a nanoelectrical engineering degree," he agreed.

"And I'm not into cooking, so steward is out."

"Do you enjoy the navigating?" Octavia asked, hopeful.

"Not really. The machine hates me. So that leaves just one thing," I said, giving them both a nod.

"Bosun's mate?" Jack smoothed down his hair. "I think Dooley would have a thing or two to say about that."

"No, silly. I'll be the ship's fighter."

They both stared at me like they'd never seen me before.

I was quite pleased to explain my reasoning to them. "See, it makes perfect sense. You can train me how to use the plasma gun, Octavia, and Jack can teach me all the martial arts stuff he learned when he was doing secret stuff in the army, and someone else can teach me how to use a sword, and bingo! I'll be the fighting expert, and the next time we run into those Black Hand revolutionary guys, I'll beat the stuffing out of them. I'll be the group meat shield."

"The group *what?*" Octavia looked confused.

"Sorry, it's a gaming term. It means warrior. Jack and I used to play video games together, and he was always the warrior, but it's my turn ... er ..." I stopped at her look of obvious incomprehension.

Octavia pursed her lips and turned to Jack.

"It was after your time, sweetheart," he told her. "They were games we used to play on a device like the autonavigator."

"Only it was fun, and not a pain in the ass, which is more than I can say about the navigator," I added.

"I can't imagine what game you could play on the autonavigator," Octavia said, slowly shaking her head. "But I'll move past that. You wish to be a warrior? But, Hallie ..." Her voice trailed away.

"You don't know how to fight," Jack pointed out for her.

I smiled, happy to explain it as many times as was needed. "I know! That's the beauty of it! I'll learn how from everyone on board, because each person here has some fighting ability in which they excel, and once they teach me, then I'll be the expert."

"I don't think it quite works that way," Octavia said with hesitation.

"Not if you're going to have a negative attitude about it, no." I narrowed my eyes on them. "That was a very pointed look you guys just gave each other. What's going on? Is something happening that you're hiding from me?"

"It's not that we're hiding anything," Octavia said reluctantly. "We just don't want you to be ..."

"Vulnerable," Jack finished for her. "Hurt. Smeared into the ground."

"OK, now I really do feel insulted." I got to my feet, waiting until Jack did likewise before socking him gently on the arm. "I could be just as good a fighter as anyone else."

"Hal," Jack said on a chiding note. "You've never so much as taken a self-defense class."

"So? You never sailed an airship before last year, and here you are Octavia's first mate."

"That's beside the point," Jack said airily.

"We are strangers in a strange land, Jack!" I said, suddenly at my wits' end to make him understand just how I felt. "This world is so different from ours, and yet, the people in it are basically the same. They need help against oppression. They need saving from dire situations. They need guidance and wisdom and assistance."

"That's exactly what we're doing," Jack protested. "We're trying to provide all those things."

"*You* are," I said, pointing first at him, then at Octavia. "And *she* is. As is the entire crew. But not *me*. I have no part in it."

Jack said nothing, but frowned as if he was going to protest.

I continued before he could do so. "What you're doing is no different than the volunteering you did back home. And yet I'm not given the chance to do the same thing."

"Do you wish to volunteer at an animal refuge?" Octavia asked, wrinkling her brow. "I know of one in England for donkeys, but other than that …"

"It's not just animals. I'd be happy to do that if there were charities I could work for. But there's nothing that I've seen. Have you?"

Both of them shook their heads. "Other than the donkey refuge, no, I can't think of a charitable organization that would welcome you," Octavia admitted.

I crossed my arms. "And that's why I'm going to have to carve my own path. That path will be the ship fighter. I will protect you guys as you steal things and distribute it to the poor folks who need it."

They exchanged yet another telling glance, and in a moment of insight, I knew Octavia was going to side with Jack against me. Drat them both.

"If you had some experience," Jack started to say, but I could tell the rest of his sentence would be a denial.

But I hadn't fought back from the biggest threat to my life just to give up when the going got rough.

"Fine," I said, looking at them both down my nose. "You want me to get experience? I will get experience. If you won't teach me how to be a kick-ass airship warrior, then I'll find someone who will. Who's the baddest ass in town?"

Octavia sighed. "Really, Hallie, your language. I realize that where you come from, bandying the word 'ass' about hither and yon is a common occurrence, but I can assure you that here polite people do not mention such words in mixed company."

"Etienne?" I asked, thinking of the Black Hand leader, whom we'd seen briefly in France half a year before. "He didn't seem to be doing much fighting. He just stood back and yelled at his people to shoot at us."

"No, of course Etienne isn't a fighter. He's a strategist." Octavia's fingers fretted with the fabric of her skirt.

"Then who is our biggest threat?"

"Prince Akbar," Jack said, his fingers twitching a little like he wanted to throttle someone. "That bastard son of a—"

"Jack!" Octavia protested.

"He is the bane of our existence, so I reserve the right to call him foul names. If I could just get him in a small, soundproofed room for about five minutes, just him, me, and a pair of electric nipple clamps—"

Octavia took a martyred breath.

"Akbar? Who … oh, the Moghul guy?" I thought about what I knew of the prince. I had a vague memory of Jack telling me how he'd fought him after we had just arrived in this alternate reality, but beyond that, and the fact that he was supposedly some hotshot warlord, I knew nothing. "Do you know where he is?"

"You can't be thinking what I think you're thinking," Jack said, shaking his head.

"What is she thinking?" Octavia asked, clearly confused.

"Sure, I can. If you guys won't teach me, then I'll just have to go to an expert." I gave Jack a long, level look, expecting that he would capitulate and order the crew to teach me their weaponry skills. Seeing as how the Moghuls had such a bad reputation, I knew Jack would rather give in than have me carry through my threat to go to the enemy. "Then, when I've learned what I need to know to be a warrior, I'll come back and protect you guys."

"Oh, lord," Octavia said, and, shaking her head, excused herself, pausing at the door to raise her eyebrows at Jack.

"Now look what you've gone and done," he said after she closed the door behind her. "You made us miss our midmorning quickie, and Octavia will be frustrated until our early-afternoon quickie time. Hal—" He took my arms in his hands. "I know you feel out of place here, but I promise you that you'll find your feet. You just have to give it time."

I hesitated for a few seconds. "Is it that you don't think I have the heart for fighting?"

His eyes were warm with affection. "I know better than anyone just how strong you are, Hallie. You are a warrior in every sense of the word ... except one."

I made a face. "We're back to experience again. Well, I'm trying to fix that. I want to be a fighter. I hate being told to go sit in my cabin whenever you guys steal stuff, or fight off those Black Hand people when they try to take our ill-gotten gains."

"We just want you to be safe," he started to say.

I punched him lightly in the chest. "Exactly! And that's why teaching me to fight is such a good idea. Then not only will I be a kick-booty steampunk chick, but you won't have to worry about protecting me anymore."

"I will always worry about protecting you," he said with a quick hug, rubbing my back just like he used to do when I was little and scared by one of the horror movies he watched.

"I want you to feel useful. I know how important that is to you. But this is not the way. We'll find something—you just have to be patient."

"I'm tired of being patient," I told him when he collected a couple of maps from the desk. "Where … uh … do you happen to know where Prince Akbar is?"

He rolled his eyes, and was about to leave when he stopped himself. "I do know, as a matter of fact. Or at least, I know the latest intelligence that was given to us at Annaba, and no, I'm not going to tell you."

My gaze slid past him for a second to where his journal lay.

"You rat fink!" I yelled, storming my way to the door, praying he wouldn't see through my sham anger. Luckily, he was a man, and thus no match for a woman. He simply followed me out and paused when I flung open the door to my cabin.

"Hal, even if Tavy and I thought it was wise for you to pick up training from someone so ruthless and violent, the brute Akbar would likely hold you for a ransom should you show up to demand he train you. That or make you part of his harem."

"Bah," I said dismissively, wishing he'd just leave. "If he's a man, he can be manipulated."

"I would be worried if I knew you weren't just expressing your discontent in the only way you know how," Jack said, giving me a quick grin before heading off.

"Shows how much you know me," I muttered, and after a couple of minutes to make sure he'd gone after Octavia, I slipped back into their cabin and read the notes he'd made from the stop at Annaba. Unfortunately, there was no concrete mention of just where Akbar was rumored to be other than a vague "southern part of Tunisia" hint.

Ten minutes later I sat on the edge of my bunk and took a good, long look at Jack's statement that when I found Akbar, he might not be willing to teach me, and decided that I had a way around that. "The only thing standing in my way,"

I said to myself when I pulled out a small chest and rifled through my sparse belongings until I found a silk envelope, "is fear. And really, the only things I'm afraid of are horses and asphyxiation, and how likely is it that I'll encounter either of those on Prince Akbar's airship?"

It wasn't until an hour later that I managed to track down the one person who had the information I needed.

"The captain won't like it if I was to pass along privileged information," Mr. Mowen said, tapping on the side of one of the boilers and listening to the echo to judge how full it was.

"I'm her sister-in-law," I reminded him. "I would never do anything that would harm either Jack or Octavia, or, for that matter, anyone on this ship."

"Well," he said, hesitating at a couple of gauges. He frowned at one, and gave it a quarter turn. "I suppose that is the truth. We're scheduled to drop supplies at three locations in Tunisia."

"Right. At Kasserine, Mahdia, and Sousse," I said, naming the towns that were mentioned in Jack's journal.

Mr. Mowen nodded.

"But those towns are in the middle and north parts of Tunisia." I stood waiting, giving him my best "eyes filled with hope" expression.

"Aye, they are. It's said that the Moghul prince has a camp to the south, around the town of Tozeur, where he makes periodic strikes upon those Black Hand scum."

"Tozeur," I said thoughtfully. From what I remembered of the map I'd studied, that wasn't very far from our first stop. "Thank you, Mr. Mowen."

"You're welcome, lass, although I hope you're not planning on doing anything that would upset the captain."

"Of course not," I told him, mentally planning the notes to Jack and Octavia, apologizing for any concern I might cause them, and one further note to the prince, informing him that I had a proposition that he would be sure to find mutually agreeable. "I wouldn't dream of doing anything that would cause problems."

"I'm sure that is the furthest thing from your mind."

I glanced at Mr. Mowen, but despite his voice being full of amusement, his face was impassive.

The next twelve hours were spent sorting through my things, packing a small bag with essentials, and fighting with the damned autonavigator.

By the time we landed at Kasserine, I was ready. I left a note to Mr. Mowen asking him to please take over the autonavigator duties, and another addressed to Jack and Octavia, which I placed on my bunk while the crew was unloading cargo.

After making sure the coast was clear, I slipped out of an escape hatch on the far end of the airship with my bag in hand. No one saw me leave, and given that I'd told everyone earlier that I had a headache and was going to try to sleep it off, I doubted if my absence would be discovered before morning.

"By then," I said from where I squatted behind a couple of large wooden crates filled with salted beef, "I should be making a deal with the prince."

When the *Enterprise* rose in the air and gently chugged off to the northeast, I felt a moment's qualm at my audacious plan. My last tie to the world in which I'd grown up was sailing off into the distance with his beloved, but after a few minutes of panicked fear, I managed to remind myself I'd been through much scarier things in my life. This was the right course to take.

"After all," I told myself four hours later, when I sat on a transport airship heading from Kasserine to points south, "I've been dragged to this world without my consent, and now I'm stuck here with no way to get back home. I refuse to live a life of uselessness. I refuse to forever be a stranger who is always on the outside looking in. No, sir! This is take-charge Hallie, and take-charge Hallie says we fulfill our destiny, and all that crap."

The woman sitting opposite me, who had appeared more than a little scandalized when I sat down on the red brocade cushioned bench across from her, now looked like she might just fall over into a faint.

"You should probably loosen your corset," I told her, taking in her highly starched white blouse, the long navy blue cotton skirt with fanciful embroidered scroll, her bright red belt, and a little straw boater that sat on top of an elaborate coiffure. She looked so much the epitome of a late Victorian-era lady that I knew I shocked her by speaking in public of such things as corsets. "It's just a foundation garment," I told her. "It's not like it's a sexual aid or something that is in bad taste to mention in mixed company. Far be it from me to judge what's right and wrong with your society, but at the same time, I begin to think that maybe a social revolution is in order. If I was to suggest you abandon your corset and free your ta-tas, what would you say?"

She weaved, a handkerchief held to her mouth, and I worried she really might faint. Luckily, at that moment two other ladies entered the cabin, which had been set aside for women and children, and their unexceptional chatter seemed to reassure my seatmate that she was safe from my heathen corset-less ways.

I spent the bulk of the flight making mental lists of things I wanted to learn. Swordplay was a must, since a lot of the people in this world used swords rather than those weird plasma-shooting guns they called Empyrean Disruptors. Naturally, I'd have to learn how to shoot those, too.

"But I rather fancy myself a bit of a swashbuckler," I told the starchy woman when our companions took themselves off to the observation deck for a few minutes. "There's nothing more kick-as—er … kick-bustle than being able to slash around with a sword, you know? Or oooh, maybe a pair of daggers. If Jack would teach me his stealthy black ops skills, I could sneak up behind people and wham! Bam! Stab, stab, stab! I'd be a dagger-assassin rogue rather than a warrior!"

The woman gurgled something, and toppled over on the bench seat, clutching a lace hankie to her face.

"I don't know—she just seemed to have some sort of an attack," I told the two ladies when they returned and asked me what happened to the other woman. I added an innocent smile for good measure.

The starchy lady squeaked, and allowed herself to be helped from the row of seats with vague little gestures toward me.

No one sat by me for the rest of the trip.

The airship steward told me that Tozeur was an oasis town, located on the edge of the Sahara desert, part of the caravan route that Berbers and Bedouins used when traveling north to the sea. The town itself was surrounded by thick date trees, a line of which also clustered around a pool of greenish-blue water fed by a waterfall that poured out of a curved wall of rock edging one side of the pool. Beyond, a few more date trees were dotted through sparse scrubland, the vegetation thinning with distance from the oasis until there was nothing but small, knee-high dusty, hardy shrubs. The land rolled in soft waves to the south into the Sahara, from whose distances periodic trains of camels and merchants emerged on their way north to the coast cities.

I disembarked (much, I suspect, to the relief of the inhabitants of the ladies' cabin) to find facing a small inn, a few scattered mud buildings, and not a lot else.

"The word 'inn' is a bit of a gross overestimation of the word," I said aloud when I hoisted my bag and entered the curtained doorway. Inside, three round tables dotted an earth floor, each table hosting four silent men bearing huge mustaches, all of whom sat nursing drinks. At one table, clearly inhabited by a livelier bunch, the men played a game of dice, their movements slow and studied as they tossed the dice, peered at the results, then took a long pull at their respective drinks before a few coins were exchanged.

For a moment, all eyes were on me, and although I'm not an exhibitionist by nature—or even terribly extroverted—I reveled in the sensation that I was on a grand adventure. For the first time in the year I'd spent in this world, I felt fully alive, possessed with a mission, a plan, a goal toward which I was actively working. It was as if I'd woken up after a year-long sleep, full of energy and enthusiasm, and I embraced the experience even though a few of the men made scandalized faces at my corset-less silk tunic and lounging pants that was my favorite outfit.

"Good afternoon," I greeted a laconic man who oozed his way over to me, his hair slicked forward in an obvious attempt to cover a balding top. "I should like some information, if you please. I understand that Prince Akbar is located near this town?"

The low murmur of voices and occasional clink of dice came to a sudden halt as thirteen pairs of eyes considered me.

"Madame?" the innkeeper asked in a French accent. He looked like he had turned into a human-sized version of the stuffed big-mouth bass that hung in my father's study.

"Akbar. The Moghul dude. He's supposed to be in this area." I glanced around the inn, wondering if I'd said something untoward. "Did he leave? I hope not, because I spent a lot of money getting out to Tozeur, and I have to save the rest of what my brother gave me."

The innkeeper swallowed a couple of times, his Adam's apple bobbing up and down in his scrawny neck before he answered, "Madame is … connected … with the prince?"

"Nope," I said, giving everyone in the room a friendly smile. They all looked like they had been turned to stone. "But that's not really a problem, because evidently he held my brother and sister-in-law prisoner for a bit, so we are kind of acquainted-by-kidnap, if you will. Is he here? In town?"

The innkeeper looked a bit dazed, but wasn't forthcoming with any information.

"Anyone?" I asked, looking at the motley gang.

No one said a word.

I sighed and reached under my tunic to pull out the little bag that hung around my neck. Octavia said it was called a Lady's Protector, but it looked like the sort of passport neck pouch I'd worn the year I went to Europe. I pulled out the collection of bills. "Right, let's see if this helps your memory."

The innkeeper seemed to come to life at the sight of the money. His gaze shot past me to the door for a moment; then he pursed his lips and let his gaze drop to the money in my hand. "There is a gentleman in the area who might fit the description of Prince Akbar, but Madame is not recommended to visit his camp."

"Oh? Why not?"

He looked almost as scandalized as the starched woman on the airship. "It is not fitting for a lady such as Madame to visit the prince in his domicile."

It was on the tip of my tongue to ask why, but I had an idea of just what was giving him so much grief. "Only ladies of ill repute visit him, eh?"

The innkeeper blinked, and murmured something about it not being a fitting subject to discuss with me.

"Right, well, I'm not a sex worker, not that I think anything is wrong with that, because women should feel completely comfortable taking ownership of their bodies and their lives, and if that's what they want to do, well then, who am I to rain on their parades? So to speak. Regardless of all that, I really do need to see the prince. If you could just be so kind as to point me in his direction, I would be happy to make a little donation to your inn."

He licked his lips when I plucked out a second bill and, holding it between two fingers, waved it in the air. "It is too dangerous, madame. I could not live with myself knowing I had led you to one who is most ruthless, most feared."

"He sounds just perfect for my needs." I added a third bill. That did the trick. He eased the bills out of my hand, saying, "To the south, the road that leads past the oasis goes to a small rise above a wadi, about a mile from town. There is a camp, and it is said the monseigneur who leads many men has a great airship the color of the darkest night."

"That sounds like Akbar to me. Is that the south road?"

He moved the finger I was pointing about fifteen degrees. *"Bonne chance, madame."*

"And to you," I repeated, and, with a little wave at the still silent and unmoving men in the inn, stepped out with a barely contained sense of excitement. I glanced at the sun, which looked likely to sink in a few hours behind the Atlas mountains that clung to the horizon, squared my shoulders, and started my trek.

"You'd just better not give me any grief, Akbar," I said to myself while I marched along the dirt road. "Because I'm through being patient. This is my time to grab life by the balls, and I mean to do it!"

TWO

Alan Dubain was furious.

That event by itself wasn't ground-shaking, Alan mused to himself, but given the number of items he was juggling, including being a diplomat in the court of William VI, being a former member of the Black Hand, and, most important, being better known throughout north, central, and southern Europe as Prince Akbar, infamous warlord son of the imperator Aurangzeb III, he felt entitled to a little more fury than someone who wasn't trying to be all things to all people.

And still keep the general population alive.

"We'll never be to El Kef in time to keep that bastard Etienne from stealing Octavia's cargo," he growled to Zand, his companion since childhood and closest friend. The two men were riding with a complement of approximately thirty Moghuls to the camp they'd set up a week before. "She'll have more than a few things to say to me if she loses any more cargo to him."

"Why is he here, in Tunisia?" Zand asked, pulling up the tail of his turban to cover his mouth, the sting of sand against Alan's face indicating another windstorm was kicking up. "His sights have been set on Prussia and your father's empire for the last eight years. Why would he come *here* when his goal is elsewhere?"

Alan thought about the last communiqué from his father, and pressed his heels into his horse, urging the great black gelding to a ground-eating canter. He felt itchy, and not just with the sand that was working its way in through his clothing. Like his friend, he adjusted the turban so that it covered his nose and mouth, squinting through the dark green glass of his goggles. "I believe he plans on meeting the imperator."

Zand looked startled. "His Imperial Majesty comes to North Africa?"

"So he says." Alan ground his teeth for a few seconds. It wasn't difficult enough to juggle two personae, and three separate commitments of time—no, now his father had to rouse himself out of Constantinople and blight him with what was sure to be nonstop interference. "We can only hope that he loses interest quickly and returns to the comforts of his palace. Damn, where is the camp? Have we gone astray hunting those revolutionaries?"

"It should be ahead of us," Zand said, consulting his compass. "Over that next dune, perhaps."

"The next time I have the bright idea to go chasing revolutionaries into the Sahara, you have my permission to knock me silly," Alan growled, relieved when, as Zand said, they crested an elegantly wind-carved sand dune and saw below in a rocky valley a dark shadow that was his temporary base. "They've lost me far too much time by evading us, and Octavia will have my head if I don't help protect her cargo."

"She has the *Falcon* nearby, though, surely, and she is an impressive airship," Zand pointed out. "Not to mention the other ship, the one captained by her father."

"Robert Anstruther is in Ireland, I believe, although, yes, the *Falcon* should be there. At least, that is what Safie told me she was doing, and she is a most dutiful captain."

"She is most definitely that," Zand said in a voice that sounded to Alan partially strangled.

He smiled into his turban, well aware that his friend had a tendresse for his oldest sister, and fully intended on talking to Safie about how they could arrange for her to marry Zand without their father beheading him. Or Alan. Or all three of them. Alan's smile faded when he thought with annoyance of his father's imminent arrival. What the devil was he thinking to prove by coming all the way to Tunisia?

As they rode, the dark shadow that was his base began to resolve itself into a variety of structures. His tent, a mammoth structure of black and gold, sat in the center of approximately twenty others, beyond which was tethered an airship, the *Nightwing*.

Another smile curled his lips under the thick black mustache he grew each time he returned to his Moghul roots. His beloved *Nightwing*, the best of all his ships. She was small as airships went, with only four envelopes, but what she lacked in size, she more than made up in speed, maneuverability, and firepower.

"We'll take off as soon as we get into camp," he told Zand, waving a hand behind him. "Az can take care of the prisoners."

"As you like," Zand said, and promptly dropped back in order to have a word with Azahgi Bahajir, one of the guards who rode alongside the seven revolutionaries they'd caught after a several-hour hunt that dragged them deep into the desert.

Alan was mentally drafting an apology to Octavia when a shout from the east caused him to pull up, one hand shading his eyes to better see the approaching horsemen.

It was the four-man scouting party who were tasked with checking the local wadis and dry riverbeds for signs of more revolutionaries, but these men rode in a tight formation, some large object hanging between them.

He frowned and tried to figure out what it was they held. The remains of a dead camel? Some other animal? It wasn't until the men were almost upon him that he realized that the scouts held a person slung between them.

"If that's another revolutionary, place him with the others, assuming he's alive," he instructed Zand, who moved up next to Alan, his eyes similarly shielded to see the oncoming group.

Alan started forward, but Zand's words stopped him. "I don't think that's a man."

"Of course it's a man. What woman in her right mind would be wandering around the desert on her own?" Despite the irritation of yet another delay, Alan turned his horse toward the scouts. To his surprise, he discovered Zand was all too correct.

"My prince," the lead scout said, leaping off his saddle to make a low bow. "We bring to you a most valuable prisoner. A spy!"

"I am so going to make you sorry!" a woman's voice croaked in English. "You're not going to be able to walk by the time I get done with you!"

Alan slid out of the saddle and froze at the words, his eyes narrowing on the woman who'd been slung between the two rearmost scouts. She was clad in some sort of long, silky trousers and tunic, vaguely green in color, but now badly stained brown by sand and earth. But it was the fact that she spoke English that made him wary.

"Let her down," he told his men, speaking in their native language while at the same time pulling around the tail of his turban. A woman who spoke English in this area could be only one of two things: a member of the Black Hand or someone Octavia had recruited. And if it was the latter, it was best that he do what he could to hide his face, since only one person other than his sister and Zand knew that Alan Dubain and Prince Akbar were one and the same.

The men took him literally. They dropped the woman, who hit the ground with a whomp that made Alan flinch. He strode forward to help her up, but she was on her feet before he could reach for her, her face yellow with sand and dirt. She spat and coughed, but he couldn't help but notice the glittering green eyes that seemed to shoot sparks of anger toward him.

"Are you their boss?" she snapped, rubbing a hand over her mouth. It just smeared the sand and dirt across her lips and chin.

He made a polite bow, not the court bow that Alan Dubain was known for, but the short, choppy bow practiced by the Moghuls, and said in the accent of his youth, "I have that honor."

"Oh, goody." The anger that had filled the woman's glittering eyes turned to pleasure when she marched up to him and slapped him on the left cheek. "Just the man I want to see."

Stunned, he allowed her to see his ire by flaring his nostrils in a dramatic fashion. "What was that for?"

"You're in charge of them, aren't you?" she said, jerking her thumb over her shoulder to the four men who clustered behind her. "That makes you responsible for the outrageous treatment I've been forced to endure for the last hour!"

He was about to tell the woman that, despite her opinion, he didn't recall giving his scouts orders to sling any women they found between them, but before he could do more than open his mouth, she slapped him again.

"Will you stop doing that!" Annoyance rode him, but he struggled to bring his temper back under control.

"They touched me!" the woman said, her hands on her hips, just as if she expected him to apologize. "Inappropriately! I swear, if I was back home, I'd have HR on their asses so fast their grubby little paws wouldn't have time to do more than clutch their termination papers!"

He pushed his goggles up onto his forehead, wondering if the time out in the sun hunting for the revolutionaries had addled his brains. She looked better than when viewed through sand-grimed green-tinted lenses, but still appeared to be much aggrieved.

"Woman," he started to say, but stopped when she slapped him a third time. He caught her wrist almost before she'd finished the slap. "You will stop these assaults upon me!" he roared at her.

"They touched me on my ass!" the woman said, and, pulling her hand free from his grip, used two of her fingers to poke him in the chest. Luckily, his leather and metal armor dulled the gesture, but he was irritated by it nonetheless. No one dared poke the prince Akbar in the chest. He was a warlord, for Christ's sake. Everyone feared him! Strong men blanched at his name! Either he'd had too much sun, or the woman was insane. Or didn't know just who he was. "That one—" The irritating, possibly mad woman turned and pointed to the scout standing in front, a big leering grin on his face. "That one copped a feel."

Alan looked from the scout to her, wondering if she was speaking in some dialect with which he was unfamiliar. She had an American accent, but her words made no sense. "What is a copped feel?" he asked, despite knowing he should consign her to the fate of the revolutionaries and be on his way.

She made a face and slapped a hand onto his leather breastplate. He looked down at her hand, confused.

"Gah. Just a sec. How do you get that—oh, that buckle there?" To his amazement, she unbuckled the shoulder strap before repeating the action to the strap that lay across his ribs, both of which helped hold the armor tight to his chest. "This," she said, sliding her hand under the armor, and cupping his pectoral. "This is copping a feel."

He stood there for a moment, the warmth of her hand on his chest, separated from his flesh only by the thin layer of linen that made up his tunic, sending a little fire that headed straight for his groin.

He eyed her breasts, and lifted a hand without thinking, but the slap that followed—which admittedly he half expected—was delivered with the warning, "Don't you even *think* about it!"

"Woman," he repeated, trying to pull his mind from imagining just how her breasts would feel against the palms of his hands. And cheeks. And possibly rubbed against his rod. "If you slap me one more time, I will instruct the scouts to return you to my camp in the same manner they carried you here. What is your name?"

"Hallie," she said, fussing with the silk tunic she wore, apparently without a corset, a slightly scandalous situation that nonetheless he found intriguing. Even the women of his father's court had adopted Western wear, and to appear without a corset was considered the height of bad taste. Or it signaled her as a camp follower. "Hallie Norris, to be specific."

He stopped imagining what he'd like to do to her, assuming she was the sort of woman who would tumble easily into his bed, and felt his blood run cold, despite the heat of the day. This was Jack Fletcher's sister, the woman he'd been engaged to save from the gallows a year before? What the devil and all his little minions was she doing here? More important, what was she doing here *now*, when he had just set up a camp? He had never met her, but the danger she posed was extreme. If she connected him with Alan Dubain, she could ruin many plans that had taken him years to lay. "I do not know this name," he lied, wondering if she would call him out on it.

"Well, of course you don't. But it's my name nonetheless."

His mind ran around like a squirrel on an iced pond, trying to remember if she had ever seen him while he was being Akbar, relaxing slightly when he realized the only time he'd seen Octavia in person during the course of the last year was some ten months before in Cairo, and then contact had been limited to just Octavia and her new husband. "What are you doing here? Where are your menfolk? Are you spying on me? Or have you come to offer your body in exchange for coin?"

That just enraged her, as he'd suspected it would, and she pulled her hand back in order to deliver yet another slap, but this time he caught her hand before she could land it. "You bastard! I'm not a hooker!"

"Hooker?" he couldn't help but ask.

"'Sex worker' is the PC term, but I don't expect you guys know anything about that. At least the men in the inn didn't seem to know what it meant, and that Mr. Piper on my brother's ship is always referring to such women as 'hoors,' but that's just downright derogatory, so I won't even bother mentioning it. As a matter of fact, I was trying to find Prince Akbar, the Moghul son of some big, bad emperor. Are you part of his group?" She gave him an obvious once-over. "You're dressed like the description my brother gave me of Moghuls."

"I *am* Prince Akbar," he said, resisting the urge to make another bow. Really, the urbane ways of Alan Dubain were starting to leach into all of his mannerisms. He reminded himself that Akbar was arrogant and uncaring of others' opinions, and so instead puffed out his chest. "I am the son of Imperator Aurangzeb."

"Oh, good." She didn't look pleased to see him. In fact, she still looked annoyed, a fact that amused him despite the situation. She glanced around and leaned in so that her breath brushed his cheek. "I need to talk to you. Privately."

Alan Dubain would have wooed the woman. He would have given her compliments, teasing her into a flirtatious mood, and only then would he allow her to fulfill all the desires she had regarding him. But Akbar was different. He didn't flirt, he didn't coax—he took. Accordingly, Alan grabbed the woman and pulled her to him, kissing her with all the arrogance he could muster.

Her mouth was warm under his, not with the heat of the cooling day, but with the fire of a woman who was filled with passion, her lips sweet if a bit sandy. He enjoyed the kiss for all of three seconds before she slapped both hands on his chest, and shoved him back, her eyes back to spitting green fire at him.

"What the hell, dude?" she snarled, wiping her mouth with the back of her hand.

He was vaguely insulted by that gesture. Akbar might be rough around the edges and very impulsive, but he prided himself that both of his personae gave all due regard to women, leaving them sated and with a smile on their respective lips.

She gave him the meanest look he'd ever received from a woman. "That is so over the line, and completely unacceptable. That's a hundred times worse than Mr. Gropey Hands back there."

"You don't wish to occupy my bed?" he asked, allowing his confusion to show.

"No!" She gave a little exaggerated eye roll. "I just told you that I wasn't a whore! I want to talk to you. Privately. About a proposition I have."

"One involving sexual congress?" he asked cautiously.

"No!" She glanced around again, and said quietly, "I want you to teach me."

He blinked three times, his mind now wholly filled with thoughts of the most erotic nature. He had a great many things he'd like to teach her, but he wasn't a stupid man. He was ready to wager that if he informed her that he was more than willing to teach her many and varied sexual acts, she'd slap him again. "Teach you what?" he asked instead.

"How to fight."

He wasn't expecting that. He considered Akbar's character, and decided that teaching this fiery, if dusty, woman to fight would be the last thing that he would expect, as well. "Why?" he felt it perfectly in character to ask.

"It's a long story," she said airily, waving away the question. "I'll tell you about it later, when we negotiate. Is your camp near here? Being strung between those hell beasts for almost an hour has made me feel like a piece of jerky."

He thought of blinking a few more times just in case it helped his somewhat muddled thought processes along, but decided that Prince Akbar would limit the number of times he blinked per day, and instead simply grabbed Hallie's arm and led her toward his horse.

"Just … uh … just how much is this going to cost me?" she asked, suddenly sounding hesitant. "I have money. My brother gave it to me, and he said it was kind of a lot, so I shouldn't just fritter it away, but honestly, what's the point in holding on to money if you want to use it for something important?"

He opened his mouth, closed it, and then, with a little shake of his head, opened it again. "I do not take payment from women in coin," was what his mouth finally managed to get out.

"No?" She looked suspicious. "If that was a not-so-subtle hint that you expect me to do the sheet tango with you just to learn how to use a sword, and shoot those gun things you guys have, and maybe some daggers, because the more I think about it, the more I think I'd do better as a stealthy, sneaky rogue than a right-out-in-the-front warrior, well then, you better think again."

"Sheet tango." He took a deep breath. His Inner Akbar was annoyed at the same time he was amused. "I tire of asking you to explain words that you are deliberately using to confuse me, but in this case I will do so. But it is the last time!"

"Sex!" she all but yelled at him, causing him to stop their process toward the horses. "I'm talking about sex, you big oaf!"

He felt mildly startled. "Are we back to that? You said you were not a camp follower, and yet now you are discussing acts of a carnal nature. I appreciate your offer of unpaid sexual congress, but not only do I prefer to be acquainted with the women who grace my bed, but also I make it a policy that I be the one doing the inviting." That former point wasn't necessarily true, since he hadn't known who Hallie was when he was thinking of all the things he wanted to do to her, but he felt that he needed to bring his mind back under control.

"I don't want to sleep with you!" she yelled.

"You just asked me to take you to a sheet tango," he pointed out. His men, all of whom were clustered around them, nodded their heads.

"You did. We all heard you," Zand said helpfully.

"I did not! And who are you?" she asked him.

He made a bow. "I am Zand, son of Abdul, and Prince Akbar's lieutenant."

"Right," Hallie said, clearly making an effort to control her temper. Alan gave his cheek one last rub, hoping she did so. "This conversation has gone into the realm of downright maddening, so I'm going to move on. I would like you to teach me, that's all. Just teach. No funny stuff. How much is it going to cost me to do that?"

"I believe that we will leave negotiations until a later time. Right now, I am anxious to return to my camp," he said, deciding that the best course of action would be to take Hallie back to her brother and Octavia. His camp was no place for a woman of her character, class, and temperament. Plus there was the fact that he couldn't stop thinking extremely lascivious things about her. "You may accompany me so long as you do not try to get into my bed without invitation, and also that you cease striking me."

"I wasn't trying to get into your bed, your pants, or any other part of you!" she yelled again, her arms flailing around in a manner that had him fighting a smile. Prince Akbar seldom smiled. "I just want to learn how to be a badass like you!"

Several of his men gasped in horror at her language. Alan struggled to contain the smile that curled the corners of his mouth.

"Oh, for heaven's sake, grow up," she told the shocked faces of his men. "Honestly, you wouldn't think men who have the reputation of being callous and brutal and marauding would be so shocked by the word *ass*."

They gasped again. Alan gave up and let the smile have its way. Carefully, he took her arm and led her the rest of the way over to where the horses waited. "You will forgive my men for having such delicate sensibilities, I'm sure. We will return to my camp now. You may ride with me."

"I mean, it's not like no one here hasn't seen an ass before—what?"

She stopped when he mounted Sampson and held out his hand for her. "I am late. Come."

"Ride with you?" she asked, her gaze skittering over the horse before returning to him. "Uh ... thanks, but I don't think so."

"We've wasted enough time with you shocking my men." He waggled his hand impatiently, very much looking forward to having her pressed up against him. "Cease delaying me."

"No thanks," she said, backing up until she stepped on the feet of one of the four scouts, who had followed immediately behind her. "I'll walk, if you don't mind."

"I do mind. I'm already delayed due to the revolutionaries, and I don't intend on wasting any more time." He gestured toward her, offering his hand again, fast losing his remaining patience. He was a tolerant man when it came to women, especially those in a vulnerable position, but this one was pushing him past his limits. "Let us be on our way."

"I don't like horses," she said, squaring her shoulders, and marching past him. "I'll walk. I like walking. I'm a very good walker."

He sighed, cast his eyes upward to see if any deity who happened to be looking might notice what he was called upon to put up with, and pressed his heels to Sampson's flanks, bending to the side and scooping up Hallie before pulling her up to sit sideways on his lap.

She screamed, struggled, and went over backward off the side of Sampson, who, being very well trained, stopped. Alan leaped down and helped Hallie to her feet.

"Are you hurt?" he asked, annoyance riding him. Damn the woman, if she made him miss the raid with her demands, he would not be answerable for his actions.

"No. I told you, I don't like horses." She brushed off her backside and, giving Sampson a wide berth, started forward again.

He sighed to himself a second time, mounted his horse, and, with a gesture toward Zand, rode forward a few steps.

Zand grabbed Hallie by her waist, ignoring her squawk of protest, and flung her up onto Alan's lap. Once again, she started fighting him, her arms and legs flailing, and this time she not only went over the side; she took Alan with her.

"What the hell is the matter with you?" he snarled when he managed to disentangle himself from her, and got to his feet.

She hastily scrambled to her own, her face red with exertion and emotion. "I told you a bazillion times now! I don't like horses."

"This foolishness ends now," he said, his patience frayed, and his temper—lauded in the court of William VI for its evenness and inability to be ruffled—well and truly lost. He grabbed her by the back of her tunic and shoved her toward Sampson, who turned to look at what all the fuss was about.

"Ack!" Hallie screamed, and turned, trying to climb him like he was some sort of a ladder.

"Woman!" he roared, giving in to Akbar's notorious black temper. "Cease this outrageous action!"

"I'm not outrageous! I don't like horses," she snarled back at him, fighting when he struggled to turn her around to face the horse. He managed to get her facing the right direction, but then she seemed to turn to stone. Or at least, that's what it felt like. When he gave her another shove forward, intending to read her a lecture, she pressed herself back into him, her body taut, her arms rigid, her expression as frozen as the rest of her body.

He was about to toss her over the saddle and mount behind her when he caught a glimpse of something in her green eyes, an emotion that reached deep inside him.

She was afraid. No, not afraid, terrified.

Instantly, the soft side of his emotions, the same one that always comforted his sisters when they were upset or anxious or frightened, came to the fore, giving him the patience that Prince Akbar allowed few to see.

He could no more bully a frightened woman than he could walk to the moon. He eyed Sampson and then said softly in Hallie's ear, "You truly are afraid of horses?"

She nodded, the movement stiff. "They're … so big. And they bite. And kick. And do other things."

"Sampson is a very well-behaved horse. I trained him myself. He will not hurt you. If you stroke him, you will see just how nice his manners are."

She shook her head and tried to flatten herself against his body. "Nuh-uh. He'll do something. They *all* do something whenever I get near them."

He had a feeling that if she could, she would merge into him. The impatience and irritation he had felt a few moments ago faded completely. He sighed to himself about what he thought of as his overactive protective streak, but did his best nonetheless to calm Hallie.

"I will show you," he said softly, and, putting one arm around her waist to keep her from bolting, tried to edge her forward to the horse.

"Nope. Not happening." Hallie refused to budge. "The words 'over my dead body' come all too strongly to my mind."

"I'm sorry you feel that way." He picked her up and carried her the four steps to the horse. She was as unmoving as a statue, but he took her hand in his, and forced her to pet the elegant lines of Sampson's neck. "There, you see how he arches his neck? He likes to be stroked there."

She made an unintelligible noise in her throat. "He's just gathering his strength to stomple me into the ground."

"I don't believe 'stomple' is an actual word," he said, unable to keep the amusement from his voice. He continued to force her to stroke Sampson's neck, letting her get used to the feel of the horse.

"It is when it comes to the things horses want to do to me."

"Now we will let him smell you. It is traditional to greet a horse by blowing in his nose, so that he may learn your scent, but since I suspect you might hyperventilate if I were to ask you to do so, we'll just let him smell you, so that he is aware of who you are, and that you are on his back."

"Oh, holy hand grenades, are you insane? Get near his mouth? The bitey end?" She moaned, her fingers digging into his arm that he still kept around her waist. He had to admit that if he were a less conscientious man, he might enjoy the sensation of having her pressed so tightly against him, as well as indulge the urge to breathe deeply of the scent rising from her hair, that of orange blossoms and exotic spices.

"Yes. You will see that Sampson is a gentleman. Not all horses are so, but he has, as I mentioned, very good manners." He lifted her bodily again, this time moving around to the front of the horse.

She began to pant when Sampson politely snuffled her torso, checking her for treats, before quickly losing interest. "He's going to bite," she whispered, not moving a single muscle.

"He would never behave in such a reprehensible manner. There, you see?" he said in her ear. "Now you have been introduced to him, and nothing bad has happened to you."

"That's just because you're here." She remained in a locked position. "The second you so much as look anywhere else, it'll be over for me."

"Hallie," he said.

Slowly, her head turned to look at him, her eyes wide.

"Breathe, little desert dove. You'll swoon if you don't, and that might startle Sampson, who, while a patient and understanding horse, has no experience with women swooning at his feet."

"Oh my god. I don't want that. Nobody move! We don't want to startle the very big horsey."

"Take a slow breath in," he said, worried she might very well faint.

"OK. I got this. I know how to breathe. I do it all the time. Yes. I will breathe." She breathed in a long, ragged breath, her head turning back to look at the horse.

He took her hand and moved it over to Sampson's soft muzzle, letting her fingers run along it. "Now, shall we try this again? This time without you throwing us off his back."

"He's gonna eat me!" Her voice was hoarse, a rough whisper that triggered a need in him to protect her.

Dammit, she wasn't one of his sisters—which was a good thing, since the thoughts that crept around the edges of his mind were wholly inappropriate—and what's more, she had a perfectly good brother to take care of her. She didn't need him to do the job.

And yet, there he was, wanting to do just that.

"Sampson doesn't eat people. He does, however, like carrots and apples. Next time, we will make sure you have such treats for him, and you will see that he is very gentle. Can you walk?"

"No," she said in a high-pitched, pathetic voice. "I think my legs are frozen with terror."

He gave a brief chuckle despite the fact that Akbar did not indulge in such things, and, lifting her again, carried her over to the saddle.

"I changed my mind. I *can* walk. In fact, I prefer it."

"You would be too slow to keep up with us," he said, nodding to Zand, who had been watching the scene with a little smile hidden in the end of his turban.

Zand immediately gave orders for the company to mount up and instructed the scouts to return to their patrol.

"I could run. I like to run, too. I'm not very fast, because I have notoriously weak ankles that I inherited from my mother, ones that were so feeble they kept me from ice-skating when all my friends had ice-skating birthday parties, but I'm perfectly happy to run now."

Alan, feeling that more than enough effort had been spent making her feel comfortable with Sampson, simply hoisted her into the saddle, and before she had time to do more than stiffen up, he mounted behind her, sliding himself to the back of the saddle in order to give her room.

As he suspected, he was very much aware of her ass pressed into his groin, and of her legs tight against his. He took the reins, and pressed his heels to Sampson, his body moving easily when the great horse leaped forward, anxious to get back to his stable.

THREE

Hallie shrieked when the horse moved, just as Alan knew she would.

What he didn't expect was the way she clutched with both hands on his arm, a stream of mumbled words issuing from her mouth. He thought at first she was cursing, but was surprised to realize she was talking to Sampson. "Oh my god, I'm going to die. We're all going to die. Oh my god, horse, this is fast, this is really fast, and Akbar is here, you know that, right? You know he's here? It's not just me, so don't even think of doing those sorts of rearing-up moves that will end up with me stompled under your feet, because the prince dude is here. He's right here, horse. You are here, aren't you?" Her voice suddenly rose in panic.

He chuckled again into her ear. "I am right here. The arm around you that you are currently gouging with your fingernails belongs to me, as a matter of fact."

"Oh. Sorry." She loosened her hold on his arm. "I ... oh, god, why is he doing that? Why are his ears moving?"

"He's listening to you talk. He's a very smart horse, in addition to being well trained."

"Hi, horsey," she said in a wavering voice. "Please don't kill me. Your boss here ... uh ... what am I supposed to call you? You're a prince, right? Are you a Your Highness sort of prince—whoa! Don't make him bend like that!"

"We have to turn a little to the north. Just relax, and move with Sampson."

"Ha ha ha ha ha," she said in a stilted, completely humorless laugh. "Oh, ha."

"You may call me Alan," he said before he knew what his mouth was going to say. He held his breath for a moment, wondering if she'd react to the name.

"Alan? Why Alan? I thought you were Akbar."

"I am. My mother, who was English, called me Alan."

"Oh. That's a nice name. Would it be racist of me if I said I liked it better than Akbar? Oh, god, it is racist, isn't it? I'm sorry. I will Akbar you if you like."

"And I will Alan you if you like," he said, once again without thinking.

She froze. "Was that an innuendo?"

"Yes," he said with a sigh, wondering what had gotten into him. It must be all the time in the sun hunting the revolutionaries. "Yes, it was, and not a very graceful one at that. I apologize for it."

"That's OK," she said, shifting against him.

His mouth was near enough to her ear that he caught another whiff of the orange-spice smell of her hair. To his discomfort, he hardened, the sensation of her in his arms, and the movement of her ass against his groin, leaving him far more aware of her than he would have liked.

It didn't help that after a few minutes she began to shift and move against him in a manner that ensured his erection remained firmly in place. In fact, he thought with martyred exaggeration even as he moved his head slightly so he could sniff her hair better, his rod was probably hard enough that it could be used to crush rocks.

"Stop moving," he commanded her at one point when she wriggled in a particularly enticing manner, one that left him gritting his teeth over the need to take her to the nearest bed and relieve his poor, tormented rod in her heated depths.

She muttered something, and tried to readjust her position yet again. He tightened his arm around her to keep her still, but she continued to wriggle, at one point her legs swinging forward.

Sampson had clearly had enough, too. He gave a little warning buck at Hallie's gymnastics, resulting in her screaming and throwing herself off the side, where she landed with a thump in the sand.

Sampson stopped, blowing and tossing his head in annoyance.

Alan counted to ten, found it didn't help, and dismounted, pulling Hallie up to her feet. His voice was tight when he asked, "What the hell is the matter with you, woman? I realize you don't like Sampson, but these antics have worn thin. You are in no danger riding with me. If you don't stop acting like a deranged person, I'll toss you over his back and you can ride like a sack of corn."

Her face was grimy, red, and embarrassed. She looked at the others who rode past, Alan having gestured them on. "It's not my fault. Your saddle hurts."

"Hurts?" He frowned, wondering how he was going to hang on to his sanity long enough to get her back to Octavia. "How does it hurt?"

She gestured toward her abdomen. "It just … hurts."

He stared at her, trying to understand what she was saying. How could one woman cause him to be so amused one moment and so annoyed the next?

"Oh, for god's sake, you're going to make me say it right out in the open, aren't you?" She buffeted him on the arm. "Women are built differently than men, OK? That bit of the saddle there, the pokey-uppy bit, presses on parts that prefer gentler handling."

He looked to the saddle horn, enlightenment dawning. "Ah. I didn't realize …" His gaze dropped to her crotch for a moment before he cleared his throat. "Just so. Very well."

"I know it's not your fault, but man alive, Alan! I'm probably chafed down there." She turned, clearly about to walk on.

He mounted and held out his hand, turning his foot toward her. "Use my foot and swing yourself up behind me."

"What? No, I can—"

"You have five seconds to decide," he said, keeping his hand and voice steady. "Either you ride behind me, or I leave you to your own devices. My camp is still a few miles away. You have no water that I can see, and no one to guide you. Three seconds."

"Gah!" she yelled, looking around her for a miracle, but just as he collected the reins, she said a very rude word and hopped a couple of times in order to get her foot onto his, clutching his arm and the back of the saddle before hauling herself up. Sampson took a side step at the unusual weight distribution, but Alan calmed him, feeling that he had endured all he was prepared to endure during the course of one single day.

"If I fall off and die, I'm going to come back and haunt you," Hallie said, wrapping both arms tight around him, her face buried into the back of his neck. "Every night. Even if you're with a woman. Or a man if you swing that way."

"I don't."

"Good."

"Eh?"

"I meant fine." She cleared her throat. "Just so you know that if I die because you insist that I can't walk to your camp, I will haunt you and make your life a living hell."

"I would expect nothing less," he answered.

There was silence for a few minutes before she said, in a much more hesitant voice, "Alan?"

"Yes?"

"I just wanted you to know … I mean, despite making me touch the horse and letting it slobber all over me … I wanted to say that I appreciate you not going all deranged warrior prince on me. I have a feeling that I may have annoyed you, which is why it's surprising that you didn't, you know, let your horse stomple me and go on your merry way. So … thank you."

"I don't make a habit of allowing my horse to trample anyone, let alone a woman," he said, warmed by her gratitude despite his annoyance.

"Still. My brother, Jack, is always telling me how annoying I can be when I get in what he calls a stubborn mood. Although he can be just as stubborn as me, but that's neither here nor there. You're not nearly so ruthless as Jack says you are."

"On the contrary, I am known for my ruthlessness," he corrected her, veering away from the subject of Octavia's new husband.

"Oh, I understand the importance of PR," she said, mystifying him.

He thought of asking her what she meant, but decided that there were only so many explanations Akbar would ask for, and instead sent up a little prayer for just a bit more patience while urging Sampson into a gallop to catch up with his men.

The usual ululating cries greeted them when they finally arrived at the camp.

"What the hell?" Hallie asked, her face having been tucked behind his head. "Are they going to attack? I thought they only did that when they attack? Don't let them scare the horse! Oh my god, we're going to die!"

"Not by my men, we aren't," he said, the urge to laugh at the outrageousness of the last half hour almost overwhelming. "Moghuls take their vocal expressions of greeting, sorrow, happiness, sadness, and assorted other emotions very seriously, and my men are no exception to that." He thought for a moment. "Although I have had to lay down a law about their habit of greeting the dawn in such a manner."

"That's the first reasonable thing you've said all day." She sounded mildly disgruntled, but at least she wasn't distraught any longer.

Men came running at their arrival, most of whom stared unabashedly at Hallie. That annoyed him, but he controlled the emotion just as he controlled the sense of frustration that he had further been delayed. "We leave immediately," he announced, swinging his leg over Sampson's neck in order to slide off the saddle, before helping Hallie down. A groom took the reins and led the horse off.

Alan eyed the lathered flanks and flecks of spittle on Sampson's muzzle, and told the groom, "Be sure to cool him down. He's worked hard today."

The groom nodded, and Alan called for water before turning Hallie toward his tent and escorting her into it.

"What are we doing here?" she asked, stopping just inside the tent to look around, suspicion on her face. "Is that a bedroom? It is! Oh my god, you're trying to seduce me, aren't you? What is *with* you? I do not want to have sex!"

"Thank you for bellowing that. You might want to repeat it a little bit louder, though, since I don't believe the people in town heard it," he said drily, gesturing when two servants entered with buckets of water, another holding some clean linens.

"Oh." She looked abashed, making an apologetic gesture. "Sorry. I get a bit shouty when I'm upset."

"You don't say." He gave her a long look.

She smiled ruefully. "All right, I deserved that. I am sorry about yelling the fact that I don't want to sleep with you. It's been a really long day. Is that water for me?"

"For us both. You may wash up first if you like. I'll take my turn in a few minutes, just as soon as I make sure that my *Nightwing* is being readied for our journey."

Hallie moved around the black lacquer screen that separated his sleeping quarters from the living space in the tent. "Your *Nightwing*? I thought the horse's name was Sampson?"

"*Nightwing* is my airship." He peeled off his goggles, turban, and armor, setting it onto a chest for his servant to clean.

"Are you going somewhere?" she asked, pausing before the water.

"We both are."

"I don't think so," she said in that outraged voice that never failed to make him annoyed. "I just got here, thank you very much."

He shrugged. He had more important things to do than to stand arguing with her if she was determined to be left behind. "It's your choice. If you wish to talk to me, you will need to be on the *Nightwing* in the next ten minutes."

"Alan?"

Her voice had him pausing at the entrance of the tent, even though he couldn't see her through the screen. "Yes?"

"Thank you again for not freaking out on me." She moved to the edge of the screen, her face red from the sun, freckles visible all over it, as well as her bare arms. She bit her lip for a moment, drawing his attention to her mouth. He wasn't normally attracted to women who were almost as tall as him, with wide mouths and a direct manner of speaking their minds, but Hallie seemed to hold a fascination that he didn't understand, and didn't particularly want.

He did not have time for a dalliance, especially not with Jack Fletcher's sister.

"My ex-husband used to tell me I was a big baby for being afraid of horses, and that the only way to stop being afraid was just to get on their back and show them who was master. It always ended up with me being stepped on, and kicked, and hurt when I fell off, and …" She waved a hand. "All sorts of horrible things. It was just bad all the way around."

He had a lot of things he would have liked to say about a man whose manner of trying to acclimatize a frightened woman was to make her more distressed, but there was no time. He simply nodded and strode out to make sure that the ship was ready, and that the men who remained behind had instructions.

By the time he'd taken care of that, the *Nightwing* strained at her mooring ropes, clearly wanting to be aloft.

He returned to his tent, automatically going around the screen, the sight of Hallie standing in front of a table bearing a bowl of water arresting him.

She'd removed her tunic, and was in the middle of washing herself, her breasts enclosed in some sort of short stays. He couldn't help but admire them for a few seconds, noting that they might not be overly large, but they looked just right to fit in his hands.

"Hey!" Hallie said, glaring. "Eyes up here, buster."

"Alan," he said automatically, but dragged his gaze off those two perfect little mounds of breasts to catch her irate expression.

"Well, Alan, you can just stop staring at my boobs. You can't tell me you haven't seen any before," she said, wringing out a cloth and spreading it to dry on the marble of the washstand. He murmured an apology while she shook out her tunic and slid it on over her head. "I take it we're ready to go?" she asked.

"Yes." He reminded himself that he was not looking for a woman, and especially not this woman, and went to the washstand, pouring out fresh water and plunging his head in it, quickly washing his face and neck before pulling off his tunic, boots, and leggings, tossing all of them onto a chair.

"I suppose I'll go with you—holy marmalade and all the little jams!" Hallie had turned to address him, her eyes wide when she caught sight of him pulling out fresh clothing. "You are starkers, sir!"

He paused in the act of pulling on leggings, looking down at himself. "If you mean I am nude, yes."

"Yes. So very. And can I just say *wow*?" Her voice took on a husky quality that thrummed within him. Although he'd managed to lose the erection her ass rubbing against him had caused, it threatened to return when her gaze crawled all over his body. To his surprise, she wasn't staring at his genitals, as most women did. Her gaze seemed to be focused on his torso and arms. "You are really buff. You almost have a six-pack."

"A pack of what?" he asked, part of him wanting to stand there and let her finish her visual examination of him, the other part wanting to lay her down in his bed and strip her unconventional clothing from her body, allowing him to stroke and taste and touch all of that smooth, freckled skin.

"Your chest. And stomach. The way the muscles ripple down to your pelvic area is called a six-pack. Can I … this is so incredibly not at all politically correct, but would you mind if I had a wee peek at your behind?"

He was back to blinking again. He thought of telling her that her attempts to arouse him weren't having any effect, but sadly, the proof of the opposite was going to be all too obvious in another few seconds. "If it pleases you, I have no objections, political or otherwise."

"Oh, thank you," she said, hurrying around to stand behind him. "Glorioski! That is one amazing behind, Alan. It's just … and that part is so lovely … I just want to put my hands right … how do you get those swoopy bits on the sides? I really … I'm sorry. You can yell at me if you like, but is it possible for me to gently, ever so gently, touch that bit right there?"

His shoulders shook with the laughter he held in. "I don't object," he managed to get out. "But I will warn you that at a later time, I will wish to reciprocate."

Hallie clearly thought about that for a few seconds before he felt her fingers on his ass. "I suppose that's only fair, although I do not have even remotely as nice a behind as you have."

Her fingers had to be made of fire, he thought. There was no other explanation for the heat that radiated out from her touch.

"Akbar, the boilers are at full capacity. We can leave whenever you are read—" Zand stopped when he came around the screen. His eyebrows rose.

Alan's shoulders shook even more.

"Er …" Zand made a little face. "What is it you're doing?"

"Me?" Hallie asked, straightening up from where she'd evidently been bent down, the better to torment his ass with her fire fingers. "Uh. Hi. Zand, is it?" She gave an embarrassed cough. "I was just ... Alan had ... er ... he had something on his behind, and I was just helping get rid of it. Nothing unsavory, mind you. Nothing that you wouldn't want to have on it. Oh, god, that sounds so awful."

Zand's eyebrows rose at her use of the word "Alan," and then moved even higher when Hallie stammered her explanation.

"She was feeling my ass," Alan explained, convinced he had somehow stepped into a farce the likes of which he'd seen on the London stage. There could be no other reason his life had suddenly become so bizarre. "She likes it."

"Does she?" Zand asked, his voice and expression now completely devoid of emotion. "I'll wait outside."

"It is a very nice behind," Hallie added, her fingers giving it one last caress before she moved around to stand next to Alan. "It's worth seeing if you haven't. Or maybe you have. Or you don't care. I don't like to presume, because I am very supportive of all types of sexualities, not just heterosexual. So if you wanted to see Alan's very nice behind, I'm sure he wouldn't mind. Would you?"

He pursed his lips, his hands fisted. He was three seconds away from just giving in to his body's demands that he throw Hallie onto the bed so he could ravish her until she couldn't talk about his ass anymore.

"I'm ... outside ..." Zand took himself off before giving in to the laughter that Alan knew was to follow, and sure enough, ten seconds later he heard Zand shouting with laughter so hard that several horses whinnied in response.

"Did I offend him, do you think?" Hallie asked, her expression thoughtful.

He pulled on his leggings and long gold tunic before wrapping a clean turban around his head. He gathered up the ornate leather and metal armor and gauntlets, not trusting himself to speak. He had a feeling if he laughed, she would be hurt.

"You're not answering. I did offend him, didn't I?" Hallie sighed. "My brother always says that my mouth will get me into trouble one of these days. You didn't mind me touching your behind, did you?"

"No." He strapped on a scabbard, placed his favorite sword in it, slipping a dagger into each of his boots. Then he took her arms in his hands, pulling her up to his chest, his lips on hers when he said, "I am very much looking forward to my turn, however. As for your brother, he was correct— your mouth is going to get you in a great deal of trouble. And I am going to enjoy every moment of it."

And then he kissed the objections he just knew she was going to make right off her lips.

He had a feeling he was greatly in over his head. The question was, did he want to surface again?

FOUR

Darkness reached across the sky with long, skeletal fingers while we flew northward. I stood on the observation deck—unlike the commercial airship in which I'd flown earlier, Alan's ship had its observation decks on the sides—and watched not only the sky grow darker and darker, but the shadows creep across the ripple of land beneath us.

"Honestly, if I'd known he was going north, I would have waited there for him," I said to myself while I watched the land slip by.

Two other crewmen were on the deck, dressed in the same gold uniform that Alan wore, complete with leather armor, turbans, and boots that went to the knee.

A third crewman joined us, standing close to me, well within the boundaries of my personal space. I edged along the railing to put a little distance between us, my mind busy with the memory of Alan standing in his tent, stark naked, flaunting his muscles and chest and arms and legs and that incredible ass at me. My fingers twitched at the memory of that ass, of the feel of it, the warm, thick muscles that gave it such lovely curves.

Then I remembered that I wasn't there looking for a sexual relationship. Alan might be tempting as hell, but it was his fighting ability that was of paramount importance to me. Without the training that Alan could offer me, I'd be lost, and would quickly find myself back on Jack and Octavia's ship, a helpless weight around their necks.

"I refuse to be that," I said softly. "Alan is just going to have to get with the program."

The crewman nearest me gave me a look, and scooted next to me.

Alan. Dear god, even now I wanted to touch him again. All of him. I slid farther down the railing, my eyes on the shadowed landscape, my mind pushing aside the problem of finding my place in this world to celebrate the glory that was naked Alan. Lord knew, the man's chest alone could drive a saint to sin, with the curling dark hair that wasn't overly abundant, but present enough to make it very clear the difference between his body and my own.

"Is there something about me that suddenly offends you?" the crewman asked, taking three steps toward me.

I stared at him in surprise, realizing it was Alan. "Oh, it's you. Boy, you guys all wear the same thing, don't you? No, there's nothing about you that offends me. Why?"

"You kept moving away from me."

He was wearing exactly the same outfit as the other men, his turban hiding his hair. His armor appeared to have a little more ornate decoration worked on it, but otherwise, he was indistinguishable from the others.

At least, he was to me.

"Have you ever heard of prosopagnosia?" I asked.

He frowned. "No. What is it?"

I shrugged, deciding that I wanted to appear in the best light, as someone who was worthy of all the things I wanted him to teach me. "It's not important. Does all your armor look like that?" I gestured toward his leather breastplate.

He looked down at, one hand touching it. "For the most part, yes. Do you have an objection to it?"

"Not in the least. It's very cool, and looks fairly comfortable. I just wondered if that design of lions and birds was something embossed on all of your armor. I take it you finally have time to talk to me?"

He was silent for a moment, his blue eyes unreadable. "You are unlike any woman I have known."

"Yeah, that's no surprise," I said with a smile. "I'm kind of unique here. Well, not totally, but mostly unique. I have a business proposition to make to you. Er …" I glanced over his shoulder at the two men who were now openly watching us.

Alan didn't even turn to look at them. He simply said a word in what must have been his native language. The two crewmen hurriedly left the observation deck.

"I didn't mean to run them off, but I really need to talk to you about what I'd like you to do for me."

"Does it involve me standing still while you torment me by touching my body parts?" he asked, leaning an elbow against the railing.

Instantly, my eyes went to his chest. I liked his armor. It looked like something I'd seen at Renaissance fairs, with lovely curved lines, lots of rivets and straps, and touches of metal at the shoulders. In the center where a long piece of leather drew a straight line from the collarbone, embossed fantastical lions and birds of prey danced along the length. "I didn't realize I was tormenting you. I did ask if you minded, and you said no."

"I didn't mind. Hallie." His voice seemed thick, as if he was choked.

"Hmm?" I dragged my eyes from his chest, wishing I'd asked him whether he minded if I stroked the lovely muscles that rippled down to his belly.

"If you keep looking at me like that, I will take you to my cabin, remove that interesting but slightly improper garment you are wearing, and take my turn touching you."

"Just because I like touching your behind—and really, you have to admit that any woman would want to once she'd seen it in all its glory—doesn't mean I want to sleep with you. Assuming that's what you were referring to with regards to your turn. Well, all right, I kind of *do* want to sleep with you, but that's because you are really handsome, and you were nice to me, and I haven't had a boyfriend in over a year now, and you know how it is. You're by yourself, so you're not getting any noogie regularly, but you have needs and urges and desires, and there's no one to scratch those itches, so you just have to either distract yourself with something else or take care of business all on your own, and although I'm not opposed to doing so on a general principle, I've always viewed that as kind of a desert-island last-case scenario sort of thing, you know? Do you?"

A number of expressions flitted across his face while I spoke. He took some time before he asked, "Do I what?"

"Take care of business." I gestured toward his groin. "Yourself, that is."

He stared at me for the count of four. "Miss Norris," he said in a lovely gravelly voice that skittered down my back, sending goose bumps along the flesh of my arms. "Did you just ask me if I indulge in onanism?"

I parsed the word, decided it meant what I thought it meant, and nodded. "It's just idle curiosity. I never know how often men do that, you see. I mean, it's not something I can ask my brother, because ew. He's my brother. I don't even like seeing him and Octavia lip-locked, other than I'm happy that they have each other. They really are madly in love, which is all sorts of sweet. I just wondered if you are hinting that you'd like to bump uglies because you were a bit needy, too."

"Bump …" He shook his head, muttering something before he said, "I would be happy to discuss my sexual needs, urges, and desires with you, but I will only do so in the confined space of my cabin, and then one or both of us will be naked."

"Oh." I made a face. "That's kind of disappointing, but I wouldn't want to make you uncomfortable with sexual talk. I know people here get all up in arms about that sort of thing."

He looked heavenward for a moment, and I had a sense that he was praying for something. Probably patience, since that's what Jack always said he needed around me. "Would you care to go to my cabin right now to discuss the matter?"

"Not really. Like I said, I'm all"—I lifted my hands and wiggled all ten fingers at him—"needy and such, but I really am not looking for a lover. I need a teacher. A trainer, really, and that's where you come in."

"You wish for me to teach you how to be a badass," he said, nodding. "Would you care to explain your definition of that last term?"

"I want to learn how to fight like you do. Everyone says you're the best," I said, feeling a little pandering to his ego wasn't out of place. "I want to be able to fight alongside my brother's crew."

"Why?" he asked. "Does your brother not have enough men to fight that he must conscript women?"

"Oh, you do not want to go down the sexist route," I told him, giving him a potent look. "Because that crap won't fly."

"I wasn't aware that crap could—"

"Women can do everything a man can do, except peeing while standing up, and we can do that if we have one of those little cup things with spouts that ladies use when camping. Plus we can have babies."

He opened and closed his mouth a couple of times, then made me a little bow. "The point goes to you, I believe."

"The answer to your question is that, yes, my brother and his wife have people to fight. But I don't have anything to do. Do you know how frustrating it is to see everyone else with a job, but no one will let you do anything?"

"Most women are content to find employment in areas other than that of combat," he said.

"I am not most women."

"I am coming to see that," he said with a little twitch of his lips beneath the thick black mustache that was much softer than it looked. I spent a moment reliving the kiss he'd given me before we got on the airship, and felt unusually warm.

"If I could learn to fight, then I'd have a use." I gave him a long look. "I don't like being extraneous, Alan. My proposition is that you teach me to fight like you, and in return,

I'll give you the money I have. I can pay you in installments as we go along, if you like. But I'd like to learn three main things: how to fight with a sword, how to shoot the disruptors, and how to use daggers effectively."

He was silent for an uncomfortably long amount of time, prompting me to ask, "Did I shock you? Do you not have any women in your company who fight? My brother's crew has two women, including his wife, and she's deadly with a gun. Er … disruptor. They both fight whenever they are attacked by the Black Hand or the Mog—" I stopped, suddenly remembering to whom I was speaking.

Alan didn't seem to notice my almost slip, however. "I am not shocked, and I count amongst my acquaintance women who have been known to pick up a sword, but that is not what gives me pause."

"What does?" I asked, heartened despite the serious look on his face.

"Does your brother know your intentions in asking for my assistance?"

I pursed my lips, thinking back to the note I'd left. "Yes. That is, I left a note."

"Ah. You do not, then, have permission to be here?"

"I'm not a child," I snapped, irritation riding me at the insinuation that I needed permission to do anything. "I'm thirty-three. I don't need to consult with anyone on decisions I make about my own future."

"You most definitely are not a child," he said, his gaze dropping to my chest for a moment. I felt a flush sweep upward from my breasts. "But I, too, have sisters, and I would not like to know that one of them went to your brother to ask for instruction without my knowledge or approval."

"Then I'm very sorry for your sisters," I said, lifting my chin to look down my nose at him. Which was basically impossible since he was taller than me. "I can assure you that I neither need nor seek my brother's permission. Are you going to teach me, or do I need to find someone else? My brother said that Etienne guy with the Black Hand isn't a fighter, but I bet he could point me to someone who is."

A muscle jumped in his jaw. After another few seconds being silent, he said, "I would be willing to teach you how to defend yourself if your brother gives his approval."

"Dammit, stop being such a stick-in-the-mud!" I yelled, then realized it wasn't going to do any good. "I'm sorry," I apologized, aware of the narrowing of his pretty blue eyes. "It's wrong of me to blame you for the society norms you were raised with, but put yourself in my shoes for a moment, Alan."

"I understand that you wish to have an occupation—"

"No," I interrupted, and moved closer to him, so close that my toes touched his. I put my hand on the part of his arm that wasn't covered in leather armor. "Imagine you are a woman. You have no skills, no talents, are trained for nothing of any use in this world. Everything you worked for in the past is gone."

"How—"

"It doesn't matter, just imagine it." I waited until he nodded. "You are an adult. You've lived on your own for more than fifteen years. You've been married, divorced, seen relationships come and go. You are a responsible, reasonably intelligent woman, and some man, a man who has had opportunities never given to you, tells you that he will not share some of his knowledge with you unless you get permission from someone else, another man who has also had opportunities denied to you. Now, how do you feel?"

His eyes seemed to see deep into me, straight through to my soul. "I would be frustrated."

"Bingo." I smiled.

"Your objection is against society, however, and not the individual from whom you seek training."

"Argh!" I yelled, slapping both hands on his armor.

"You will write to your brother to tell him where you are. If he poses no objection to you being in my company …" The muscle in his jaw worked a couple of times. "Then I will train you."

Protest after protest rose, but I kept them behind my teeth. He was right in that I couldn't change societal norms simply because I didn't like them. I would just have to give in to the absurd notion that my brother had a say in my life ... and immediately pushed down the uncomfortable notion that Jack would never agree to letting Alan teach me.

I'd cross that bridge when I came to it. "As it happens, I don't have to write to Jack. He should be at El Kef. At least, that's where they were going, and I believe the plan was to spend the night somewhere near there before moving on."

"Indeed." His eyes turned speculative.

"If you were thinking about attacking my brother's ship," I said, buffing a fingernail, "you should be aware that they have some pretty big guns. They picked them up in Cairo. They're some sort of superpowerful guns that are the latest in aether technology."

He pursed his lips, which just made me look at his mouth, thinking about that kiss, and how soft his mustache was, and whether I wanted to be so hasty in my no-sex policy. Once I got the agreement from him to teach me, perhaps then I could indulge in a little dalliance. "Thank you for the warning. I will keep that in mind."

"Plus they don't have any valuable cargo," I said hastily, feeling I'd better toss that out in case he thought I was exaggerating the firepower of the *Enterprise*. "They dropped that off at Annaba. Can we start now?"

"Start ... training?" He looked startled, but recovered quickly. "You have not yet spoken to your brother."

"No, but come on. It's going to take, what, another four hours to get to El Kef? Once we're there, I'll find Jack and talk to him, but what were you planning on doing until then?"

His eyes seemed to go liquid. "I thought we might go to my cabin and resume the discussion of sexual needs and desires."

I thought about it. I really thought about it. I eyed the width of his shoulders (impressive), the strength of his neck going down to that chest (drool-worthy), and on down to the legs that were even now braced apart so as to move with the ship (his thighs were a work of art). "Would you be offended if I said I'd rather have you start the training instead?"

He laughed, actually tipped his head back and laughed a long, hearty laugh, one that was filled with so much humor that it made me smile.

"My male pride is wounded, yes," he finally said, wiping the corners of his eyes, "but I believe I will survive. Very well, we will have an introductory lesson, but if your brother does not agree to your plan, that will be the only one."

"Deal," I said, and followed him when he gestured. He didn't take me to the hold, as I expected, but to one of the rooms in the crew quarters.

I hesitated at the doorway of the cabin when he strode in and looked around, his hands on his hips, before he said, "Ah," following which he glanced at me. "Come in, come in."

"We're going to train in here?" I asked, reluctantly entering the small cabin.

"No." His gaze raked my body. "You can't fight in that bit of nothing."

I brushed a hand down my silk and linen tunic. "This is a very nice outfit. I had several made based on the original. It's flattering, and easy to wear, and yes, it gets wrinkled a lot, but nothing that a little steam can't take care of."

"I have no complaints about the aesthetics of it," he said with what was very close to a leer, "but the practicality of it is another matter. Let's see what Leila left."

"Leila?" I felt annoyed just hearing the name. I had absolutely no doubt that a man as handsome as he was, one with such a fabulous butt, and who came damn close to steaming out my tunic wrinkles with just one kiss, had any number of castoffs left by old girlfriends. "One of your harem?"

He knelt down before a wood and leather chest, digging through the contents, pausing to slide me a speculative look. "What do you know of my harem?"

My eyes widened. I had been joking, but to have him confirm it left me feeling prickly and itchy. And spoiling for a fight. "The only thing I know is that I'll never be one of them, your insanely gorgeous behind aside. I don't really want to wear clothing left by one of your no-doubt countless lovers."

"That's a shame, because I think this might very well suit you," he said, pulling out a leather breastplate, one clearly meant for a woman. He eyed me again, then gestured toward his chest with both hands. "Although I think she had bigger … er …"

I crossed my arms, just daring him to make a comment about my breasts. "My breasts are not lacking, if that's what you're about to imply."

"I wasn't. I happen to prefer women who fit nicely into my hands than those who overflow."

I seethed at him, positively seethed as he laid a couple of long gauntlets on the bunk, digging around until he pulled out a scabbard and a narrow box.

"My breasts are not a subject of jokes," I said stiffly, wanting to both yell and cry. I hated it when I was emotional like this, and wondered if I was hormonal.

He cocked an eyebrow at me. "Take them that seriously, do you?"

"Considering I had one removed due to a cancer scare, yes, I do." The words were out before I realized it. I rubbed my arms, looking away from him, asking myself what the hell I was doing telling him something so personal. It was a fact that only a few people knew.

I felt his gaze on me. "I meant no insult," he finally said, and I looked back expecting to see … I don't know what. False sympathy? A glint of humor? What I saw instead was earnest regard. "Although I am confused. When I saw you in my tent, you appeared to possess both … er … attributes."

"One was surgically reconstructed. It's quite common where I come from. They even managed to save my nipple, which was nice." I shook my head at myself. "I don't know why I'm telling you. The only person here who knows is my brother."

He was silent for another moment, then rose to his feet. "I see I was wrong about you."

I stopped mentally yelling at myself, and frowned. "About what? That my breasts are worthy of your hands? Because let me tell you—"

"I was wrong in thinking you did not have it within you to fight. You have already fought and won a most valiant battle."

A sudden moment of epiphany struck me. "You know someone who has cancer."

"Had. My mother. It affected her elsewhere, but she, too, fought well." His gaze dropped to the narrow wooden box he held.

I moved before I realized what I was doing, putting my hand on his. "I'm sorry. My mother died of breast cancer when Jack and I were very young, so I know what it's like."

He handed me the armor. "Leila is my sister. These belong to her, but I don't think she would mind you using them while you train."

"Oh. Thank you."

"There is clothing in the chest, as well. I suggest you utilize it lest you ruin what you are wearing. When you are ready, I will be in the forward hold."

He left without saying anything more, leaving me feeling oddly deflated.

"You are not looking for a man. Just concentrate on what's important, and stop thinking about his butt. And chest. And holy horticulture, his mouth," I reminded myself while I took off my tunic and pants, sorting through the unfamiliar clothes bundled at the bottom until I found a pair of tight-fitting gold leggings, the material soft and slightly clingy when I pulled them on. Leila must be a little bit shorter than me, but I figured that Alan would just have to cope with seeing a bit of ankle. The tunic was a shorter version than the one the men wore, this one falling to midthigh.

There were also a couple of what looked like floor-length tunic-dresses, but those I ignored, pulling out an item wadded up into the bottom. There was a small red pillbox hat, the sort I mentally connected with Jacqueline Kennedy, but attached to it was a long swath of white material. I realized that it was very similar to the turbans that the male Moghuls wore, and promptly plopped it onto my head, wrapping the white cloth around in a fashion that I hoped emulated their headwear.

I found Alan standing in the hold, which was mostly empty, although he stood talking to Zand next to three dirty bales of hay that were stacked on top of one another. They stopped talking when they saw me, Zand blinking at me for a moment before he pulled the tail of his turban across his mouth. He made me a little bow, but before I could say anything, he hustled out of the hold.

Alan watched me with an indescribable expression. "What … uh … what have you done with the lay?"

"The what, now?"

"The scarf women wear instead of the turban," he said, staring at my head. "It is called a lay."

"Oh. I have a Muslim friend who said hers was called a shayla, but she didn't wear it on top of her head. Is this not right? I tried to make mine look like yours."

"It's not meant to duplicate a turban."

"Wait a minute," I said, stopping him when he untangled the cloth from the top of my head and was about to fix it. "Women in the Moghul culture don't cover their faces, do they? Because while I respect everyone's right to do what they like with their body, I am not of that mind-set."

"You surprise me," he said in obvious amusement. "No, our women do not feel the need to hide themselves from view. The lay is used by women just as men use the turban: as protection in environments where it's desirable to keep sand out of our noses and mouths. It goes around your face like this, with a tail that hangs down your shoulder, which you may pull across your face and tuck in when desired. My sister likes it because she says she has to wash her hair less often, but she doesn't wear it often now."

He did a little draping of the soft cloth, then stepped back and eyed the armor.

I ran a hand down the leather of it, doing a turn for him. "Does it look OK?"

"I am more concerned about the fit," he murmured, tightening the straps on the sides. "I was wrong about the … er … front. It seems to sit well there."

"That's because I took a pair of her leggings and stuffed it there to fill it out. And provide padding," I said, wiggling to adjust myself to the tightness of the leather. Like Alan's, this one was ornately made, with a long inverted-triangular piece that ran from the breastbone to the bottom of the armor, but unlike his, which had three rings of leather that cascaded down his pectorals, this one had one ring, which ended at the under-breast mark. The rest of the armor, going down to the waist, was made up of leather scales, reminding me of dragon armor I'd seen at the local science fiction conventions. The gauntlets also had scales, and ran from wrist to elbow. "It's very pretty. I hope your sister won't mind me wearing it."

He said nothing, just moved over to pull out the scabbard I'd seen him with earlier, handing it to me. I buckled it around my waist, beneath the bottom of the armor. "This is a falchion. Have you seen one before?"

"Yes, Mr. Ho, the assistant steward on my brother's airship, has one. I asked her to teach me to use it, but she was always too busy. Hers was much plainer than this, though."

He held out a short sword that was straight until the very point, where it had a curve to the tip. Birds were inscribed down the length of the blade, and it bore the same birds on a black-and-gold crosspiece. It looked deadly as hell, and my hands positively itched to hold it.

"This is the cross guard," he said, pointing to the crosspiece. "Also known as a quillon. The blade only has one edge to it. That's so that you can use the dulled side in order to block attacks. This sword is particularly good for hacking, less so for stabbing."

"It's pretty," I said, doing a little anticipatory dance. "Can I hold it?"

"Not just yet. I'm going to show you a few basic attacks. These bales of hay will serve as your target."

"Come on, Alan, let me hold the pretty sword," I said, following him to the hay bales. "I promise I won't gut you with it. Or geld you."

He shot me a startled look.

My smile included a whole lot of teeth.

"A sword is not a toy. This is a weapon, a weapon that can take a life easily. You need to respect the power it can wield," he said in a lecturing tone that Jack so frequently used with me. He went on like that for a few more minutes, showing me a few basic moves on the hay before handing it over to me.

"Right," I said, saluting him with the sword in the best Errol Flynn fashion.

"No, not right! Hallie—" He looked exasperated, taking it from me. "I just finished telling you that it was not a toy. Do not raise it to your head unless you are parrying a blow. You could have injured yourself by treating it in such a frivolous manner."

"I'm sorry," I said, trying to appear contrite. "Can I have my pretty sword back, please?"

He made mean eyes at me. "Do you promise to treat it with the respect due a weapon that could easily maim or kill you?"

I made an X over my heart. "Cross my heart. Please, Alan. I swear I will be absolutely serious and careful."

"Very well." Grudgingly, he handed it back to me. I eyed the hay bale, and tried to duplicate the slashing motions he had shown me, using my body to add power to the swings.

"If you attacked me like that, I'd have your arm off in five seconds," Alan told me. "You're not slashing at a tree branch—you're trying to disable someone intent on harming you. Try it again, and remember to remain balanced. If you lunge forward, you leave yourself open to disemboweling."

"Urgh. OK. No disemboweling lunge, keep non-sword-arm out of the range of attacker, and slash and twist, not twist and drag down," I said, trying to remember just how Alan had showed me to use the sword to sever a muscle in the attacker's upper arm.

Two hours later, Zand returned to find me flat out on the floor, my arm over my head as I struggled to breathe. I was a blob of sweat, exhaustion, and aching muscles, while above me, Alan paced, his voice going on and on. "—and if you ever try that spinning move again, I will not only take the falchion away from you for good; I will also tie you to a horse and deliver you to your brother with a sign pinned to your back warning that you are a danger to yourself. What is it?"

I moved my arm to see whom he was talking to, lifting a wan hand to wave at Zand. "Alan is pissed," I explained to Zand when he looked from me to Alan.

"So I see," he said, studying his friend. I could swear his lips started to make a smile, but evidently Zand had excellent self-control. "We're about to arrive," he told Alan.

"Good." The two men exchanged glances that looked to me to be pretty fraught with meaning, but as I painfully got myself to my feet, I couldn't interpret just what that meaning was.

I followed when they climbed the spiral metal staircase that all airships used to get between floors, sheathing my sword and hoping Alan wouldn't demand I give it back because I was fairly inept with it. I had a horrible suspicion he was about to do just that when he turned toward me. I forestalled him by saying brightly, "Are we landing? I'll go watch on the observation deck," and then scurrying off to do so.

I breathed a sigh of relief when he didn't object, and remained on the deck, watching as the airship descended toward a medium-sized town. The moon was high enough to glow dimly on the white stone buildings that were scattered around crooked streets in what seemed to be a haphazard manner. There was one large central square that I barely caught a glimpse of before the airship descended too low to see into it.

"And that's my cue," I told myself, straightening my borrowed clothing, shifting my leather breastplate so that it was a bit more comfortable, and putting one hand on the hilt of my sword.

FIVE

I trotted down the stairs to the cargo area, finding most of the crew gathered at the great doors that opened to allow cargo in and out of the hold. I searched through the men, looking for Alan by examining the decorations on all the armor.

Two men who were speaking in a language I didn't understand paused when I passed by before one of them said in English, "I hope you don't intend on doing what I think you intend on doing."

I turned back, my gaze first on the man's armor, moving up to meet a pair of frowning blue eyes shadowed by a turban. "Oh, there you are. Of course I don't intend to join you fighting, assuming there is fighting, and given the few seconds I saw of the main square, I'd say there was."

"There is fighting," Zand said, his voice recognizable despite it being slightly muffled by the cloth over his lower face. "The Black Hand is here."

All the men gathered had the tails of their respective turbans tucked across their faces, as well. I gathered this was the style de rigueur for combat, or other stealthy actions. "I've only had a few hours' worth of lessons. I'm not a complete idiot, Alan."

He looked momentarily surprised, then gave me a sharp nod. "I'm glad to hear you realize your limitations."

"I do have to find my brother if he's still in town, but I can wait until you guys cream the revolutionaries."

"Cream?" Zand asked, his eyes smiling.

"Beat to a pulp. Pound into the sand. Wipe all over the ground," I explained.

"You're that sure of us?" he asked, glancing at Alan.

"Of course. You guys are the baddest of the bad. Why else would I ask Alan to train me?"

Alan gave what nearly amounted to a roll of his eyes, taking my arm when the big double doors were opened, and a couple of ramps slid into place. Beyond the doors, darkness lay. We had moored just at the end of the town. "Hallie, I wish to speak to you briefly."

"If you're going to lecture me about staying out of trouble—"

"I don't lecture. I give orders."

"Oh, I *really* do not like orders," I warned, prying his fingers off my arm. "That said, I have no intention of doing anything reckless. I'll wait a bit before I go look for Jack."

He tried to pull me aside, but I resisted, getting annoyed. I realized he didn't trust me to not behave in a manner that would leave me open to being hurt, but the sooner he understood that I wasn't a fool, the happier we'd both be. "Will you stop fighting me?" he snarled when he grabbed me and tried to push me against the wall.

"I will if you stop treating me like I'm a brainless child!" I snapped back.

"That's because you're acting brainless. I'm trying to move you out of the way, woman!"

"Out of the way of what?" I asked, rubbing my arm when he pushed me back.

"Horses," he said, turning so that he stood directly in front of me. I was aware then that the dull rumbling sound I had heard was coming from inside the airship. From the aft hold, the doors suddenly were thrown open, and a screaming white horse charged through, all flashing black hooves, two men holding his bridle while he more or less dragged them forward.

I pressed myself against the wall, thankful for Alan in front of me, although just as the horse was passing by us, his mouth frothing, eyes rolling, and hooves kicking at someone who got too close, Alan did the stupidest thing I've ever seen.

He marched forward to the insane, killer beast, and punched it on the shoulder, saying, "That's enough."

The horse reared up. I watched in horror, sure that Alan was about to be slaughtered before my eyes, but to my amazement, he simply snatched the horse's bridle perilously close to teeth that I knew could take off his hand, and pulled the horse's head down to waist level. "Stop this. You're scaring Hallie. She doesn't understand you like to put on a show."

I squeaked something that was meant to be, "Holy shit, Alan. Holy everlasting shit."

"She's going to think you're mad when you're just full of valor," Alan said to the horse, still holding his head down, but now stroking the beast's neck with one hand.

"Oh, I know he's mad, but not as batshit crazy as you are," I managed to say. "Alan, he's vicious."

"No, he's not. He's just high-spirited." Amazingly, the horse seemed to calm under his influence, at least enough that the two men still holding on to him managed to lead him down the ramp and onto the ground without anyone losing life or limb.

Alan returned to me, watching as three other horses were led past us—all of them calm in comparison with the white devil—before saying, "I want you to stay here to guard the *Nightwing*."

"Wow, that wasn't quite what I was expecting you were going to say," I said, surprised despite seeing through his ploy. "Although I will point out that I know full well you're doing that just so I'll stay here where it's safe."

He said nothing, just tugged me after him when he walked down the ramp, thankfully stopping us a little distance from the horses. "The only place you would be safe, as you put it, would be locked into my cabin, with four guards on the outside of the door." His eyes seemed to burn into mine with a blue fevered light that left me shivering. "Understand this—I value the *Nightwing* very highly indeed, but with the Black Hand's presence, I have to take as many men with me as possible. I can only leave two men to guard her, so despite your belief that I'm trying to keep you out of trouble, I do need your help protecting my airship."

"Oh," I said, squaring my shoulders a little, trying to exude confidence and reliability. "I appreciate that, Alan. But I have to find Jack—"

"I will help you find your brother, never fear of that," he said grimly, turning and raising a hand when Zand, already mounted, called something to him. For a moment, his eyes were filled with an emotion that made me very aware that he was a man, and I was a woman. One gloved hand brushed a strand of hair from my cheek. "Do not engage anyone. Call the guards if you see anything untoward. And do not, under any circumstance—"

"Try that spinning move, I know." I bit my bottom lip for a moment, glanced over his shoulder at the men who were waiting for him, then grabbed his armor and pulled him to me, kissing him with a sudden rush of emotion. "And you take care of yourself, too."

His lips smiled against mine. "I thought you weren't looking for a lover?"

"I'm not." I let go of his armor, the heat of his lips still burning mine. "I just don't want to go to the trouble of having to find someone else and convince them to teach me how to fight."

He tucked the tail of his turban across his face, but I could tell by the way the lines around his eyes crinkled that he was smiling. "Stay safe, woman."

I saluted, watching with no little admiration the way he strode to the horses, punching the white demon on the shoulder again when the horse lifted a back leg in warning. Then he was gone, the three other mounted men followed by a dozen more who trotted after them on foot, all of them armed to the teeth.

"Hoo, does he know how to kiss," I said aloud, then became aware that one of the two guards was standing on the other side of the open hold doors. I smiled and, with my hand on my sword, began to patrol the perimeter.

I was under no delusion that despite Alan's pretty words, he had come up with this guard job as a way to keep me out of action, but since I knew full well my nascent fighting skills stood no chance against anyone who'd had more than a couple of hours at stacked hay bales, I didn't protest.

"One day, though," I promised myself, "I'll be going out with the rest of them, filled to the rim with badassery."

Just as I was making my fourth circuit of the airship, I caught sight of a familiar dark shape gliding overhead, the moonlight glinting off the painted silver compass that marked the forward envelope of the *Enterprise*.

"Jack!" I said softly, watching the ship descend on the far side of the town. "Oh, thank god, the cavalry has arrived."

I hurried over to the guard who stood in front of the open hold, a long aether-fueled rifle in his hands, two swords crossed over his back. "I know Alan said I was to stay here and help guard the ship, but it looks pretty quiet here, and it's super important that I talk to my brother. That's him, there," I told the man, gesturing toward where the *Enterprise* had disappeared over the domed tops of the mud and stone buildings. "I'm just going to go talk to him really quickly. Then I'll be back to help guard again."

The man stared, clearly not understanding me.

"If Alan comes back before I return, tell him I'm not being irresponsible, but I have to talk to my brother. To Jack. OK?"

The man frowned.

"Oy. Never mind. I'll just make sure this is quick."

I dashed off, skirting the edges of town, knowing the action—assuming there was some, and with the Black Hand present, I couldn't imagine how there weren't some shenanigans going down—would be sparse to nonexistent on the outskirts. My heart beat wildly at the thought that someday—when I'd had training—it would be me in the middle of the skirmish.

The moon was higher now, giving me enough light to see the crooked streets and dim shapes of buildings, but not a whole lot else. I followed first one street, then another, twisting and turning, but trying to keep myself pointed in the direction of the *Enterprise*. In the distance, sounds of fighting were audible: shrieks, screams, and shouts in languages I didn't understand, a couple of small explosions, the dull splatting noise that indicated someone was firing disruptors, and the general cacophony of noises that accompanied bodies struggling with other bodies.

To my irritation, I turned a corner, trying to align myself by the moon, and saw two people standing ahead of me, right at the edge of the central square.

"Dammit," I swore softly to myself, and flattened against the shadowed wall of a building when a third person joined the other two. They were nothing more than silhouettes, but since I had no idea of who they were, I skulked down the side of the building, ducking behind a stone oven when two of them separated. I caught just the barest snatch of conversation. "—we can't with the Moghuls. The prince himself is here, Etienne. He's already taken three prisoners."

Etienne? I peered around the round stone oven and looked at the tall, wiry man who remained in shadow. The leader of the Black Hand was there, right in front of me?

Glorious visions of me hauling an unconscious Etienne into the middle of the square blossomed to life in my brain, the look of admiration that would surely be plastered all over Alan's face warming me to my toes. I might be unlearned in the ways of the warrior—or rogue, since I really wanted to acquire a pair of daggers—but by god, I would show him what I was made of! I pulled around the bit of the lay that hung down my back, hiding my lower face like Alan and his men.

"Just do it," the man named Etienne snarled, and the two others made jerky bows, then hurried off to the right, disappearing into the shadows.

I couldn't see anything of the open space beyond Etienne, the bulge of a large square building blocking my view, but I crept forward, keeping to the shadows, and peering around every few feet to make sure no one was coming.

I was almost on Etienne, my sword reversed in my hand so that I could brain him with the hilt, when he spun around and lunged at me, knocking me backward onto the soft sand. He swore in French, his hands going around my neck, tightening painfully so that instantly black blotches crawled across my vision.

"Argh," I tried to yell, but the word came out garbled and strangled. Literally. Self-preservation was strong in me, however, and I brought my knee up as hard as I could right into Etienne's crotch. He swore profanely, releasing my neck for a moment while he clutched himself. I rolled off him, intending on running like hell to the nearest friendly person, preferably one who was armed to the teeth, but Etienne kicked out, knocking my foot out from under me. I fell forward, pain burning across my scalp when he snatched the lay from my head, twisting the long scarf between his hands like a garrote.

I lay in a beam of moonlight, causing Etienne to pause for a moment when he realized I was a woman; then he spat out, "Moghul bitch," before lunging at me with the garrote. I didn't even think about it—I rolled away and spun around, punching him as hard as I could in the face. I doubt if that would have stopped him but for one thing—I was still holding my sword. The metal hilt slammed into his face as I punched, causing his head to snap back, a cracking noise following that indicated some bone had broken.

I snatched up my lay, and was off before he could do more than grab blindly for me. I ran to the left, praying I could circle around the square without entering it, but luck was against me, and after two turns, I found myself bursting out into a scene that looked like something Hollywood would be proud of. The square clearly did double duty as a marketplace, with wooden carts and little stands shrouded in long curtains clinging to the edges. In the center squatted a well, around which at least forty people were engaged in combat. I could see frightened faces in the glassless windows of the buildings that formed the perimeter, the occupants of the town clearly favoring the wisdom of staying inside rather than joining the fray that had erupted around them.

Smoke rose beyond the rooftops, probably from one of the explosions I'd heard, but I didn't see signs that anyone here was using disruptors—judging by the madness of bodies fighting, twisting, being thrown, leaping, and flinging themselves willy-nilly, it was likely deemed too hazardous to fire in those conditions, at least not without harming people with friendly fire.

I caught sight of a familiar head of red hair, and ran toward it, wrapping my slightly torn lay around my head. Octavia was in the process of leaping onto a cart, a tall man at her side, giving her a hand up.

"Jack!" I yelled, trying to make myself be heard over the noise of all the screaming and shouting. "Octavia!"

A man bearing the Black Hand logo on his chest spun around at my words and, with a snarl, headed for me, a wicked-looking curved sword in his hand, one that dripped red.

"ALAN!" I screamed at the top of my lungs, throwing myself behind a small donkey cart that was parked outside a house, quickly scrambling underneath it when the revolutionary tried to follow me. "ALAN, WHERE ARE YOU?"

A cry lifted in the air, the same one that the Moghuls had made when Alan rode into the camp, quickly picked up by others, but I didn't have time to stop and see if Alan had heard me. I crawled out from the donkey cart, kicking when my attacker grabbed at my leg, getting to my feet, and bolting to where I'd seen Octavia.

I'd just reached the fruit cart she had climbed, when someone slammed me from behind, throwing me forward into the cart. I dropped my sword, having forgotten I was holding it, the breath knocked out of me.

I was spun around, a man's furious face blotting out everything else as he lifted a sword, clearly about to skewer me. "Jack!" I gasped, and snatched up my sword to block his attack. He paused a second, his eyes narrowing. "Hallie?"

"Yes, it's me." I pulled down the bit of lay that clung to my mouth and nose. "Holy cheese, Jack, you almost killed me. Duck!"

The man who had chased me loomed up behind him, but Jack wasn't trained by the army in all sorts of covert fighting techniques for nothing. He spun around, slashing as he did so.

The man fell with a gurgle, thankfully facedown.

"What the hell are you doing here?" Jack demanded, grabbing me by the arm. Beyond him, a wave of men in gold was moving toward us. I had a feeling Alan was trying to get to me, but I had no way to tell him that the man with me was my brother, and that the Company of Thieves were no threat to me. "Why are you dressed like one of those damned Moghuls? Dammit, you really did find him?"

Octavia appeared behind me, saying in a rush, "Hallie? Is that you?"

"Ala—Prince Akbar is training me. He's agreed to teach me, and he's very nice, really. Surprisingly so, given his reputation—" I flinched when, on the perimeter of the town, an explosion lit up the night sky, leaving dirt and stone to rain down around us.

"Jack, Etienne is bombing the town," Octavia said, gesturing toward him. "We have to get back to the ship. All of us," she added with a glance toward me.

"Are you insane?" Jack asked me, ignoring her. "Why would you go to our enemy—"

Just then a couple of Black Hand members rushed toward us. Both Jack and Octavia moved in front of me, their swords flashing in the moonlight. To my right, three men in gold fought their way through another wave of revolutionaries.

"Hallie!" one of them demanded, gesturing for me, obviously Alan.

"I have to go," I told Jack when he dropped one of the Black Hand men before turning to help Octavia.

"What? Hallie, no!"

I grabbed Jack by his arm. "I know you won't understand, but I have to do this, Jack. I feel in my bones that this is the way my life is supposed to go. Prince Akbar isn't the bad guy you think he is. He's been very nice to me, and he says he'll teach me to fight if you say it's OK, which is something that infuriates me, but ... oh, I don't have time to go into it. I just don't want you to worry about me, OK?"

"No, it's not OK. Wait, he's being *nice* to you? Why is he being nice—" Jack started to say, but Octavia took him by the other arm, saying, "Jack, we must leave."

"I can't abandon my sister," Jack growled.

"You're not abandoning me. I have Prince Akbar to protect me until I can do it myself," I told Jack, giving him a swift kiss on the cheek. "I've made my choice, brother."

Before he could protest any further, I ran to where the man I assumed was Alan fought with one of the revolutionaries, knocking a disruptor out of the man's hand before slamming the hilt of his sword down on the man's head. I leaped over his slumped form, taking the hand Alan offered me, wanting badly to pull out my own sword and join him, but knowing that I would be more of a hindrance.

"Take your damned hands off her," Jack roared, starting toward us.

"Jack, no," Octavia cried, both hands on his arm, trying to pull him back.

"I love you both," I called to them. "And thank you for giving me permission for Prince Akbar to train me!"

"We have to leave," Alan told me, not sparing a glance toward Jack, who was sputtering indignantly over the lie I'd just yelled, but he couldn't do more since Octavia was hauling him backward. Alan called to his men, hustling me in the opposite direction. "Etienne is opening fire on the town."

"Are you insane?" I heard Jack ask Octavia when she pulled him back. "That's Akbar! He's brainwashed my sister into thinking he's nice!"

"She'll be safe with him, I promise you," Octavia said, her voice drowned out at a horrible chucking sound. One of the buildings on the square exploded with a force that threw us all backward.

Alan dragged me to my feet, pulling me after him as he ran to the west, away from the square, calling orders as he did so. Ahead of us, one of the men who was holding the horses ran into view, the great white beast rearing and snorting viciously.

"You don't think—" I started to say, but Alan didn't wait for me to finish. He simply picked me up and threw me across the saddle, quickly mounting behind me.

I screamed and would have struggled, but decided that would mean certain death not only for me, but for Alan when the revolutionaries bombed him while he was trying to scrape me off his horse's hooves. Instead, I clutched his leg with both hands, praying I wouldn't vomit or fall off.

Lights from torches flashed past us as we barreled up the ramp and into the *Nightwing*'s hold, the horse skidding to a halt.

"We leave now!" Alan bellowed before switching into his native language of Kazakh.

Hands grabbed my waist, pulling me off the horse. I weaved a little with all the blood that had rushed to my head, but Alan was there, one arm around me as he more or less dragged me up spiral stairs to the upper decks.

"Charge the guns!" he yelled once we reached the main deck, releasing me before dashing up one more flight to the gun deck. "Fire at will!"

I'd been in a couple of air skirmishes during my time with Jack and Octavia, so I was familiar with how their crew acted when prepping the ship for battle, but it was nothing like Alan's men. They moved quickly, the aether cannons being primed and charged in less time than it took for Jack's crew to decide which cannon would be fired first. It was a ballet, a grim ballet to be sure, but one that I had to admire. The roar of the boilers indicated that they had been ready to pump maximum steam into the envelopes and propellers, and I clutched a nearby metal girder when the ship lifted off at a sharp angle. Crewmen ran past and around me, no one the least bit panicked, but every man intent on his job at hand.

I waited until the ship righted itself, then raced up the steps to what I assumed was the captain's observation deck, the one used for battle.

Alan paced the length of it, holding a pair of binoculars to his eyes as we circled around to put ourselves in a better position to open fire. He glanced briefly at me when I emerged onto the narrow metal deck, clutching the railing when we lurched to the side, making a sharp turn to the south before swinging east. "I would prefer you go to the safety of my cabin, woman."

"Yeah, well, that's not going to happen. Why is Etienne trying to destroy the town?"

"He's not. He's trying to destroy me."

"By shooting up the town? That's ridiculous," I said, horrified as I watched another explosion strike the square, this one sending bits of wood spinning into the night sky. "He's killing innocent townspeople! For the love of Pete, his own people are down there!"

"He doesn't care who he murders so long as he thinks he can kill me," Alan replied. His voice was rough, almost hoarse, and filled with what I thought was impotent fury. He muttered something, then turned and strode back into the airship.

I trotted after him, the adrenaline of the scene in the square leaving me itching to do something, anything. He went down to the deck with the cannons, the bulk of the men there, pumping air into the long iron cannons that had been rolled out through open portholes.

"Are they in sight?" Alan demanded, striding down the gangway, his haste making me run to keep up with him.

"Why aren't we firing?"

"Not yet," Zand said, leaning out of one of the unoccupied portholes, binoculars to his eyes. "Another five degrees and we should have them."

Alan turned to say something, but I was right behind him. "I thought I told you to go to my cabin," he growled at me.

"I am not a delicate little flower who has to be protected," I snapped.

He narrowed his eyes at my neck, which I suspected showed signs of where Etienne had tried to strangle me.

"All right, I need some protection, but only until I learn how to fight better. I want to help, Alan! Let me help with the cannons."

"Do you know how to prime them? How to set the inclination and range? How to clean the tube so the aether doesn't explode in the barrel?"

"No, but I'm a fast learner," I said, then added softly, so that only he could hear, "Please, Alan. This is important to me. I can help, I swear I can."

He snarled something and grabbed my wrist, hauling me down the gangway until he stopped at the last gun, shoving me at the man who paused in the middle of turning a handle at an open panel on the side of the cannon. "Show her how to prime the gun, Az."

The man straightened up. He must have been over seven feet tall, as big as a brick building, and probably half as yielding.

The man pursed his lips for a moment, then shrugged, and handed me a Z-shaped piece of metal. "The priming mechanism is there," he said in a thick accent. "You must inject air into the aether in order for it to be ready to ignite, following which you set the flow through the tube. These guns take a thirty-three-milliliter burst, so you have to set both the air and the flow to that level. Then the priming pins must be set. There are four of them along the length of the gun."

"Air, flow, thirty-three, priming pins," I repeated, praying I'd remember it. In the distance, the sound of an airship's guns firing could be heard, but I couldn't tell if they were from Etienne's ships or the *Enterprise*.

Az moved a few feet down the cannon, flipping open another panel, showing me a flat metal piece into which several adjusting pins had been set. "Don't touch anything but the priming pins, else you'll blow us to kingdom come."

He showed me how each of the four sets of pins needed to be set (all different, of course, because anything else would be too easy), and after making me repeat it twice, told me to go ahead and set it. He hovered over my shoulder when I reached for the air-injection knob, but just as my fingers were tightening around it, we must have come into range, because the airship gave a little lurch when three of the six cannons on that side started firing.

Aether cannon fire had a peculiar property to it. There was an initial rushing noise, which I realized was the gun sucking in air that mixed with the aether, then a moment of silence, followed by an odd roaring noise as the resulting plasma tore through the air. Jack had told me that he thought the aether affected air on a molecular level, changing the makeup of the atoms as it ripped through them. Whatever the heated aether did on a molecular level, the results were deadly and horrible.

Alan strode up and down the gangway while the cannons were fired, tossing out orders, and pitching in to help more times than not. The cannons, like the gunpowder version of the normal world, grew hot with use, and periodically had to have the barrels cleaned. In the case of the *Night-wing*'s guns, they needed to have a big stick with a white bit of cloth on the end rammed down the barrel after it was fired a half-dozen times. Az attended to that on our gun, reminding me of a man holding a giant Q-tip. Two younger men, probably in their late teens, assisted him, in both rolling the gun back when it needed to be cleaned and setting the directional gauges on the cannon. I didn't have time to ask them their names, and wasn't sure they spoke English even if I had been able to.

If I'd thought training with Alan earlier was exhausting, it was nothing to being trapped in the gun bay, the sound of twelve guns firing, the heat from the aether as it spat out into the night; the nerve-racking task of making sure I primed the gun properly had sweat rolling under my armor, but there wasn't time to do more than wipe my sweaty face on the bit of lay that dangled down between my damp shoulder blades, and then the gun was rolled back, ready to be primed again.

The fight seemed to go on forever, but I learned later it took only about half an hour before Etienne decided that his ship wasn't going to be able to take out Alan and the *Nightwing*, especially with the *Enterprise* hanging above us.

"Why aren't Jack and Octavia shooting?" I paused at one point, when Alan ran to a speaking tube that led up two decks to where the pilot waited next to the autonavigator to issue maneuvers. "They've fought the Black Hand before. They should be firing with us."

"Theirs is a cargo ship," he answered after giving orders into the bell-like receiver that clung to the wall. "Their guns are defensive only. The *Nightwing* was built to attack."

Fear pinched me. "Are they in danger hanging overhead like that?" I asked.

"Not unless they get in range of Etienne's guns. I have no intention of attacking them, and their position is such that Etienne can't harm them." Alan gave me an odd look. "Hallie, there's—"

A blast beneath us caused the ship to wobble. Alan swore and ran to the porthole.

I wiped my face on my sleeve, relieved Jack and Octavia were safe. I would have followed Alan to see what exploded beneath us, but just then Az called curtly for me.

When the battle was over, and the guns fell silent, I tottered backward until I hit a wall, sliding down it to plop into a puddle of exhausted Hallie. I sat there trying to catch my breath, watching as Alan, who had stripped off not only his armor but also his tunic, moved amongst the men and cannons, checking on both. His chest was shiny with sweat, one side smeared with the red residue that aether left in the cannon after firing.

Dear goddess, he was a gorgeous man. His hair, standing in clumps after he'd evidently ripped off the turban, was blue-black in the gaslights that ran along the ceiling. His arms had delicious muscles that indicated a man who lived a physical life, without going into the—to me—less savory area of bodybuilder. My wild heart rate started to slow as I let myself watch the play of muscles in his back when he bent and helped one of the younger men up, one arm around him until Zand hurried over to lend his aid.

And then there was Alan's chest, with the black curls now damp and subdued, the soft ripple of muscles disappearing into the waistband of his leggings.

Why shouldn't I take the opportunity to satisfy my cravings with him? He'd agreed to teach me how to fight—my mind skittered over the way I'd yelled to Jack in order to give Alan the impression I'd received permission to do so—so it wasn't like I was giving in to my lust without regard to my plan.

After all, what was wrong with a little honest lust? Alan was clearly not averse to it, judging by comments he'd made earlier in the day. But that brought a question of its own— was I prepared to be the sort of woman who climbed into bed with a man she just met?

He bent to pick up his turban and armor, dumped into a corner, the material of his leggings pulling tight across his divine ass.

"Oh, you bet I am," I said, trying unsuccessfully to get to my feet.

Alan turned at my words, smiling when I waved my hand toward him. "Problems, dove?"

"Just help me up, you big oaf," I said, telling my legs they had to work just a little longer before I let them collapse onto a bed.

Preferably Alan's.

He pulled me up, catching me when I teetered forward, almost falling on my face. "Sorry. Legs are a bit wobbly."

"That was a bit more work than you thought, eh?" he asked, then drew me to his side and walked me over to the staircase.

"Yes. But at least I helped, and I didn't blow us up, and Az said that although I was the slowest person he ever had under him, that if I got more experience, I could be a creditable gunner." I felt no little amount of pride at the (faint, to be true) words of praise from Az and, with a groan, hauled myself up two flights of spiral stairs until we reached the crew deck.

"You're filthy," Alan said without a comment on my performance.

"Gee, thanks, Mr. Sweaty," I responded, eyeing his chest. I wanted so badly to touch it, even moist as he was.

"Want a bath?"

"Uh …" I gave him a wide-eyed look. "By myself, or together?"

He smiled a long, slow smile. "Alas, the bath on the *Nightwing* is not big enough for two. The one back at my camp, however …"

"I can't wait that long," I said, pulling off one of the gauntlets. "I'm a giant ball of sweat, myself, so yes, I'd love a bath."

To my disappointment, he deposited me in his sister's cabin .

"Feel free to use whatever you find in the chests," he told me, moving aside when a small, round tin tub was brought in from his cabin, located next to mine. Almost immediately, men started hauling in buckets of water, steaming hot, no doubt straight from the boilers. "Leila won't mind."

"Thank you," I said, sighing at the sight of the steam rising from the tub as it was filled. While it was true there were times when I greatly missed the conveniences of life in the world I knew so well, I wasn't about to spurn the offerings that this world had.

"We won't be back to Tozeur until midmorning, so get some rest if you can," he added, nodding to the bed.

I dipped my fingers into the two buckets of water set alongside the tub. They were cool, there so I could adjust the water temperature to my desire. When I looked back to the door to tell Alan that I appreciated his thoughtfulness, he was gone. I peered down the hall, but he was nowhere to be seen.

I closed the door and, after a moment's thought, locked it, quickly peeling off my clothing before sinking with a grateful—and exhausted—sigh into the water.

"The only thing that would feel better on my body is Alan," I said, leaning back, letting the heat of the water seep into my bones while I thought about everything I wanted to do to him.

SIX

I waited until Alan's men had hauled the tub out before collapsing on the bed. I'd found a second chest that also contained clothing, one that had books in French, English, and a third language that looked like a cross between Persian and Turkish, and which I assumed was the Moghuls' native Kazakh.

"This smells like …" I sniffed the long dress I was holding. "Hmm. Frankincense? Carnations? Something spicy. I hope it's not leftover perfume." The idea of wearing something that held the scent of its previous wearer was mildly disturbing. "Oh, thank god," I murmured, pulling from the bottom of the chest two little bags of dried flowers and spices. "Well, that makes the decision much easier."

My tunic and pants lay draped over a chair, filthy, stained brown, and with a long smear of dried horse slobber where Alan's Sampson had investigated me. "I am so going to have a talk with Alan about his men throwing away the pack with my clothes just because they didn't see any value in it … oh, pretty."

I wasn't much for dresses, and especially not the long Victorian skirts the ladies in this world wore, but I pulled out a nice midcalf tunic dress in soft sky blue with intricate beaded embroidery along the collar, sleeves, and hem, complete with a belt that had little bells on it. The dress itself was made in a silky material that flowed over my hand like water. It had slits on the side that went to midthigh, making walking easier. A pair of sandals were too small for me, so I set them aside, and although there were a few undergarments of the knicker class, I hesitated at using them. I had washed my underwear and bra in the bath with me, and they were now hooked over a knob on the opened porthole, hopefully drying in the air as we flew.

"They'd just better dry, because I don't really want to go commando in this dress." I set it and its twin in a lovely forest green aside, then replaced the clothing in the chest, all except a pair of navy blue pants, which, when I tried them on, were more leggings than actual pants. They fit my legs snugly, and although they were a bit short in the crotch, they fit well enough that I could use them in an emergency.

After a quick look around the cabin, I gave in to exhaustion and climbed into bed naked, praying my undies would be dried in the morning.

I was just drifting off to sleep wondering what Alan was doing, whether he expected me to join him in his cabin, and what he tasted like, when a little breeze rippled in the room, accompanied by a rustle.

I'd left one of the gaslights on, since I'm not fond of the pitch-dark of airship cabins, which allowed me to watch as one of the tapestries that hung on the wall moved and Alan emerged.

"Ah, you're not asleep," he said, holding a decanter and two glasses. "Excellent. I feared you might be."

"Did you just come through the wall?" I asked, sitting up, immediately pulling up the sheets to cover my bare breasts. I peered at the hanging.

"In a manner of speaking. There's a connecting door there. Do you like brandy?"

"I don't drink," I told him, narrowing my eyes when he sat at the foot of my bed, and poured himself a tot.

"Do you mind if I do?"

"No. I got a bit … carried away … last year when Jack

and I first came here, and I decided that if I didn't want to end up an alcoholic, I'd better stop drinking altogether. Why do you have a connecting door to your sister's cabin, Alan? Is there something you want to tell me?"

He laughed, swirling the amber liquid in the glass, his eyes glittering in the gaslight. He was dressed in what looked like sleeping pants and another of the ubiquitous tunics, this one in black. "I have many things to tell you, my dove, but I don't think you're ready to hear all of them. I have no improper designs upon my sister, which I can see is what you are about to ask. I had originally planned to make this a ready room but, after the airship was built, decided it would better be used as a cabin. Did you enjoy your bath?"

"Very much so. Alan, are you here to just indulge in a little polite chitchat before bed, a kind of unwinding after an exciting and harrowing afternoon and evening, or are you planning on seducing me?"

"That depends." He swallowed the brandy, and set the glass on the floor next to its partner and the decanter. "Do you want to be talked to, or seduced?"

I thought for a few seconds. "What if I want both?"

"Then you may have both, although I can't guarantee the quality of my conversation when before me I see such delectable temptation."

I looked down to where the sheet had slid down my boobs, almost exposing them entirely. I hiked it back up, clamping it down with my arms. "Then we'd better get the talking part done fast. I hope you heard me thanking Jack for that permission business you insisted on." I kept my eyes steady on his, hoping to bluff my way through that statement.

"I did." His head tipped a little to the side. "I also noticed that you had left the *Nightwing*."

"Ah. Yes. About that." I gave an embarrassed cough and tried to summon a confident smile. "I apologize about leaving when I knew you needed guards, but it just seemed an opportune time to find Jack, and I planned on being back as soon as I told him I was training with you. Things … er … didn't quite work out the way I thought they would."

"Indeed." His eyes appeared to study me. I squirmed, unable to shove down the resulting guilt at my deception. "I take it that your brother had no issues to you remaining with me?"

"No issues," I said quickly, and cleared my throat, but after a few seconds of silence, my shoulders slumped. "Damnation. I can't do this. I'm a horrible liar. What I yelled at Jack wasn't quite true. I did tell him about our agreement, though."

"And he gave his permission?"

"He didn't deny it," I said with all honesty. "But we really didn't have time to go into details."

Alan frowned. "That's not explicit permission, however."

"It might not be explicit, but the fact that he let me go off with you is," I said, realizing that in this case Jack's actions spoke more than words. "My brother has always been very protective, and if he was dead set against me staying with you, he would have moved heaven and earth to get me away from you. So, you can take the fact that he did nothing more than shake his fist a few times as tantamount to approval."

"Hmm," Alan said. I thought for a moment he would refuse to train me without an actual letter from Jack, but after a moment he gave a little shrug. "I believe you are right in that estimation. No doubt Octavia will have words with him."

"Probably," I said, relieved to have the subject cleared. Now I could go forward and train without being burdened with a lie. "She's very good that way. Is there anything else you wanted to talk about?"

"There are a great many things, but none that need immediate attention," he said, his eyes glittering in the gaslight.

I warmed myself in their look for a few seconds. "I wasn't going to sleep with you, you know. I'd told myself that I didn't want to, didn't need to, and had no real reason to do so except for being able to touch your magnificent behind, and I was willing to bet you'd let me do that anyway. Would you?"

"Yes," he said without a moment's hesitation. "I assume you changed your mind?"

"I did. I keep thinking about kissing you, and your chest, and arms, and I didn't even get to appreciate your legs."

"Most women—I say this merely as an observation, and not as a comment on you, personally—most women tend to look at my cock when I'm naked. I noticed you did not."

"Oh, I glanced," I admitted. "But you know, there's only so much to be seen in the genital area. Once you've had a gander for general size, shape, and color assessment, there are so many other areas worthy of time."

"Interesting," he said, his eyes going to my chest again. "Would you consider me crass if I asked to have my turn touching you now?"

I thought about that for a bit. "I suppose not, although it seems awfully clinical to stand there and let you touch my butt."

He smiled, a wicked smile, one that touched his eyes, making them shimmer with desire. "This will be anything but clinical, my dove."

"Reeally," I drawled, my body seeming to come alive just with the intent in his voice.

He stood up, pulling off first his tunic, allowing me to admire all those delicious muscles of his chest and arms and belly. His chest hair was fluffy again, indicating that he, too, had a bath. "Just so you know," I told him when he pulled the drawstring on the soft pants, allowing them to slide down his legs to the ground, "I don't normally go to bed with someone I just met."

"I am of the same mind," he said, pulling back the sheet. "I prefer to know the women with whom I have an intimate knowledge."

"And yet here you are," I pointed out, dragging my eyes from his chest to admire his thighs when he knelt with my ankles between his knees. "Wow, you have really nice legs. I noticed them before, and wholly approved of them, but now that I see them up close and personal, I can say that they are very, very nice legs. I'm going to want to touch them, Alan."

"Oh, no," he said, pulling one of my legs out from between his. He bent down and kissed a spot just behind my anklebone. "This is my turn. You don't get to touch me until I'm done with you. And you, my fair little dove, are unique amongst women."

"That is so sweet," I said, shivering a little when he kissed his way up one calf. "Oh, and just so you know, oral sex is off the table."

He paused while snaking his tongue in the crease behind my knee, his eyebrows up. "It is?"

"Yes." I waved at my pubic mound. "For me, that is. I have no problem doing it to you, though. I know a lot of women think of it as kind of a necessary evil, but I, personally, like being able to give pleasure. It's kind of a power trip, you know."

"I do know, which is why I like to reciprocate."

"Yeah, well, I don't enjoy it at all. My therapist says it all stems from the bad self-image I had as a teen. I don't recall anything about my girl bits being traumatized, but my therapist was very good, and she got to me to realize just what a dickwad my ex-husband was being, so she's probably right."

He pulled my other leg out so that he was kneeling between them. "I will not ask you to do anything that you don't want to do, but I would like, at some point, the opportunity to show you that there is pleasure to be had in both giving and receiving."

"Maybe," I said, shivering again when he kissed my other ankle, and started working his way up to that knee. A slow burn started in my deep, secret parts, a burn that was spreading outward, filling first my belly, then my limbs with a strange sensation that made me feel both languid and restless at the same time. "I do like this. This is nice. You can just do this without going all the way up to my personal parts.

With your mouth, that is. I'm totally go for you visiting with your own personal bits."

He pressed a kiss to my inner thigh, pulling my knee over his shoulder. "I'm so glad you approve. Do you mind if I touch you in your … er … personal parts?"

"No mouth?" I asked suspiciously.

"No mouth," he agreed.

"All right, but I'll be watching you."

He grinned, then continued to nibble his way up first one thigh, then the other. "I wouldn't expect you to do anything else. Do you like this?" He rubbed his cheeks on my inner thighs. He had a little stubble on his cheeks and jaw, which meant that what were once perfectly mundane thighs were now a highly erogenous zone.

"Oh, holy handbells, yes!" I squirmed at the feeling of his mouth and stubble, the warmth in my female parts growing hotter until my muscles cramped wanting him in their depths.

"Good. I like it, too. You are so soft, so smooth and tempting. I can use my tongue here, yes?" he asked, just before he licked my inner thigh. I tensed a little when he got close to ground zero, but he stopped, and moved over to the other leg. "And you smell like spices and flowers."

"That's the sachets your sister put in her clothes chests. I found one in the sheets, too." I slid a quick glance to his groin, and saw that he was aroused and ready for action. "I don't suppose you're go for the main course now?"

"Why rush when there are so many delicious appetizers to partake of?" he murmured against the crease of my thigh, kissing it before moving up to my hip.

"Well, I just thought you might—Alan!" I squirmed when he bit my hip at the same time his fingers visited some very sensitive flesh, his thumb rubbing a little circle, while the rest of his fingers danced.

"Like that, do you?" he asked, smugness rich in his voice.

I pointed a finger at him. "I will exact my revenge, just you see if I don't. Oh, goddess, yes, please do that again. No, not with your thumb, the other thing. Oh, yes. Yes, yes, yes." I clutched the sheets with both hands, my legs tensing up as my body raced toward an orgasm.

Alan must have sensed I was very close to the edge, because he withdrew his fingers from the magic they were stirring in my depths, and spread his hands across my belly.

"Your hips," he murmured, kissing my belly before licking a path over to my other hip, which he nipped. "Your hips entrance me. They weave a spell around me—they beckon me like no other hips have. They promise so much, and stir my blood until all I can think about is possessing you."

"My grandmother always told me they were good birthing hips," I said, my breath coming short and fast when he moved upward. "But then there was the cancer and chemo and ... oh. You're going to ... uh ..."

I stopped squirming when he reached the bottom of my rib cage and was rubbing his cheeks on the underside of my breasts. I felt a moment of awkwardness. He looked first at my breasts, then up to my face. "I was going to, but if you would prefer I not—"

"No." I swallowed hard, then saying quickly when he rose up, obviously taking that as a negative, "Sorry, that should have been no, I don't mind if you do touch my breasts, but I feel like I should point out a few things. You'll notice they aren't a matched set."

He studied first one breast, then the other. "I can see that. Does it bother you?"

"Not at all. Does it ... uh ... does it weird you out? Usually the men I'm with—not that there have been vast huge herds of them like, you know, a harem's worth—but the couple of men that I've been with have felt that my reconstructed boob is not worthy of the same consideration as the other one, and then that makes them feel even weirder, and they just usually leave my boobs alone, which is a shame because my repaired boob doesn't have the same number of nerves as the regular one, so it likes extra love. So to speak. Am I babbling?"

"No, you are simply explaining to me that the men you have been with are inferior. I am not them. I will pay homage to both your breasts equally, and if your warrior breast would like extra attention from me, it shall have it."

I smiled at him, arching my back so my breasts—which were now impudent little blobs that were demanding I stop explaining and just get them into Alan's hands already—could present themselves for his review. "Warrior breast. I like that."

"I like *them*," he said, and lowered his head to prove to me that he did. He allowed a little stubble to get them stirred up, then stroked them with both hands, my nipples hard against the palms of his hands while he kissed along my collarbone, my leg between his, his penis pressed against my belly. Then he carefully took first one nipple in his mouth, then the other, sending streaks of sheer, unadulterated pleasure rippling through my body.

If I was restless and needy before, he pushed me into a whole new level of frustration. "I think if you continue with many more appetizers, I may spontaneously combust," I said, shifting underneath him, trying to will him to the spot I wanted him most. "Please, Alan."

"Please what, my demanding little dove?" he murmured against a spot behind my ear that made shivers run up and down my arms.

I reached between us, taking him in my hand, gently scraping his testicles with my nails.

He shot up off me, his hair standing on end, his eyes blazing. "Woman, you push me too far."

"You pushed me too far first. Finish it, Alan. Finish me before I die, because if you don't, you'll have to tell my brother that you killed me because you weren't inside me like you were supposed to be."

He spread my legs, now quivering with the strain to wrap around him, the tip of him nudging into me, making all my intimate muscles stand up and cheer with happiness. "Tell me what you want, Hallie," he murmured, edging ever so slightly into me.

"Are you daft?" I almost yelled, tightening my legs around him at the same time I thrust my hips up, pulling him into me. "I want you! Right now! Now do your job so I can have my turn at you, because I am so going to make you insane by the time I'm done with you."

He chuckled as he slipped a little deeper in me, the chuckle quickly turning into a groan of the sweetest pleasure. He moved slowly in me until I flexed my hips again and started tightening my muscles on him, mentally thanking my gynecologist for making me do Kegels.

He murmured things that I didn't understand, his hips moving faster, his mouth hot on mine, his mustache tickling first my shoulder, then my neck, and finally, his tongue sashayed into my mouth just like it owned the place.

By the time he lost his rhythm and was starting to pound hard and fast, the tension inside me was beyond bearing, and I burst into what seemed to be a million pieces, my body rippling with pleasure. He swore, and pressed hard into me, his hips bucking a couple of times before he collapsed on me, his chest heaving. Almost immediately he tried to push himself off with a murmured apology, but I wrapped my arms around him.

"You're not hurting me," I said in between gasps for air.

"Your breasts—"

"Are fine. They like you being pressed against them. Holy orgasm to end all orgasms, Alan. That was the most amazing thing."

His breath was rough as he rolled us over with me still holding him, but he must have underestimated the size of his sister's bed, because he fell off the edge.

I peered down at him, my heart still beating frantically. "Are you OK?"

He laughed, his legs splayed, his big chest still desperately trying to suck in enough air. "I forgot we weren't on my bed. Yes, I'm fine."

"Good. You want to come back up here where it's nice and comfy?"

"No," he said, and with a groan got to his feet, then without stopping to pick up his clothes, marched around the bed, scooped me up, and took me over to where the tapestry hung. "Open the door, please."

"I can't believe you have the strength to actually pick me up and haul me around," I said, doing as he asked and opening the door. He ducked as he entered the room, closing the door with a foot before marching across the room and depositing me on his bed.

"That's because I am a superior sort of man, one who enjoys paying attention to warrior breasts, women with hips that could talk me into doing anything, and green eyes that right now are almost smoky with passion." He leaned down and kissed me again, making me want to purr.

I scooted over since it was obvious he preferred to sleep on the left side, secretly relishing the fact that he wanted to spend the rest of the night—or, rather, morning—together. I always hated it when my previous lover remained only for as long as was polite before leaving. "I'm not going to dispute any of that," I said, smiling to myself when he got into bed and immediately pulled me up to his side before heaving a sigh of happiness.

"Good. Go to sleep, dove."

"Since you've left me wrung out and boneless with your mind-numbing lovemaking, I don't think that will be an issue." I rose up on my elbow so that I could look down on him.

His eyes were closed. I put a finger on his mustache, giving it a little pet. It was such a thick black thing, and yet was incredibly soft. "Hmm?"

"I told Jack you were nice to me."

"I'm sure that reassured him." His voice held more than a little sleepy amusement.

"Oddly enough, I think it did. Like I said, he wouldn't have let me go off with you if he was truly worried." I stroked Alan's eyebrows, lovely curved black lines above his eyes, then traced my finger down his nose.

"Mmhmm."

I studied his face for a minute, taking in all the lines of his jaw and chin, his cheeks, and those glorious eyes.

I snuggled into him, closing my eyes and trying to visualize the face I'd just seen. My mind skittered away to other things, like the sweep of his hair off his forehead, and the line of his shoulders.

Mentally, I shook my head, and told myself that I couldn't change what life had dealt me.

Besides, right now, my life was anything but unpleasant. My way was clear to get the training I needed, which of course was of paramount importance. I pretended I didn't hear the whispered thought that Alan was fast becoming just as important to me, instead enjoying the sense of fulfillment that I was finally taking charge of my life, and making it what I wanted.

I just hoped that Alan wouldn't mind me writing him down for a whole lot of participation in said life. At least for the present.

And who knew what the future would bring?

SEVEN

"Alan."

A weight pressed down on him, pulling him to the surface of sleep. His hands immediately went to discover what it was that had settled upon him. It was a soft, silky, warm weight, one with delightful curves.

One that giggled when he tickled its ass, asking in a husky voice, "Did I wake you?"

He cracked an eye open to examine the green eyes that were watching him with the bright interest that seemed to draw him into their depths. He rolled the eye over to see the clock on the desk. "Yes, but I should be up now anyway. I must have been more tired than I thought I was."

Hallie smiled, a purely feminine smile that instantly filled his groin with blood. "You worked very hard last night. Do you always do such lengthy foreplay?"

He frowned as he thought about that, his hands stroking the lines of her hips, those delightful hips, on down to the curve of her ass. He loved her ass almost as much as the swell of her hips. "Was it lengthy? It didn't seem unduly so to me."

"It's just longer than I am normally used to. Not that I'm complaining, because holy hasenpfeffer, you made me feel like I was made of fire. Needy fire." She gave a little shiver that he took immense pride in. "I figured I ought to tell you that if you were doing it because you think I need a long warm-up, it's not necessary. Just looking at you has my motor running, and I've never been one to take long to get to the fun zone."

"I'm delighted to know both that you are aroused easily and that I don't need to spend copious amounts of time pleasuring you, but I assure you that I don't view a single second touching and tasting you as anything but the purest enjoyment."

"OK. Just so you know that if you want to have a quickie now and again, I'm totally on board with that."

"Thank you," he said gravely, smiling into his mustache. "I will keep that in mind."

"There is one other thing I feel merits discussion," she said, one finger stroking his mustache. He made a mental note to shave it off, since ladies, he knew, preferred to be kissed without feeling like they were doing so with a hairbrush, as one former lover had once complained. "I want to talk about this harem of yours."

It was on the tip of his tongue to ask what harem, but then he remembered that he was Akbar, and Akbar was just the sort of man who had a harem stashed away back at his father's palace. "You wish to join it? I don't think you'd like the life, dove. You wouldn't be able to learn to fight."

She slapped a hand on his chest, her eyes narrowing on him, her expression decidedly disgruntled. Even her freckles looked annoyed with him. "No, I do not want to be a part of it. The very fact that you have one is disgusting, Alan. I realize we jumped into bed without knowing a lot about each other—"

"On the contrary," he interrupted, his hands moving up her sides to where her breasts were pressed against his chest. "I knew a great deal about you before we engaged in sexual activity."

"Like what?" she asked, clearly distracted.

"I knew you were passionate, intelligent, curious, had a desire for knowledge, gloried in your unconventionality, weren't overly concerned by what others thought, and you had an overestimation of the quality of my body, specifically my ass. It's just an ass, Hallie. It's functional. It does what I need it to do. It is pleasant to sit upon. That's it."

She made a face and waved away his statement. "Your behind is beyond the range of mortal man and into the realm of godlike, but that's not the point. And thank you for all those nice things you said about me. I like you, too. A lot. But that doesn't mean I'm going to share you. Regardless of your insight into me, you clearly didn't know that I'm not the sort of woman who shares her man. So I'm willing to be reasonable, and not rail at you now because you have a great big herd of who knows how many women at your home waiting for you to get back so they can do all sorts of things to you that I want to do, and instead tell you that you have a choice: You can have the herd, or me. But not both."

He pretended to think about this, his fingers drawing symbols on her breasts, causing her to arch her back so that he could take them into his hands properly. "You will naturally honor the proprietary nature of the relationship, as well?" he asked, wanting to laugh and sing and kiss her until she lay panting.

"You mean I won't have any other lovers than you? Of course. What's good for the goose is good for the gander."

"Very well," he said after half a minute's pretend thought, allowing a smidgen of faux reluctance to creep into his voice. "I will dismiss the harem so long as you remain a fixture in my bed."

She looked disgruntled for a moment, then smiled, the warmth from it filling him with a sense of happiness that he realized had been missing from his life for some time. "I have a lot of things I want to learn, Alan. That might take a while."

"And I have many things I wish to teach you," he said with a little leer, his thumbs brushing her nipples.

She shivered again. "We have a deal, then?"

He had no idea why she felt like putting what was

promising to be a very enjoyable relationship on such a businesslike term, but if it made her happy … "We do."

"Excellent." She sat up, her legs astride his hips, his cock—now hard and desirous of attention—pressed against her thigh. "That means it's my turn, and I get to seduce you."

"I am all yours," he said, watching with interest and no little amount of hope when she slid back onto his knees, and eyed his cock. She pursed her lips at it, frowning slightly.

"Why are you frowning at my cock?" He lifted his head to look down his body to where it stood at attention, clearly waiting for her to notice it. "Is something wrong with it?"

"No," she said slowly, then nibbled on her lower lip for a moment. Dammit, he wanted to nibble on her lower lip. It wasn't fair that she do so when she wasn't within his reach so that he could stop her and take over the job.

To his immense surprise, she slid off him and padded naked over to the door that connected with Leila's cabin. "Stay there. I'll be right back."

"What's wrong?" he called after her, looking back at himself, and asking his cock, "What did you do?"

It bobbed at him, looking innocent of all wrongdoing.

"Aha! I thought I saw this when I was poking around your sister's things." Hallie returned, her hips swaying in a manner that made his mouth water, his hands twitch, and his cock harder than it had been a second before. She held up a small blue stoppered bottle. "Your sister evidently likes orange oil."

"She uses it in her bath, I believe," he said, watching as she retook her seat on his legs, pouring a little bit of oil onto her palm before replacing the stopper and then rubbing her hands together. "What is it you're doing?"

Her eyebrows rose. "You don't know about massage oil?"

"No," he said, the pleasant scent of oranges filling the cabin. "Is it something American?"

"Er … yeah, let's just say that." She smiled. "I think you're going to like this."

"I have no dou—hrng!" He gasped when her hands slid along the length of him, the oil warm and slippery and causing a friction that he hadn't known was possible. His hips bucked when she slid her hands up and down a few times before pouring out a bit more oil, which she used to rub into his balls and surrounding area.

He had no idea why she felt like she had to oil all of him up when it was just his cock that wanted the attention, but the second she wrapped one hand around his hard length while using the other hand to gently pull on his testicles, he decided she was wise beyond her years. "Lord, woman, where did you learn to—would you do that again? No, with your left hand. Hrng. Where did you learn to do this?"

"My last boyfriend. He taught me something else you might like. Let's see. … I think it's just about here."

She slid her fingers back from his testicles, and for a moment, he thought she might be about to breach an area he preferred to remain unbreachable, but she stopped short of that, and did a little circular rubbing motion that, when joined with the strokes her other hand was making, almost had him crossing his eyes. "No one has ever—lord, yes, right there—touched me like that."

"You've never had a hand job, or no one has done the perineum massage?"

"The latter. You're not—you're going to—" Words jumbled up on his lips as she bent her head and licked the underside of his cock, the warm, soft swirl of her tongue damn near making him lose control.

"My ex-boyfriend used to swear by two knuckles. Let's see if you are go with it, too," she said, gently pressing two knuckles in the pleasurable spot near his testicles while her mouth engulfed him, the slight negative pressure combined with her tongue teasing the tip of him suddenly too much.

He had her on her back with her legs spread before he realized that he'd even moved. "I am go with it. Very go with it. Too go, as a matter of fact. Tell me you're ready for me."

"Sweetie, I was ready for you the minute I woke up," she cooed, sliding her hands down his back, using her nails just enough to push his need for her over the edge. He thrust hard into her, relishing the moan of pleasure that he caught in his mouth, his hips pistoning, his mind filled with the feel of her, and taste of her, and the warm, familiar scent of orange wrapping around them.

"Is this too much for you?" he managed to ask, tearing his mouth from where he was nibbling on her neck. "I will slow down if it is. It may kill me, but I will do it."

"God, no. I told you, I'm very quick off the mark. I like it hard and fast. ..." Her words trailed off into yet another moan when he slid his arms under her legs, pushing them up against her body, his hips moving with a rhythm that seemed to match the beat of his heart. Her legs tightened, her pelvis arching up, her eyes wide with the pleasure that consumed her. Muscles gripped him with a strength that pushed him beyond what a mere mortal man could bear, causing him to buck wildly while he poured himself into her, every muscle, every sinew of his body straining to join with her in the most fundamental way he knew how.

"Boy," she said some time later, a long time later, possibly an eon or two later. "You sure liked the two knuckles."

"Yes," he answered, lying exhausted on his back, Hallie draped over him, feeling as if someone had replaced every bone in his body with sodden noodles. "You have my permission to use both knuckles on me whenever the urge strikes you. Nightly is good. Possibly mornings, as well, and if I'm able to get away from my duties, afternoons, early evenings, and that time in late morning when you're a little hungry, but it's not quite time for a meal."

She giggled, and kissed the nipple nearest her mouth. "You're on."

A thought struck him then, one that he, as a gentleman—even if Akbar was not, Alan most definitely was—should offer. "We did not use a French preventative. Would you care for me to do so in the future?"

"A French—oh, that's the name for condoms here. Thank you for offering, but I don't think it's necessary. Unless you have a venereal disease that you want to tell me about. But chemo did a number on me, so I don't have to worry about anything else happening."

He wasn't familiar with a preparation called chemo, but he assumed it was what American women used to prevent unwanted pregnancies. "I'm glad to hear that we won't need to use them. I would if you desired, but it is much more pleasant for both of us if we can dispense with them."

"I suppose we should get up," Hallie said, stretching in a way that reminded him of a cat in a pool of sunshine.

"We should. I have many things to do." He continued to lie there, boneless, his entire body sated and thrumming with the glow of lovemaking.

"Maybe after a quick nap," she said, yawning, and snuggled into his side, one leg draped over him.

A nap sounded exactly like what he needed.

He was in the mess a few hours later, telling Az that he wanted a security detail to be assigned to Hallie. "She's not to leave camp on her own. The revolutionaries would take her in a second if they found her—"

He heard the intake of several breaths and turned to look down the length of the mess to see what suddenly had his men, most of whom were hurriedly consuming breakfast, so shocked.

Hallie strolled into the room wearing one of Leila's gowns, a favorite blue one that he decided looked much better on Hallie.

She gave him a bright smile before greeting the men seated, moving over to where a table had been set up with a variety of foods. "Oh, it all looks so good. Is that yogurt? Awesome. I love yogurt."

And that's when Alan noticed that she was wearing just part of the blue ensemble, just the long tunic, and no trousers. Hallie's legs, her deliciously smooth, silky legs, were clearly visible up to midthigh as she moved, the side slits on the tunic allowing flashes of flesh to tantalize anyone with a pair of eyes in his head.

His gaze moved over to two long tables around which his crew sat. They all, to a man, stared unblinking at the sight of Hallie serving herself a dish of yogurt and fruit before she hesitated over a plate of sticky buns. "What the hell do you think you're doing?" he roared, feeling every inch Akbar. He marched over to her, wanting to wrap her in a blanket or two.

"Jesus!" she said, jumping a few inches. "Just scare the crap out of me, why don't you? Are these your personal sticky buns or something?"

He stared at her, wondering if she was doing this on purpose, or if he'd suddenly gone stark, staring mad. "What?"

"The buns," she said, gesturing toward them. "I won't take them if it's not allowed, although you should put a sign up saying they're for Your Holy Royal Imperial Majesty. Sheesh!"

"I don't give a damn if you eat every last one, woman," he snarled, glaring at the narrow line of leg he could see through the slit in her dress. "I do, however, object to you exposing yourself to my men."

"I beg your pardon?" She looked first at her chest, then peered to the side where he was looking. The movement caused the material of the dress to swing back, revealing even more leg. "Where? Is it tucked up in the back?"

"Your legs," he said, reminding himself that she was not used to Moghul clothing, or even, heaven help him, the limb-covering clothing worn by ladies in Europe. He had no idea of the sorts of garments that women wore in the Americas, but he suspected they were of the type that would raise his blood pressure. "They are exposed so that anyone might see them."

She was silent for a moment, then looked down at the tunic. "That's how this came."

"You are supposed to wear trousers under it."

"You're kidding."

He thinned his lips at her.

"Wow. You're not kidding." She glanced around the room. The men, who were still, he was unhappy to note, watching her with an avidity that annoyed him to the utmost, hastily turned back to their meals upon receipt of a pointed look that he sent to each and every one of them. "I'm sorry, Alan, I thought this was a dress. I'll put on some pants after I eat, OK?"

He crossed his arms over his chest, biting back his body's demand to take her straight back to his bed, where he could sate himself in her heat.

"Fine!" she said, handing him her bowl of yogurt and fruit, and a small plate with a sticky bun. "Hold that for me."

She left the room, muttering things under her breath.

"Nicely handled," Zand said as he passed by, en route to the door. Alan quite clearly heard the laughter in his voice. "Smooth, very smooth."

"I can have you beheaded, you know," Alan called after him. "My men would be happy to do it. Wouldn't you?" He directed the last sentence to the men at the tables.

They all avoided meeting his eyes. He sighed to himself, realizing that he was going to have to apologize to Hallie.

She returned a half minute later, wearing a proper pair of trousers under the tunic. The men all looked disappointed by this, but he was much happier.

"Honestly, I knew you guys are really narrow-minded when it comes to women's rights and all, but I would have thought you could have borne up under the horror of a little leg." She held her arms out and did a spin. "Better?"

"So far as allowing others to view your bare legs? Infinitely so," he said, handing her back her breakfast, then leaned down to whisper, "I like yogurt, too. I look forward to licking it off of those legs that you insist on showing to everyone. I will happily do so tonight. I have a couple of things I'd like to show you that I can do with two knuckles, as well."

He left her fanning herself with a napkin.

Less than an hour later, they landed at Tozeur, having

stopped during the night to take on some supplies that he'd arranged for in advance, which Zand oversaw while he was busy with Hallie.

He ordered Leila's things to be taken to his tent, telling Hallie that she would stay there with him.

"Assuming you approve of that plan," he said, gesturing toward the bed that sat in the tent.

She eyed first it, then him. "Thank you, I would like that."

"You may consider this your home, then, at least for so long as we are here," he told her, wanting badly to take her to bed despite the fact that she'd damned near killed him earlier that morning with the intensity of her lovemaking. "Feel free to use any of my things as you like."

Her eyes lit.

"Except my weapons," he said quickly.

She made a face at him. "Spoilsport."

"No, just prudent. You aren't ready for anything with a sharp blade yet."

"Ha! Shows what you know. I almost gutted Etienne last night," she tossed casually over her shoulder as she went to examine herself in his shaving mirror, fussing with her hair.

"You what?" The words came out at a louder volume than he intended. He was on her in a second, staring down into startled green eyes. "When did you see Etienne? Do you know him? You're not part of the Black Hand, are you?"

"Of course not. He swore a vendetta against all of us when he kicked out my sister-in-law, although admittedly she did steal the best of his airships." She eyed his chest, her lips twisting. "Is that what you're going to wear today? No armor? Just the gold tunic?"

"Yes, this is what I'm wearing, and when did you see Etienne that you almost gutted him?" He gave her a little shake.

"I don't suppose you'd like to get an ear pierced or something? Maybe a tattoo on a visible spot ... hmm? Oh, last night, right before I found Jack. He was lurking in the shadows while the rest of you were fighting in the square, which you have to admit says a lot about the sort of man he is. I can't imagine you ever lurking in the shadows while others fought for you."

Alan's blood went from its usually heated state when around Hallie to one that icebergs could have safely floated in. She had seen Etienne? Been close to him? His stomach tightened unpleasantly as he imagined what Etienne would have made of a woman wearing his colors.

"Did he see you? No, he couldn't have." He shook his head. She wouldn't be here now if Etienne had her in his grasp. "You should have told me this earlier this morning."

"I didn't think it was important. And he did see me. He tried to strangle me, but I kneed him in the noogies, and then whacked him on the head with the hilt of my sword. I thought of stabbing him with it, but it just seemed so bloody, and besides, smacking him on the head let me get away," she said in a matter-of-fact voice, just like it was nothing.

Alan felt a distinct need to sit down and have a mild case of apoplexy. "He tried to strangle you?" he asked in a voice that sounded like he was gargling stones. "You hit him on the head?"

"Yup." She smiled with obvious pride, and spread a hand on the open vee of his tunic, her fingers gently stroking the dip in his collarbone. "So you see, I'm not quite as inept as you make me out to be. Hey, have you ever thought of getting a distinctive haircut? Maybe have the sides shaved short?"

He turned around and walked away at that point. He had to, lest he yell at her, forbidding her to ever leave his tent again. That or have the fit of apoplexy that right now was looking pretty damned good. He went straight to Az and told him to double the amount of men that were to be assigned to Hallie.

If Etienne had seen her, known her to be a member of his company, he would show absolutely no mercy the next time he encountered her. And that, Alan swore to himself, would happen over his cold, dead body.

Two days later, he was still thinking darkly about the close call Hallie had had with Etienne. The only time he seemed to be able to put it aside was when she was in his arms, or writhing beneath him, or riding him like a well-lathered horse. Or, in the case of earlier that morning, sliding around on him in the lemon-oiled water of his large bath, her knuckle massage causing him to lose control once again, which left most of the water on the rug beneath the bath, and them both exhausted, lemon-scented, and sated almost beyond human ability.

"Is something worrying you?"

Alan stopped planning a sunken pool in the house that he'd been thinking of building, realizing with a start that for the last ten minutes he'd been standing next to where the horses were pastured. He glanced at Zand, standing beside him. "Why do you ask that?"

"Because for the last few days, you've been quiet. If you were another man, I'd say you were pensive. Or moody."

Alan shot his friend a cold look. "I am not moody or pensive. If I'm quiet, it's because teaching Hallie how to use a weapon without her managing to kill herself on it is taking all my ingenuity, attention, and effort. It's exhausting. The woman has the most hair-raising ideas of ways to attack. It's adding years to my life, if not decades."

Zand laughed, and punched him in the arm. "I would think it was worth it just to have the nights you've obviously been having with her."

"Yes, well, those are good," he said, smiling at the thought of the bath, but that smile faded when he remembered her actions of two hours after that, his finger on his now-bare upper lip. "She leaves me feeling unbalanced, Zand. I never know what she's going to say or do."

"She is a bit odd, but she's American. That might explain it."

"Some, yes. But take a couple of hours ago. After I shaved, I went to find her so that we could work on her defensive moves, and she ignored me until I asked her what was wrong, and then she got mad at me because I shaved off my mustache." He thought over the scene again. "She actually demanded that I grow it back, saying that no one else had one the exact shape and size. Most women want you to be clean-shaven, but not Hallie. What the hell is wrong with her?"

Zand shrugged and rubbed his own mustache. "She seems to be pretty fond of you. Maybe she liked it?"

"I don't know. And then there's her insistence that I teach her stealth moves, so she can be a rogue. A rogue what?"

Zand looked confused. "Should I know?"

"I sure as hell don't. It would be nice if someone did." He sighed. "It all just leaves me feeling … bah. It doesn't matter. What did you want?"

"Maybe," Zand suggested, obviously ignoring the last question, "you are at odds with yourself because you're no longer happy being Akbar."

Alan stiffened. "Are you saying you wish to take over?"

"No, no," Zand said with a laugh, holding his hands up in a gesture of peace. "I'm not so foolish as that. I simply mean that now that you have found Hallie, perhaps the time of Akbar is drawing to a close?"

Alan thought about that for a few minutes. "It is true that I have grown tired of juggling Alan's and Akbar's lives. If it were possible for me to give up my duty to the imperator … but too many lives depend on me to buffer them from his wrath. No, Akbar will have to remain until such time as I can do no more to keep the imperator from wreaking havoc."

"Have you told her about Alan?" Zand asked.

"Not yet," Alan answered, ignoring the voice in his head that reminded him he should be acting far more like the arrogant Prince Akbar and less like the diplomatic Alan. So long as he could be his true self with Hallie, that would have to do. At least for the time being, until his father … he stopped that thought, and turned away from the horses, his eyes automatically scanning the camp. People bustled hither and yon, tending animals, mending armor and equipment, hunting, cooking … all the usual happenings of his camps, and yet there was something else in the air, something beyond his personal issues. It was an awareness that prickled along his skin. "Is there any word on my father's movements?"

"Nothing since last night. Will he stay with you?"

"He'll demand my bed, I'm sure. Make sure another tent is set up for me."

"And Hallie?"

His eyes narrowed. "What do you mean by that?"

"I meant, where will she sleep?"

"With me," he snapped, and strode forward.

"You don't think your father will want to … er … enjoy her charms?"

Alan stopped dead, fury making his blood go into an immediate boil. "He wouldn't dare."

Zand shrugged. "He's demanded—and received—whatever woman you were partaking of during other visits. Hallie is lovely. I don't see a reason why he wouldn't assume you'll share her, too."

"I don't share. Those other women he took to his bed never returned to mine," he ground out through teeth that he was surprised to find were clenched tight. "Hallie is not available."

Alan marched past a line of bales of hay that had been set up as Hallie's practice area. His eyes went to her as Amir, one of the best of his swordsmen, was now armed with a wooden sword while he engaged in sparring with her, supposedly giving her much needed practice in the art of defense.

She was really quite horrible at it. Alan closed his eyes when Amir checked himself in midswing. Had he a real sword, he might have taken off Hallie's arm, and what was she doing while she was supposed to be parrying the attack? She was making odd little jumping moves and yelling, "Hiya!" and "Take that, you marauding bastard!"

If she didn't kill him with all the worry about keeping her safe from Etienne, she was going to kill herself with the belief that she was fast approaching the status of master swordsman.

"You've got it bad for her, don't you?" Zand asked, watching and grimacing when Amir accidentally allowed his sword to connect with her shin. She limped around him doubled over, clutching her leg, and threatening him with dire repercussions.

"Apparently," Alan muttered, trying to force himself to turn away. He had things to do, important things, things that must be done to prepare for the visit of his father.

"Is this a permanent arrangement?"

Alan slid him a glance. "If you were anyone else, I'd have your head for such impertinence."

"Nooo," Zand drawled. "Prince Akbar might, but not Alan Dubain. When are you going to tell her about that?"

He shrugged. He'd started to tell her the truth while they were on the *Nightwing*, but the time wasn't right. Even so, the fact that he was keeping Alan Dubain a secret from her was starting to rankle. He knew the time was coming when he'd have to reveal the truth to her. "Whenever the time is right. It's not important now."

"It will be if you plan on returning to William's court after the imperator's visit."

"I'll deal with it then. Right now, I have to survive her training. And my father."

"You might want to mention Alan Dubain sooner rather than later," Zand said, walking with him when one of the men arrived bearing messages that had been forwarded to Tozeur. "You know how women are about that sort of thing."

"I doubt if she's even heard of me," he answered, guilt pricking at him. "Octavia isn't likely to talk about me to anyone."

"Not even her new husband?"

Alan smiled. Despite his initial reservations, he liked Jack Fletcher. The American was head over ears in love with Octavia, a fact that pleased Alan, since Octavia remained high in his estimation, a former lover who had become a cherished friend. "I doubt if she's told him, although it wouldn't be the end of the world if she had. He can be trusted."

Zand was silent for a few minutes while the messenger dismounted and hurried over to Alan with a satchel. "Have you thought of sending her away?"

"Hallie?"

"Aye."

Alan eyed him, wondering if his friend had taken a sudden aversion to the woman who was fast dominating all his attention, but after a moment's thought, he understood. "I don't think it's necessary."

"She's American. If you're serious about her—and frankly if you're not, I'll take her—your father is sure to make a scene."

"So I should tell Safie that you're no longer pining for her?" he asked, his voice a little acid at the idea of anyone else being the recipient of Hallie's inventive attentions.

Zand glared. "You do, and I'll—"

"You'll what?" Alan asked, his voice mild.

"Do something that would have Prince Akbar calling for my head on a platter. All right, you can stop bristling at me—I don't have designs on your woman. Safie is all my heart wants, as you well know."

"I also know she's just as mad for you," Alan said, taking the three letters the messenger had been waiting impatiently to deliver.

"Then it shouldn't be a problem killing her."

"Not just yet." He studied the message from his informant in London. The emperor was getting restless with his excuses for not making an appearance in court for almost six months. Dammit. He was going to have to don the mantle of Alan Dubain in the very near future. "Once we find someone else to captain the *Falcon*, we will arrange for my father to learn of her untimely and much-mourned artistically devised demise, and then you can marry her and have several sons all named for me. Blast it to hell and back."

"Problems?"

"Ysed writes from Constantinople that a Black Hand representative has been cozying up to the imperator."

"A truce, do you think?" Zand asked as they considered the repercussions of one of the two enemies of the empire suddenly becoming an ally.

"I hope not. I wouldn't trust him any further than I could piss. Did you know that Etienne almost strangled Hallie back in El Kef?"

Zand looked suitably shocked when Alan told him Hallie's recounting of the night.

"You'd better redouble your efforts to teach her to defend herself," he said, nodding as they strolled by the area where Hallie was now on her back, slashing out wildly with the sword, attempting to strike Amir's ankles. "I doubt she'll have such an easy time getting away from him should she encounter him again."

"You're not telling me anything I haven't told myself a hundred times. Woman! What the hell do you think you're doing? You're not a beetle that's been flipped onto its back!" Alan strode into the practice area and gave Hallie his hand, righting her and dusting her off before giving her yet another lecture about the importance of proper defense.

"It's this falchion," she said, smiling at Amir when he bowed and murmured something about attending to other duties. "Thanks for all your help, Amir. I think it's time to move to daggers, Alan."

"I don't know what types of combat they have in the Americas, but daggers are not a particularly effective weapon for close combat," Alan said somewhat desperately. The fact that he was even considering doing as she asked said a lot about just how frazzled he was when it came to teaching her to protect herself.

"Please. I know I'll be better at it. I always play rogues in video … er … that is, I'm very familiar with the rogues who live in America, and I just know that if I had a couple of wickedly sharp daggers, and you showed me some stealthy moves, I'd have a lot more luck with that than the sword."

"Very well. But if you cut off a hand, I don't want you complaining to me about it," he said, realizing just how ridiculous that sounded, but unable to keep from saying it nonetheless.

She giggled. Then her gaze lit on his naked upper lip, and her brows pulled down. "Are you growing it back? It doesn't look like you are."

"I shaved it off a matter of two hours ago. My whiskers don't grow in that fast, dove. What are your plans for this afternoon?"

"I was going to go into town for a fitting with the local seamstress, but if you want to start teaching me the effective use of a dagger, I can see her tomorrow, instead."

"No daggers today. It will take some hours for one of the men to dull a couple suitably for you to practice with."

Her eyes narrowed, and her lips thinned. She poked him in the chest with two fingers. "That is offensive, Your High and Mighty Prince Asshat."

"Akbar, and the proper term of address is Imperial Royal Highness."

"If the asshat fits, wear it," she snapped, and would have turned on her heel and made a fine show of stomping away, but he caught her arm.

"There is something I must discuss with you." He glanced around, then signaled for horses. "I will escort you into town."

"What sort of something?" she asked, looking nervous when he led her over to where grooms were hurriedly saddling Sampson, and an ancient cart horse he'd purchased in town the day before. Hallie had reluctantly named her Delilah. "It's not about the fact that I fell off Delilah yesterday, is it? Because I maintain she did it on purpose. Also, I don't think it's fair for you to insist I have one riding lesson for every fighting lesson you teach me. Those were not our original terms."

"If you wish to remain here, you need to learn how to ride, and considering I could put a baby on Delilah's broad back and it wouldn't so much as tip over, you need the lessons."

Hallie muttered something that sounded like "asshat," but he ignored it, instead patiently helping her to greet the horse and stroke the old mare's neck (both acts of which he insisted she do until she could approach the horse without making a fuss), before assisting her up onto the saddle.

Four men accompanied them as they set off toward the town, Alan having to slow Sampson's ground-eating gait to an amble so the old mare could keep up. He made a mental note to find Hallie a nice little Arabian mare, one with a bit more spirit, but still gentle and easygoing.

"What was it you wanted to talk about?" she asked after fifteen minutes, the time being spent by her clutching to the horse's mane, her back hunched, her legs swaying.

"You have to keep your feet in the stirrups," he said, ignoring her question.

"I don't like them there. I feel trapped. This way I can move if I have to," she answered.

"You have better balance with your feet in the stirrups." He stopped and waited until she regained the proper riding attitude. "Hands low. Back straight. Head up. Don't look at where the horse is going—look ahead," he reminded her.

"You are a tyrant, do you know that? You're a horse dictator, and I, for one, resent you thinking you can tell me what to do. I don't know how your men put up with you telling them how they can sit on a horse, and where they can look. Honestly, Alan—"

She had dropped the reins to gesture with her hands while she railed at him, and the old mare dropped her head, shifting as she did so.

Hallie promptly squawked, kicked her feet out of the stirrups, and fell off.

The rest of the trip to Tozeur was spent with Hallie riding behind him on Sampson while one of the men walked the old mare back to camp. At least this way, Alan thought as they cantered for the scant mile to town, it wouldn't take them hours to get there and back.

He stopped outside a small inn, taking Hallie aside while one of the men watered the horses at the pool that formed the oasis proper. "Sometime in the next few days, my father is due to visit this area."

Her eyes widened. "The emperor?"

"Moghuls refer to him as an imperator, but yes, it is the same thing as an emperor."

"I see." She was silent for a moment, her expression one of concern. "I take it you aren't particularly thrilled by this visit?"

"No. My father and I don't always see eye to eye." He picked his words carefully. "With regards to many subjects, not just those of an imperial nature. He is … there's no polite way to put this, but I want you to be warned so that you can take steps to protect yourself if I am not around. He is a man of many pleasures, one of which is women. He will expect me to provide him with a choice of women, and I will contact the local bawdy house in order to do so, but he may well set his sights on you."

She stiffened, outrage visible in every line. "Well, he can just stuff his sight where the bawdy house don't shine!"

"I will tell him you are my woman, but he may ignore that. Hallie, I know you don't like the guards that accompany you when we are separated, but you must not go anywhere by yourself while my father is with us."

He thought she was going to make a flip comment, and was ready to explain to her that about this she must heed him, but once again she surprised him. "Are two guards going to be enough? I mean, Yussuf and Ajay are nice enough, but they aren't overly beefy. Maybe I should have Az, too. Your dad would have to be insane to try to go against Az."

"That isn't a bad idea at all," he said, making a mental note to reassign Az's duties to now focus on protecting Hallie.

"And if I had nice sharp daggers, then I could—"

"No," he said firmly, giving her a look to let her know that she wasn't going to slip anything past him. "Practice daggers until I see how you do with them."

"Fine," she said with mock irritation, but her eyes glowed with a warm light as she tipped her head back to kiss him. She wrinkled her nose and glared at his upper lip, saying when she turned, "You better work on growing that mustache back, buster, because it's either that or a nice big tattoo right on the middle of your forehead."

He nodded at Yussuf and Ajay when the two men followed her down to one of the houses where a local woman was making Hallie some clothing, and went into the inn in order to write replies to the letters he'd received. He had plans to put into action before his father arrived. He just hoped it would be enough.

EIGHT

"Right," I said a few weeks later, sitting on the edge of Alan's bed while he knelt before me, my foot resting on his thigh. "So, daggers are out."

He dabbed at the blood, using a wet cloth to wipe the small puncture hole I'd managed to make on my own damned foot, before spreading a little ointment on it, and then wrapping a white linen bandage across my instep.

He did all that without saying a word. I knew he was angry, but I hoped not too angry. The last three weeks had been—with the exception of the horse lessons—wonderful. Fulfilling. Exciting and marvelous and heart-stoppingly fabulous.

We'd worked out an easy pattern, with nights spent in sensual exploration of what made us both writhe in delight, while the days were spent with me learning how to defend myself with swords, two dulled daggers, and a bow with a quiverful of arrows, all the while Alan tried hard not to throttle me with exasperation.

I slid my noninjured foot up his thigh to his groin, wiggling my toes provocatively. "You know, we could skip the lesson with Delilah and instead you could use the orange oil on my breasts. And belly. And ... well, I was saving this for a special occasion, but I think that if you wanted to try a little oral sex on me with the orange oil—just a little, because I'm still not sure I'm going to like it—then that would be just fine."

He sighed, his gaze still on the top of my foot. "Just tell me one thing, Hallie."

Oh dear. He sounded weary. He sounded that way only after my lessons.

"I don't know how," I answered, knowing exactly what he was going to ask me. "It just slipped and the pointy tip went smack-dab into my foot."

"Those blades were dulled. You couldn't even cut butter with them." He looked up, and I saw a mixture of amusement and regret in his eyes. "You are the only woman in the world who could stab herself on something that literally could not cut anything else."

"Well, it's not literal if it cut my skin, but I know what you mean. I was thinking about it while you were carrying me in here, and maybe I'm not meant for melee fighting. You haven't seen me use the bow yet, but I'm really pretty good with it. Maybe if I got some of the big arrows, the kind with metal tips on them—"

"No," he said, sliding on my sandal that I had bought from a local shoemaker. "No metal-tipped arrows. Nor, and I know this will be your next suggestion, are you getting a disruptor."

"Oh, come on," I said, smiling my most beguiling smile when he stood up and held out his hands for me. "I'll just shoot targets, I promise. And I really am quite good with the bow. You'll have to come out and watch me practice."

He was going to say no—I just knew it—but instead, he led me outside to the horses, stopping where one of his men was saddling the bony old horse that he'd bought for me. "Very well. I will make a deal with you."

I groaned. "It's going to be something to do with the horse, isn't it?"

"Yes."

"Metal-tipped arrows?"

"Absolutely not. But I will teach you how to shoot a disruptor—only targets, and only when I am present—but you must ride Delilah at a trot."

I bit back the need to whine that I'd fall off, and thought about it for a minute before shaking his hand. "Five minutes of trotting for an hour of shooting practice."

"An hour for an hour," he countered.

"Ten minutes trotting for half an hour shooting."

"One-to-one, dove. For every minute you learn how to ride at a trot, I will allow you a minute shooting."

That seemed like the best deal I was going to get, so I agreed to his terms.

I survived a whole twenty minutes of going around in a circle at a trot while Delilah was on a long lead, Alan on the other end, before I made him stop, claiming my butt had suffered enough.

He'd just set up a bit of cloth with marks on it, attached to one of the hay bales, and was instructing me on how to prime and ready the disruptor before firing, when one of the men guarding the perimeter shouted.

Alan swore when he turned, holding a hand to his eyes.

In the distance, the long shape of an airship could be seen. It was black, like Alan's, but it looked much bigger, one that was clearly suitable for an emperor.

"Damn him, he's early," Alan said under his breath, turning back to me.

"Lesson later," I said, turning the disruptor's charge switch to off, and putting it back in the holster. "Where do you want me?"

He thought for a moment, his eyes going to the tent that he'd recently had erected, and which he'd told me would be our temporary home while the emperor claimed his.

"By my side," he said at last, and, taking my hand in his, started flinging orders to everyone. Our clothes and effects were moved to the smaller tent, while other men and servants ran to ready the meal that the imperator would expect upon arrival.

I rode at Alan's side, aware of a sense of tension that seemed to hum through the camp. It left me feeling itchy and uncomfortable, but I didn't want to say anything to Alan. He had enough on his plate, and I had promised myself that I would do everything I could to ease his mind. If that meant keeping my mouth shut while his father was here, then so be it.

I did leave him long enough to go into our replacement tent and change out of the reproduced version of my silk tunic and pants to don one of Leila's dresses, the loosest one, as well as the baggiest of her pants. The more I looked like a shapeless frump, the happier I'd be.

"Are you up to this?" Alan asked, ready to help me onto Delilah's back. "I would prefer to have you with me, but if you wish to stay behind—"

"No, if you want me with you when you meet your father, then I'll be there." I eyed Delilah, taking a firm grip on my resolve. "It won't be a long ride."

He said nothing, just hoisted me up into the saddle before taking charge of the white monster. I rode behind him as we went out to meet the imperator's entourage, Delilah's trot slow enough that we'd drifted to the back of Alan's company by the time we stopped where the airship had landed.

I noted that one of the men led Sampson, but didn't have a chance to ask why before Yussuf, a guard Alan had assigned to accompany me, helped me off Delilah. I was just thankful I'd managed to not fall off despite her bone-shaking trot, and even steeled myself enough to pat her neck twice before moving up to where Alan stood, his arms crossed, his legs braced wide. With his turban, and the rich gold fabric embroidered with birds of prey, he looked every inch the fierce Prince Akbar.

He didn't turn his head when I stopped next to him, but he did poke one elbow out. I tucked my hand in it, feeling oddly touched by the gesture. From what Alan hinted, I suspected his father would not be any too happy seeing him with me, but the fact that he didn't try to downplay our relationship—burgeoning as it was—warmed me to the tips of my toes.

"Dammit," I said under my breath.

"What?" he asked just as softly, his eyes firmly fixed on the people who streamed out of the airship.

"I think I'm falling in love with you."

He said nothing for a moment, then turned to glare at me. "You choose now, this moment, when my father is literally seconds away from us, to tell me that?"

"Sorry," I apologized, patting his arm. "It just kind of burst out of me. I didn't mean to discombobulate you when you're distracted."

"I don't even know what 'discombobulated' means, and yet, it doesn't matter, because I have no time, absolutely no time to deal with the fact that you are deliberately trying to make me insane with words I don't know."

"I wouldn't do that," I said out of the side of my mouth when he turned his attention back to the incoming group of people. "Think of it more as something to chew over when you're bored."

He gave a little snort of laughter that was immediately stifled. I slapped a serene expression on my face, moving with him when he strode forward, the entourage having halted about ten feet in front of us. He stopped in front of a large, fleshy man in white-and-gold robes, poufy harem pants, and a fierce grizzled beard.

"You are welcome, Father," Alan said, bowing, then released my hand and stepped forward to kiss his father's cheeks. The imperator studied him with black, shiny eyes that instantly filled me with distrust.

"My son, you look well. But why do we speak English?"

"Thank you, I am well. You do me great honor with your visit," Alan replied, and then gestured back toward me. "My woman is American. She does not speak Kazakh, and I would not have her miss a word from the great Imperator Aurangzeb III. Hallie, I would present you to my father, the Imperator."

Smooth, I thought to myself, taking the hand Alan offered me, and made my best curtsy, not that I was exactly sure how to make one. "It's a pleasure to meet you, Your Imperial Majesty," I said, hoping I was remembering the form of address correctly.

"Ah, indeed," the imperator said, his eyes crawling over me in a way that left me wanting an immediate bath. I kept my smile, wanting to do Alan proud. "She is a beauty, my son, even though she is unfortunately marked."

I opened my mouth to tell him that I didn't consider being freckled as "unfortunately marked," but snapped my teeth closed, remembering that I was there to support Alan.

He acknowledged the compliment with a bow of his head and, with my hand firmly in his, turned to lead his father to the horses, but stopped when the imperator spoke again.

"I have with me a most important visitor, one whose comforts I know you will see to as well as you do my own."

A man sidled out from the collection of twenty or so courtiers and guards, all of them male. I stiffened at the sight of the long face and coppery hair of the man when he stopped in front of us, his eyes widening at the sight of me.

"Etienne Briel is the leader of those who would see the British emperor brought to heel," the imperator said, his voice fat with pleasure. "We have drawn up an accord so that we might better work together to bring an end to William VI's influence on Europe."

"What?" The look of mingled fury and horror on Alan's face said a lot, but although his grip on my hand turned painful, he managed to get himself under control quickly. "You take our enemy to your bosom?"

"Is it not said that an enemy held close cannot strike without harming himself?" the imperator countered, and I knew, I just *knew* he was enjoying Alan's discomfiture.

Alan could not protest his father's actions. I made sure to drop my gaze to the ground in hopes that my hair would hide my face from Etienne. He couldn't have had much of a glimpse of me at El Kef, so perhaps he wouldn't put two and two together.

"Indeed," Alan said at last, and stiffly gestured toward the horses. "We have much to discuss. Would you care to try out my stallion, Father?"

"Naturally I would, but I believe we should allow that honor to our esteemed guest," the imperator said.

Etienne made a smarmy little bow, and was about to reply when the white devil reared up, screaming and thrashing the air with his polished hooves. Once the two grooms had him under control again, Etienne murmured that he would not dream of denying the imperator the pleasure of such a fine beast.

"Chicken," I murmured softly. The jerk of Alan's hand in mine showed he heard me, but he said nothing, just led me back to where Delilah stood with her head hanging low, looking more than half-asleep.

The imperator evidently possessed Alan's way with horses, because he charged past us, the white horse prancing and tossing his head, but more or less in control. I could feel his gaze on Delilah, scorn curling his lips. And it was at that moment that I threw fear to the wind and, with head held high, didn't wait for Alan to walk me through the usual procedures. I patted Delilah on her nose, slid my hand over to her neck, and then got into the saddle before Alan could hoist me up.

He stood with his hand on my thigh for a moment, his gaze as blue as a sapphire in a pool of clear water; then he mounted Sampson and rode after his father.

Yussuf immediately rode to my side. I was about to ask him where Ajay was when Az, the behemoth who I knew was devoted to Alan, moved up to my other side. I shot him a grateful glance, which he acknowledged with a little nod.

We were the last to arrive in the camp. I assumed Alan and his father were already in the big tent, and so took myself off to our temporary home, figuring I'd be sent for if I was wanted.

Alan came into the tent about an hour later. I was curled up in a chair reading one of the few books his sister had in

English, amazed that even though this world's society had evolved differently than mine, the literature was very similar, but set it down at his furious scowl.

He ripped off his tunic and threw it onto the rug that covered the ground, snarling something in Kazakh while pouring water into the big washbowl, and splashing much of it on his chest and face.

I rose and picked up his tunic, shaking it out and folding it before putting it on a chest. "That bad, was it?"

He swore in French.

"I take it you had no idea your dad was joining forces with Etienne?"

"No." He stood for a moment with his hands on the water bowl, looking at the mirror he used to shave, his gaze locked on mine. "I have to get you out of here."

I froze. "Did he recognize me?"

"No, I don't think so. At least, he made no mention of it."

"Oh, good." I relaxed a little. "If it's not because of Etienne, then it must be your dad. Was he so overcome with my charms that he demanded you hand me over on a silver platter?"

"Yes," he said, surprising me.

I slid my arms around him, pressing myself against his bare back, reveling in the feeling of all that warm flesh. I pressed a kiss to one of his shoulders. "Sweetie, there's no way in hell I'm going to sleep with anyone but you. I meant what I said, you know. You've gotten to me the way no one else has, not that I want to talk about that now. I just want to reassure you that I'm here for you, and no one else."

He sighed, then turned around, pulling me against his damp chest, burying his face in my neck. "And I thank god for that. Hallie—what you said—"

"No," I interrupted, putting two fingers on his lips. He gently bit them. "Let's leave the relationship talk for another time, OK? Everything is still so new and, honestly, kind of confusing, and I feel a bit self-conscious even talking with you about it."

"There are times when you drive me almost to insanity with your ideas, and then there are times when I want to praise your wisdom to the skies," he said, kissing my fingers.

"Uh-huh. Men are always happy to avoid talking about relationships, so don't give me that crap." I smiled to take the sting out of my words. "Now, the important stuff: what does your dad want you to do that has you so irate?"

"Too much to talk about now. The feast is ready to start, and I must be in attendance. If I were to ask you to take the *Nightwing* to your brother, would you do it?"

I thought about that for a good fifteen seconds. "Do you really think I'm in danger if Etienne doesn't realize it was me in El Kef? With Az and Yussuf and Ajay guarding me?"

He ran a hand through his hair, making it stand on end. "I don't know. In this, my father is the least of my worries. He will not like me refusing to let him use your body, but he knows he can't force me to do so. But Etienne ..."

"Is an asshat, but I doubt if he's the kind of person who'd keep quiet if he recognized me," I said, nodding. "The answer is pretty clear, then. No, I won't go to Jack and Octavia. If all you're really worried about is Etienne, then I'll just stay here, and will become besties with Az, Ajay, and Yussuf. I promise that I won't so much as use the latrine without having at least one of them with me, all right?"

He hesitated, his breath warm on my neck. I hugged him as tightly as I could and added, "I've got a warrior boob, remember? And I know how to use a sword, and daggers, even if I'm not super awesome with them, and maybe I'll have my threesome teach me to shoot a disruptor while you are doing things with your daddy and Mr. Nasty."

He laughed, kissed me hard and fast, and then set me from him so he could don a fresh tunic. "The last thing that's going to convince me to let you stay here are your credentials with weapons, little dove. But I will trust that you will not place yourself in any situation where you're at risk."

"Cross my heart," I promised, suiting action to word. "Am I to come to this feast?"

"Yes." His voice was grim. "I want you in my sight as much as possible."

"Oooh, that sounds promising," I said, then hurried over to the chest that contained my new clothes, and pulled out a modified version of Leila's dress that I'd had made in a pretty shade of moss and gold. Alan was outside the tent when I had put it on, brushed my hair, and, after a moment's thought, rubbed one of Leila's sachets over my dress in hopes of giving me a little aromatherapy boost.

The tables that Alan's men ate at had been pushed together and supplemented by the one from his tent. Since only a few of his men were actually at the table, I gathered that this event was for the imperator's entourage. Aurangzeb himself sat at the head of the table, sitting in a massive throne-like chair that must have been hauled out from his airship. He was already seated when we approached, with Etienne sitting on his right. He gestured toward the chair to the left. Alan pulled out the chair next to it, seating me first before taking his own.

"You say your woman is American?" the imperator asked, giving me another oily look that left me feeling soiled. "Have you made sure she has no ties to William? I have heard that he uses many women, and when he is done with them, he sends them out to his enemies to act as spies. Have you tortured her sufficiently to know she can be trusted?"

I looked at him in shock for a moment, and then did the unthinkable. I burst into laughter.

Alan sighed, and I immediately apologized. "I'm sorry, I really am. It's just that it was so funny the way he said … never mind." I was aware of the fulminating looks of everyone around me. I cleared my throat and addressed myself to the food put in front of me, biting my lip to keep from laughing more.

"Your woman thinks I am funny?" the imperator said, working himself up to an outraged state. "She would dare mock me! You will strip her bare and flog her before us, one stripe on her back for every second of her reprehensible actions."

Etienne smirked. "What an excellent idea. It's been far too long since I've seen a good flogging."

I stiffened, but Alan's warning hand on my leg kept me silent despite the need to tell the annoying, slimy, overbearing ass what he could do with his attitude. The urge to ask Etienne how his broken nose was doing was almost as strong, but I kept Alan's need for peace uppermost in my mind.

"I will not do anything so heinous," Alan said in a voice that was smooth and unemotional, but I wasn't fooled. "She did not mock you; she simply responded to your outrageous comments, as you knew she would." He leveled his father a long look. "In the future, if you wish to goad me, I would prefer you do it directly, rather than going through Hallie."

The imperator grunted and, to my relief, turned his attention to Etienne.

"Ah, I have a bit of news that will interest you, my son," the imperator said toward the end of the meal, giving Alan a very toothy smile. "I have arranged for a marriage between you and Constanza, the Duchess of Prussia."

"The hell?"

Everyone looked at me in surprise, and I realized that not only had I shrieked the word, but I was on my feet.

"Uh … sorry. Something nasty just stung me," I said, pretending to rub my arm, and quickly retook my seat.

Alan shot me a look before turning back to his father. "I've told you in the past that I have no desire for you to arrange a marriage for me, and that continues to be true."

"Bah," the imperator said, waving away his objection. "You are my only son. You are not getting younger, and Constanza is young. She will give you many fine sons."

I took a piece of flatbread, laid it carefully on my plate, and stabbed it with my fork. It felt so good, I stabbed it twice more, and was seriously considering getting my blunted daggers to do a better job of stabbing until Alan, without looking at me, took away my fork.

"Do you think I'm interested in another man's leavings?" Alan said, his voice full of arrogance. "She was to wed

William, but he shunned her on their wedding day. When I marry, it will be to a virtuous woman, not one who was spurned because she was caught in the arms of a guard."

I wondered if that was true, and looked at Alan with speculation. Just how did he define virtuous?

"You will marry her. I have decreed this. The marriage contracts have been signed." The obnoxious old man signaled for more wine. "She will meet us in Bohemia, where you will be wed, and then you will control all of Prussia and Bohemia."

"I have signed no marriage contract," Alan said calmly. "Any agreement you have made is not with my consent, and I will be sure to tell the duchess that."

"You will do as you are ordered," the imperator snapped. "You forget who I am!"

"I have forgotten nothing," Alan answered, his voice getting a bit ragged around the edges. "I have served you and the interest of your empire my entire life, but about this, I alone will have the final say."

"You are letting your cock talk for you," the old man said, glancing at me. "There is no need to give up your woman if you choose not to. You may have her and any others so long as you wed the duchess. Heed me well, Akbar! I will not allow the lands she holds to slip through my fingers."

I wanted to tell the old coot off—oh, how I wanted to tell him off—but the promise I'd made myself to keep my lips zipped kept me sitting there without saying anything. This was about Alan, and supporting him while he was in a difficult position. So no matter what utter rot his father spewed, I'd sit there and not say a damned thing.

Even if it killed me.

Alan must have read my mind, because he stood up and murmured something about me retiring for the night.

"Are you sure?" I whispered to him when he pulled out my chair. "If you need moral support, I will stay. I want my fork back, and several more pieces of bread, but I'll stay."

"This will take half the night," he said, suddenly looking tired. My heart went out to him, and I wanted nothing so much as to put my arms around him, and kiss him until he forgot his worries, but instead I nodded and, without a word to the others, left the feast.

NINE

Before going to our temporary home, I made a brief stop at the tiny tent Alan had set up for my use as a private toilet, for which I was infinitely grateful, since the rest of his company simply used open latrines.

"Thanks for being my bodyguard," I told Az when he escorted me back to our temporary digs. Beyond the row of tents, I could see Alan still sitting at the long table, talking to his father and Etienne.

"It is my pleasure," he said in his deep, thickly accented voice. "I will guard the falcon's dove with my life."

"The falcon. Is that what you call Alan?"

"Aye," he answered, making a little bow in Alan's direction. "Since he was a young boy, he has ever had a fondness for birds, and spent many a long hour in with the falconer, learning his ways."

"Interesting. It explains why he has bird decorations everywhere. Well, thank you again. I appreciate you taking the trouble to follow me around. Good night."

He held open the flap for me, waiting until I lit an oil lamp before dropping it. I had a quick wash, brushed my teeth with the repulsive tooth powder I'd bought in town, and got into bed with Leila's book, wondering how long the imperator would keep Alan, and how hard the former was going to fight to get Alan to marry the duchess.

I remembered hearing about her from Jack. She was set to marry William the day we were going to be hung for treason, but then the Moghuls attacked, and evidently the wedding was delayed. I guess they called it off after that. I had no idea why, and frankly, I didn't care so long as Constanza kept her grubby hands off Alan.

The question was, could Alan outright defy his father? "If he can't, it'll be over for us," I told the book, not seeing the words on the pages. "I won't be anyone's bit of fluff on the side, not even Alan's. Oh, goddess, why is everything so horribly tangled up?"

I resigned myself to a long night, one filled with doubts and worry and heartache.

Warmth at my back woke me up. I froze for a moment at the feel of something pressed against me, my brain muzzy with a disturbing dream. "Alan?"

"Did you think I would never return?" he murmured, one hand around my front, caressing my breasts, the other sliding down to my hip, and lower to my thigh. "My father enjoys hearing himself talk, but even he has limits."

"What time is it?" I asked, arching when his hand stroked up my thigh, and teased flesh that was more than happy to wake up and party with him.

"About three hours from dawn. My father wishes to go hunting once the sun is up, but I must have you before I leave."

"I like the sound of that … whoa. New position? This is … oooh!"

Alan pulled my upper leg back over his, positioning my hips so that they were tilted, giving him access to where he knew he would find a welcome, and welcome him I did when he eased into me. "I'm sorry, love, but all I could do was think of you while that Etienne droned on and on. I know you said you were fast, but perhaps you're not—"

"Oh, yes I am. I so very am. Do it now. Right now," I moaned, desperately wanting to turn so I could touch him, feel him against my chest, but at the same time enjoying this new angle. He seemed to reach places that he'd never touched before. "I think … oh, god yes to the hip swivel … I think you found my G-spot. Holy hamsters, yes, that's definitely it."

"I don't know what that is, but since you seem to enjoy it—" His hips flexed with strong, piercing movements, his hand on my abdomen, pulling my hips to him with every thrust. He built an amazing pressure inside of me, one that seemed to make my whole body tighten around just one point, the fullness of him combined with the different angle hitting all the sensitive spots inside pushing me inexorably into an orgasm that had me tightening all my muscles in spasms of absolute pleasure.

Alan groaned my name as he, too, found his release, pressing deep into me a couple of times, which was enough to generate little aftershocks in me.

"So, that position gets an A plus from me," I said, turning so I could kiss him, his lips warm and sweet. "Mmm. You've been drinking mead."

"My father favors it," he said, pulling me close, his chest drawing me in as it always did. "And yes, that is now a favorite position. I hadn't tried it before, but we will add it to the list of preferred methods of lovemaking."

"It's right up there with orange oil in the bathtub. Do you have to go hunting in the morning? If it's so close to dawn, you'll only get a few hours of sleep."

"Unfortunately, yes. It is something my father enjoys, and he requested it specifically. Are you going to yell at me now about Constanza?"

I smiled against his mouth, nipping his lower lip. "You know me so well. I won't yell, but I do want to ask you one thing."

"No," he said, pulling me against him. "I do not want to wed her."

"Silly." I pinched his side, breathing deeply of his delicious scent. It was very masculine, now tinged with the results of our lovemaking, but even without that, he smelled like … I had a hard time pinning down the scents that teased me. Something faintly spicy that I assumed was his shaving soap, but there was another layer, something that made me feel very feminine. "I was going to ask if you can defy your father."

"I can, I have, and I will continue to do so if I need to," he reassured me.

"Good." I sighed, and pressed my face into his shoulder, twining one of my legs between his. "Then I have nothing to yell at you about."

"I'm sure you'll find something, but not concerning Constanza. Hallie, promise me that you will not go anywhere without all three guards."

"I have no intention of doing so. I *was* going to go into town, because I really want to start an anti-corset league for the ladies there, to show them that they don't have to be slaves to the steel-caged fashion, but I can have a day reading in bed instead."

"I think that might be a better idea. Do not stir from the tent without the guards."

"All right," I said, yawning, and snuggling into him, strangely happy despite the threat of having the imperator and Etienne breathing down our necks.

I trusted Alan to keep us both safe. He was, after all, a famous warlord. Who else could keep others from messing with us?

It's amazing sometimes just how wrong I can be about things.

What seemed like ten minutes later, but was probably a couple of hours, Alan shook me awake. "Hallie."

"Mmrf?" I cracked open an eye to see him pulling clothing out of the chest belonging to his sister. I wondered if he'd even had time to sleep, since he was fully dressed. "Are you going off to slaughter animals now?" I made kissy sounds before snuggling back into the feather bed. "Have fun."

"You have to get up. Here, these look like they go together." He shoved a couple of pieces of clothing at me.

"What?" I sat up, frowning. "Why do I need to get dressed? I don't want to go hunting with you or anyone else. I'm against blood sports."

"You're going into town." His voice was grim and flinty.

"Why?"

"Because I've changed my mind. Etienne may not have recognized you, but I don't trust him not to make some excuse while we're out and return in order to do you harm."

"Why would he do that if he didn't recognize me?"

"I said he *may* not have recognized you. I don't know for certain that he did not do so. If he did, and hid it, it must be for some foul purpose."

I thought about that for a moment, then hurriedly pulled on the clothes Alan held out, snatching up the soft linen bag I usually wore under my shirt that had the remains of my funds, and tucked into it the book I was reading before slinging it across my chest. "Normally I would say you were being overprotective and a worrywart, but from what I've heard of Etienne, if he knows it was me in El Kef, then I'd really rather not tangle with him. Where am I going?"

"The house of the headman. I've paid him to keep your presence quiet. You must be quick, though. I don't want anyone seeing you leave."

We crept out of the tent after Alan had a quick look around first; then we booked it to the line where the horses were tied, Alan leading me past them and out into the wilds for another five minutes, before he stopped at a large outcropping of dusty rocks. Az waited there, along with Yussuf and Ajay, all three of them mounted, with Delilah looking particularly dejected.

"Go," Alan said, kissing me hard and fast. "I'll bring you back later, when the hunt is over. Do not go anywhere alone."

"Are you kidding? I just know if Etienne does me in, your dad will have you married to that Constanza chick so fast, your head will spin. I have to stay alive just to save you from that horrible future."

He smiled, and heaved me onto Delilah's back. "I will hold you to that, dove. Now, fly."

We flew, if by "flying" you mean trotting, which was more than fast enough for me. We hit the town of Tozeur just as the sun's peach fingers stretched across the sky, and made it to the headman's house without anyone seeing us but a couple of goats and a small boy who was herding them to a field filled with scraggly shrubs.

The headman turned out to be a very nice old man, white haired and with a lined face, his wife just as ancient, but they made us at home, offering me the only private room in their house. Neither of them spoke anything but the most primitive English, and since my only other language was French, we didn't communicate until Yussuf offered to translate.

I helped the woman, whose name was Hiba, make some of the flatbread consumed locally, petted the small dog who followed her around until I caught a flea leaping off the dog and onto my arm, then sat in their minuscule bedroom and read for a few hours.

By midday, I was bored, and going nuts.

"Would it be OK if we went to the oasis and had a swim?" I asked Az.

He sounded scandalized when he answered, "You wish to bathe in the oasis waters?"

"Not bathe, swim. I could wear my undies and ... right," I said, realizing that although I badly wanted to help emancipate women, I wasn't going to be able to do it starting with Az. "OK, so a swim is out. What about a walk? Can we take a walk? Just the four of us?"

He shook his head. "The prince would not like it. He wishes for you to stay here until he returns for you."

"But Etienne isn't here. Even if did want to hurt me, he has no idea I'm in town. What if we walked to the north? That's the opposite direction of the camp, and it's even less likely that we'd run into Etienne there. Plus, I'll have all three of you to protect me."

It took a good ten minutes of wheedling, but at last Az agreed that I could take a short walk, but only to the north, and we had to stay off the road.

The region around Tozeur was filled with dried river-beds called wadis, sharp, dusty rock outcroppings, a variety of scraggly shrubs that seldom grew taller than three feet, and numerous date trees.

To the south, beyond Alan's camp, the terrain turned to undulating waves that transitioned into the sand dunes of the Sahara, while to the north, the land was arid and un-inspiring. But I was determined to take pleasure in every minute of it as we strolled along the middle of a wadi, taking delight in the few birds that flitted high overhead playing hide-and-seek amongst the date trees.

The wadi swung to the east, and Az stopped us, saying we needed to turn back.

"You're a party pooper," I said, unwilling to go back to house arrest. "All right, all right, I know, it's not safe. Let me just pop up to the top for a second so I can see what the landscape is like—then we'll go back."

Az grumbled, but pulled out a skin containing wine, taking a pull on it while I scrambled up the wadi bank. As I crested it, I stopped, staring with first surprise, then horror at the white-and-black airship that was moored about fifty feet away, my appearance startling an armed guard who spun around to look at me.

I looked at the guard. I looked at the giant Black Hand image on the forward-most envelope. I looked at the group of people who were lounging around outside open cargo doors, all of whom stood and gawked at me.

"The prince's woman!" one of the men said in French, pointing at me.

"Oh, shit," I swore, and for a fraction of a second, the immediate future was laid out before me just as if some-one had filmed it. I saw my three guards streaming up over the wadi bank, only to be slaughtered by the approximately fifteen Black Hand men. That I was caught was not disputable—they had me, and I knew it. But I'd be damned if I sacrificed Az, Yussuf, and Ajay because I had to take a walk.

All that went through my mind while one second passed to another, and then I was running, racing away from the wadi at a speed that I had not, to that point in my life, ever achieved.

There was a shout that I feared was from Az, but I didn't slow down to look back. I ran like I was trying to qualify for the Olympics, leaping over small rocks and shrubs, heading, for some reason that I couldn't explain, for the road that snaked northward. If I could just get the Black Hand guards far enough away from Az and company, then perhaps they would survive.

As best I can figure it, I lasted about a quarter mile; then the fact that I wasn't in the shape of someone qualifying for the Olympics caught up to me.

As did Etienne's men.

The first one to reach me launched a flying tackle that ended up with me flattened, the breath knocked out of me, and my mouth full of dirt. I limped and swore as the full contingent of men hauled me back to their airship, but even though I spat out dirt and invectives equally, I didn't see any bodies near the wadi. I sent up a little prayer that Az and company had gotten away, my mind so busy with that, I didn't even object when I was tossed into a small, airless storeroom on the airship.

I sat there for what seemed like an interminable time, guilty, angry with myself, trying to think of an explanation for Alan—assuming I ever saw him again—and in general utterly miserable. The incarceration reminded me of the time a year before when I'd been imprisoned on a trumped-up charge. I'd survived then by going over the acts of revenge I would perform on my captors, lovingly detailing them, as well as thoughts of what I'd do when I returned to my own world.

This time, my thoughts spun around Alan, just as if he was a lodestone. If the guards had gotten away and told him

I'd been captured, what would he do? Would he come after me? Try to take down Etienne? Would his father stand for that?

I was confident that Alan wouldn't just wash his hands of me, but realistically, was there anything he could do? "If his dad is so damned insistent that they work with the Black Hand, then he won't be able to do anything against Etienne without causing a civil war, and Alan isn't stupid. He knows he can't win that."

I gnawed on my lower lip while I worried, suddenly sitting upright when I realized that not only had I fallen asleep, but the floor under my feet was vibrating in a familiar manner.

The airship was moving. I peered out a small, grimy porthole, barely able to see a few wispy clouds and rolling brown earth sliding away beneath us.

At that moment, the door behind me opened, and Etienne himself stood with a smug smile on his face. "How very thoughtful you were to deliver yourself to me. It's almost as if you know of the many plans I have for you."

I slumped back on the narrow cot, my heart sinking. I was well and truly in it this time.

TEN

"I want you to remove to France as soon as you can."

Alan looked at his father in surprise, wondering what the old fox had in mind. "Why France? You wished for me to move inward to Spain, once we had cleared the British empire and revolutionaries from Tunisia and Algeria. I have only just begun to do so."

"Our plans have changed," the imperator said, waving a hand backward, toward where Etienne rode with Soroush, his father's confidant and vizier. Alan didn't trust Soroush any more than he did Etienne, well aware that for the last ten years or so, the advice given by the vizier went counter to Alan's attempts to de-escalate his father's hostilities and brutality. "You have difficulty embracing our new alliance."

"Of course I do. It's a foolish plan. Etienne Briel is the consummate liar. He spills honeyed words in your ear while stabbing you in the back. To believe he will honor any agreement you make with him is to not just make yourself a fool, but to damn our people."

"I will allow you to speak such hasty, ill-thought words because I know my passion flows through your veins," his father said, obviously well pleased with himself.

Alan wondered why that was, since he had steadfastly refused the demands that he wed Constanza. He turned to look back at the company that rode with them. Thus far, the hunt had yielded little, only two hartebeests, and one ancient gazelle that had looked like it was about to die even before his father shot it. Etienne was still there, conversing with the vizier.

That didn't dissipate the uneasy feeling that gripped Alan. Something had made his father happy, and Alan had come to view that emotion with much misgiving. It seldom boded well for him or his plans. "What am I to do in France?" he asked, deciding he needed to know the worst.

"We will stop here for a meal," his father said, raising a hand. Immediately, the servants leaped off their mounts, placing rugs, pillows, a small table, and a chair for the imperator's pleasure. Alan dismounted, handing Sampson's reins to his groom, reluctant for any delay. The longer his father dragged out the hunt, the more time Hallie was out of his protection.

He told himself he was being nervous over nothing, and stood before his father, waiting as patiently as possible for the instructions that were sure to come.

"Sit, my son, sit," the imperator said, waving him to a cushion. Around them, men and servants bustled, unpacking food and drink, watering the horses, and taking their own meager rations to whatever comfortable rocks or bare patches of earth that could be found. "You wish to know about France, eh? Well, these are my thoughts. I will lay them before you, and you will see just how clever your father has been. Our brother-in-arms Etienne has discovered that William has a plot to lay claim to the Hungarian empire by means of France and Germany. He has convinced the queen of France to give him free passage through her lands, and is stockpiling men and resources in Marseilles. From there, it is evident he will launch attacks east, through Germany to Bohemia, while the fool Iago will bestir himself from Rome and also move to the east, attempting to reclaim Turkey."

"Then why are you here?" Alan asked, the memories of how many lives were lost retaking Constantinople still all too fresh in his mind. He had fought hard against his father's plans to take that city, but had been unable to keep the resulting destruction from wiping the city bare. "Why do you not defend your own borders instead of looking to fight for others?"

"Because now we have the Black Hand giving Bohemia to us," his father said with a satisfied chuckle, peering at a plate of cold roast fowl that was offered. He wrinkled his nose and waved it away, examining instead a bowl of spiced sweetmeats. "And all it cost me was a little time—Etienne was adamant that I should see for myself the potential that North Africa holds for us, but I see little here that is worthy of our concern—and one easily granted boon."

"What boon is that?" Alan asked, shaking his head at the food offered to him. He damned near itched to get moving, to make sure Hallie was safe, but he knew there was no hurrying his father.

The imperator smiled, and popped a bit of sweetmeat into his mouth, saying around it, "Your woman."

"What?" He was on his feet before he realized it, a great wave of fury boiling out of him. "What have you done?"

"What needed to be done," his father snapped, his dark eyes narrowed on Alan. "For too long have I let you run free, furthering my cause as you saw fit, but now is the time when I call you to heel. Etienne demanded your woman as compensation for eliminating William's forces from the Hungarian empire, at which point it will be mine. She is a spy, my son, working for some rebel group. Etienne said she attempted to strike at him recently, but ran away when his superior strength became apparent. It is a small price to pay—"

Fear, anger, guilt—a horrible mixture of emotions gripped Alan's gut, but he was moving even before his father had finished speaking, searching through the people who were scattered amongst and around the horses.

Etienne was nowhere to be found.

The vizier sidled up to the imperator, but Alan knew then that he had been played for a fool, and idiot that he was, he'd walked into it blindly. Sick almost to the point of retching at the knowledge he'd failed his dove, he prayed that Hallie's hiding place wouldn't be discovered before he returned.

He called for his horse and his men.

"Akbar! You will not defy me in this," the imperator yelled, getting to his feet with a grunt. "I have labored long to set these plans in motion, and you will fall in line with them."

"I have done as you've commanded all my life," Alan told his father, striding toward him in a manner that had the vizier, who had been whispering in his father's ear, backing up until he stumbled over a footstool. He fought against his emotions, his voice harsh with the effort of control. "I have fought for you. I have watched as friends, family, and entire towns were slaughtered on the altar of your greed for power, and not once did you listen to my advice. You were too bound up in visions of your own glory. I have fought my entire life against William's empire, but you have become a hundred times worse than him. You have become an insatiable monster, willing to sell your very soul in order to conquer what you do not possess. I will not be a party to that. No longer. You have gone too far this time."

"You dare!" his father roared, his face red with anger. "No son of mine will speak to me so!"

"Then I am no longer your son. Akbar dies here, right now," he snarled in return, and would have walked away, but at that moment, a black-and-red pain exploded in his head, and he slipped unwillingly into an abyss of misery.

The pain was what pulled him out of the abyss, that and a nagging feeling that he needed to be doing something. He swam in the pain for a bit, trying to get his mind to focus, but thoughts kept dodging him, sliding away just when he thought he had them in his grasp.

And then suddenly, the blackness ebbed, and he was left with pain and the memory of what had troubled him.

"Hallie!" he said on a long, gasping breath, sitting upright, and immediately regretting that movement when the world wobbled around him.

"Thank the gods, you are not insensible," a voice said behind him. "Az was convinced the imperator had bashed your head in hard enough that he'd left you an idiot. You look like you're going to vomit."

Alan gripped the side of the bed he sat on, his eyes closed as he fought to keep the contents of his stomach where they were. It took a few minutes, but at last the pain ebbed enough that he could open his eyes and face his friend. "Where is she?" he asked Zand.

"I'm sorry to say that the revolutionaries have her."

"When?" he asked, closing his eyes for a moment, the sickness rising again in his throat as he thought of his dove, his sweet, unconventional, endlessly fascinating Hallie, in the hands of Etienne Briel.

"Yesterday. It is almost morn. Your father's men struck you down, thinking you were going to attack him. You have been insensible for more than twelve hours."

"Christ," Alan swore, wanting to get his hands first on Etienne, and then on his father. "And Hallie?"

"She ran into the revolutionaries' airship outside of town." Zand recounted the happenings of the previous day. "She deliberately led the Black Hand away from her guards, Alan. Do you think she wanted to be captured?"

The pain of imagining her having been taken from him was almost too much to bear, but he pushed his emotions down, knowing he needed his wits to be sharp. "She loathes Etienne almost as much as we do," he answered after a moment. "It's more likely that she thought she could lead the revolutionaries away from them in order to protect them."

"Why would she be so foolish?" Zand asked, shaking his head.

Alan met his gaze with one filled with pain. "Because she values the welfare of those around her."

"My prince!" Yussuf, who had evidently been lurking outside the tent, threw himself at Alan's feet. He was almost immediately followed by Ajay, who followed suit, leaving both men now prostrated before him. Slowly, Alan stood, fear gripping him with sharp, razor-like talons.

Azahgi Bahajir entered the tent and moved to stand before him, before he knelt, his head bowed. "My prince, we have failed you. We have shamed ourselves and our families, and we humbly ask that you relieve us of our heads, for we do not deserve to live."

For a moment, Alan's hand itched for a sword. He had placed Hallie in his trusted guards' care, and this was how they repaid him? But even as that thought flitted through his head, he realized that short of handing Hallie over to Etienne, his men were no more to blame for her capture than she was.

"You have indeed committed a grave sin," he said after a suitably weighty silence. He knew the men's pride was at stake, and since he, too, valued those who served him, he said in a voice that was harsher than he felt, "Henceforth, you owe me a debt that will be fulfilled by your service until such time as I say it has been redeemed. Now rise, and get your things packed. Send a servant in to pack mine. And you," he said, turning to Zand when the other three men, with stunned looks on all three of their faces, bowed and hurried out. "You can tell me what's happened while I was lying with a broken head."

"Etienne returned before your father from the hunt," he said, watching Alan while he got into the familiar gold tunic and leggings. "I couldn't have stopped him if I had wanted to, since most of the men were with you, and the imperator left behind a good two dozen men. I had a few men trail him—they reported that he entered an airship that was moored north of Tozeur and left almost immediately. That was after noon, yesterday."

"We've lost a whole day," Alan said, wincing when, without thinking, he tried to don a turban. "At least I know where he's headed."

"Bohemia?" Zand asked.

"France. Marseilles, to be exact." Alan caught sight of a flash of yellow in his shaving mirror and stood for a moment, looking at himself.

"What are you going to do? Other than go after her, of course. One of the men said that you told your father that he was dead to you, and that you would no longer do his bidding."

"Akbar is dead," he said slowly, still eyeing his reflection. "He was killed by the imperator."

Zand said nothing, but his eyebrows rose. Slowly, deliberately, Alan removed the gold clothing of the Moghuls. He threw it on the ground, then turned to a chest that was seldom opened, pulling from it the Western clothing that Alan Dubain wore while he graced the court of William VI.

"So that's what you're thinking," Zand said, watching as Alan donned trousers, shirt, and waistcoat before attaching a collar to the shirt, and pulling on a short suit coat. "Akbar dies, and Dubain lives?"

"I do not ask you to follow me," he told his friend, turning to face him. "My actions will be irrevocable. My father will send assassins after me for daring to defy him."

Zand grinned, and punched him on the shoulder. "Since when has there been any love lost between the imperator and me? He would have beheaded me for daring to ask for Safie's hand had you not intervened. I will follow you in this as I have in all other things."

Alan gripped Zand's arms for a moment, grateful that his old friend would support him no matter the risk. "I will see to it that you are not sorry."

"Please tell me that Safie is about to join her brother in heaven, because I can't live much longer without her."

"You may take her with my blessing," Alan answered, and, as a servant entered, directed him to packing up the necessary items.

"What will you tell your father?" Zand asked, having ordered a servant to do likewise with his effects.

"That Akbar is dead," he answered, glancing at the big tent. Four guards stood at attention at it. The sky was lightening, but it wasn't yet dawn. "Have the horses loaded. If anyone tries to stop you, kill them. Yussuf! Gather the men, but be quiet about it. Don't disturb the imperator's people."

It took time to get the *Nightwing* loaded with supplies, horses, tents, and personal effects, but Alan felt infinitely better for doing something. He spoke to his men, gathered outside the camp, and told them that he was resigning from serving the imperator, but that he would leave the decision of what they wished to do up to them.

"If you wish to join the imperator's forces, he will welcome you. If you want the freedom to pursue your own course, you may do that with my blessing. Those of you who wish to join me in a fight against tyranny are more than welcome to gather under my banner."

"What banner would that be?" Zand asked.

Alan looked at the men gathered. Most of them he'd known for at least five years, but some had been with him since he'd been a young man, newly put in charge of a small force of men and given trivial tasks to undertake, until his father had deemed him worthy of more responsibility. "Freedom," he said at last. "Our symbol will be the falcon and the dove."

The men bustled off to get the last of the items loaded, and Alan, knowing he couldn't delay it any longer, marched into the big tent, pausing at the guards. His men moved behind him. He waited for a moment, then entered the tent, moving around the screen until he stood next to the bed where his father slept. A woman, one of the prostitutes he had arranged to be available, *eep*ed and slid out of the bed, gathering up her clothing and scurrying into a corner. The movement woke the imperator.

Alan looked at the man who had sired him, for whom he had fought so hard and long, and felt nothing but a sense of regret that he'd wasted so much time. So many lives.

The imperator squinted at him, grunting. "So you live, eh?"

"I do, but your son is dead. You saw to that yesterday when you sold him for a piece of land."

His father sat up, snarling vicious oaths, his face flushing with anger. "You ungrateful cur! So my son is dead? So be it! I am young yet, and virile still. I will wed the duchess, and beget sons with her, sons who will have the untold riches that Akbar never could have imagined."

Alan was silent for a moment, shaking his aching head. "The fact that you believe wealth is all I sought simply shows me that Akbar never would have pleased you."

He left the tent with his father hurling curses at him, sputtering and calling for his guards to come to his aid. Since all four guards were now unconscious, stacked neatly behind the tent, no one came to answer his demands.

Ten minutes later, the *Nightwing* lifted off just as the imperator's entourage was waking up. Three of Alan's men had opted to leave his company to follow their own paths, and he had given them a sizable amount of money with which to start their own lives. The other men he also paid ahead of the normal date. "From this time on, we will do things differently," he told the gathered crew in the mess. "No longer will we be acting for the glory of the empire. We will, if they will have us, join with a small group who devote themselves to profiting from those who would subdue the general populations."

A word whispered through the crew. *Pirates.*

"We will take a cut of all profits, naturally, just as the Company of Thieves does, but the bulk will be used to ease those whose lives have been negatively affected by the imperator, the Black Hand, and Emperor William." Alan felt a lightening of a burden that he hadn't been aware had bound him so tightly. He wanted badly to explain the feeling to Hallie, pushing down again the pain that threatened to overwhelm him if he let it. "I consider us in a state of war with all three of those entities. We will therefore no longer use any ports or resources friendly to the imperator. Are there any questions?"

There were, and Alan spent another half hour explaining just who the Company of Thieves were, why he had chosen to join his lot with theirs, and what their future held. "As to that, I can't say other than I will do my best to stand by the code of honor to which we have always held, and if you wish to leave my company, you may do so at any time. Az?"

Az stepped forward, bowed to Alan, then turned to the crew and started roaring out orders for them. There was a stampede, and then Alan was alone with his friend.

"You're sure about this?" Zand asked him, then made a face and spread his hands. "I sound like I'm trying to talk you out of it, and I'm not, because this means that after seven long years, Safie and I can be together. But are you sure you wish for Akbar to die? Your father's pride won't let you ever go back."

"He swears he will marry Constanza and breed himself a new crop of sons," Alan said, gently feeling the large lump on the back of his head.

Zand considered that, then shrugged. "I suppose he feels that would give him a claim on Prussia and Bohemia. Are you certain that Etienne is going to Marseilles?"

"That's what the imperator said," Alan said, leaving the mess and heading for his cabin. He had letters to write, ones that would be sent at the first refilling stop. "We're going to need to gather what intelligence we can from our spies. Can you handle that?"

"With pleasure," Zand said, and, after a moment, clapped him on the shoulder. "She'll be all right, Alan. She's a fighter. A poor one, but she has spirit."

Alan gave a grim little laugh, but he made no reply. Worry about Hallie was uppermost on his mind, and he'd already given the navigator the command to get them to Marseilles by the most direct route, taking as little time as possible with stops to refill the boilers and purchase supplies.

Six days later, mail caught up with him in Valencia, Spain. They were flying up the east coast, still roughly two days out of Marseilles, but he eagerly opened the letter written in a familiar concise hand.

Alan, this is a brief note to acknowledge that we have received your letter of the fourteenth. Jack and I are both horrified that Etienne has acted in such an underhanded manner. Of the imperator, the less said the better. Of course you may count on our assistance. Whatever you need, we will provide. Unfortunately, Robert Anstruther is in Ireland, visiting family. Safie is, as you know, in the north of Italy, but I am sending her a message to meet us in France. We are at present in the south of Spain, but are setting off within the hour for Marseilles. We will likely reach there before you, and you can be assured that we will immediately ascertain the location of Etienne, and the status of Hallie.

Jack, needless to say, is beside himself. I'm afraid, my old friend, that the time is nigh to let him in on your secret. I fear for his sanity otherwise, since he is swearing he will slaughter Akbar for handing his sister over to Etienne. I won't reveal your secret to him until I have your permission, but please, do not delay in giving it to me. Jack is suffering, and it pains me greatly to keep anything from him.

There is much more I wish to say, but I will close now, so that this may be sent. Have heart, my friend. The Company of Thieves has your back.

Alan felt a modicum of relief from the letter, but fretted nonetheless at the time that was passing. He didn't expect to be in Marseilles before Etienne, but with luck, the *Nightwing* would arrive shortly thereafter. His ship was faster, and he had bypassed the normal airship routes in favor of speed.

He stood staring out as the land slid by beneath them, his heart filled with emotions that he couldn't deal with. He had a strong suspicion what he'd find when he did look into his feelings, but he pushed it all back, and shoved it out of his mind. He had to remain focused.

He would find Hallie first; then he could breathe again.

ELEVEN

"I really hate you, you know that, right?" I asked when Etienne came to deliver what I'd come to think of as his daily taunt, one where he stood in the doorway of the cell in which I was locked, and said mean things to me.

He sneered at me, his lip curling back in a manner that I found wholly repugnant. "Your thoughts matter little to me, Moghul bitch. As you will find out as soon as we land."

"Yeah, yeah, you're going to torture me, and force me to tell you all of Prince Akbar's secrets, and I'll suffer the most intense torments known to man before you finally put me out of my misery. Heard it for the last seven days, have the T-shirt." I strove for a bored tone, and in truth, it wasn't too hard to achieve.

He snarled something very rude in French, and once again I mused on the fact that he hadn't, in fact, so much as struck me.

Not that I wanted him to become violent, but for a man given to daily visits in which he took great delight in telling me just how he was planning on torturing me, I found it a bit odd that he didn't raise a finger to me. It might have been that he was all bluster and no action, or perhaps the fact that on the day when I was abducted, he had stridden into the cabin where I was confined, only to have me throw up on his feet.

"Hey, while you're here, can you please have your steward cook something that isn't rancid? I've barfed up the meals of the last three days, and it's getting a bit old. Maybe stop for a few fresh veggies? How about some eggs? I wouldn't balk at a steak, even though I don't eat much red meat anymore."

Etienne slammed the door shut, leaving me with nothing but my own company. I sighed and scooted back on the narrow bed, picking up one of the books that I'd begged from a friendly guard. It was in French, and detailed the glorious history of France, but since it was significantly different from the France I knew, I plowed my way steadily through it.

Dinner was served by Armand, the apologetic second steward, a gangly teenager with what I thought at first was acne scars, but later figured out was from smallpox.

"Your food," Armand said, sliding a tray of reddish-brown slop before me, along with a glass of room-temperature goat's milk. He had insisted on bringing me ale the first few days, but I quickly figured out I could barter it to him for milk, so at least now I had something to drink. "It's ragout."

"Eh," I said, poking at it with a spoon. There was a lump of gray mystery meat in it. "A ragout of what?"

He shrugged before digging out from his pocket a heel of bread, set it on the tiny table that was bolted to the wall and floor, and left, locking the door behind him.

I ate around the meat lumps, nibbling on the bread, but regretted the action a few hours later when the ship gave a lurch. My stomach lurched with it, and then seemed to flop over. I dived for the closestool that sat in the corner, and heaved up my dinner.

"I swear to god, that damned Etienne is poisoning me. I'm just going to have to stop eating until I can get away," I told myself after rinsing my mouth out with a tiny bit of water I'd saved from the daily allotment. "It's probably arsenic. All the mysteries I've read say that it makes you ralph. Ugh.

I hope all this barfing isn't bad for my teeth. I really need a proper toothbrush."

Once the poison had been ejected from my stomach, I felt much better, and moved over to open the small porthole window to let a little fresh air into the small cabin. The air was salty, with a tang of the sea on it that raised my spirits.

Below us, a town slid past. We were landing in Marseilles, Etienne's destination according to the chatty Armand. The airship turned to the north, drifting over buildings, streets, and tiny ant-like people. Etienne wasn't likely to land at an airfield, but he probably had some arranged spot where he could land and hide the airship. Jack and Octavia had one not far from town, I mused, doing a swift calculation in my head. According to Jack's notebook that I'd read before I left them, they were due to be in Marseilles soon. I prayed they had arrived early, as they sometimes did in order to research whatever cargo they were planning on liberating.

"Time for the escape plan," I told myself, watching when we skimmed lower, over the tops of a few trees, heading not into a rural area but toward the industrial part of town, one where a couple of massive warehouses held items for the many ships that visited.

I waited until we were within a few minutes of landing, then, according to the plan I'd perfected during my seven days of confinement, started banging on the door of my cell, yelling loudly for someone to help me.

Thankfully, it was Armand who answered my call, not one of the other crew members who sometimes attended to me, and who treated me in a hard, unyielding manner. "Madame? You are unwell again?"

"Oh, yes, Armand," I said in an exaggerated manner, sagging against the doorframe just as if I couldn't stand. "There is … there is … in the corner." I gestured, and swooned backward against the door.

He stepped into the cabin, glancing in the corner that I had indicated. "What is there, madame? I see noth—"

I shoved him hard with both hands, then whirled around

and was out of the door, snapping the lock into place before he realized what I'd done.

"That was far too easy," I said softly, hurrying down the gangway toward the rear of the ship, secure in the knowledge that the attention would be focused on the front, where the cargo doors were located. During a discussion with dear, gullible Armand, I'd discovered the location of the emergency hatch, the doors cut into the bottom of the gondola where the crew could parachute to earth if the airship was too damaged to fly.

I ran down two flights of rear stairs, pausing when a crewman rushed ahead of me, a coil of mooring rope on his shoulders. I counted to five, then dashed across the broad lower-level gangway, and into a small storeroom, quickly pulling up the ring that swung up the trapdoor.

The airship was dropping quickly to the ground, the forward thrust disabled, as steam was let out of the envelope.

I swung my legs out, trying to steel myself to jump, knowing if I waited too long, the exit would be blocked when the gondola settled on the ground.

"One, two, dear god don't let me break a leg, three!" I leaped, hitting the ground hard, trying to immediately roll onto my shoulder like I'd seen my ex-husband do when he attended skydiving school. The impact knocked my breath out of my lungs, but I hurriedly scrambled out of the way just as the gondola settled with a soft whoosh.

We were outside one of the gray warehouses, a few men sitting on wooden crates, pipes in mouth, observing the proceedings while the crew scurried around to use mooring lines to drag the airship into the warehouse.

I didn't wait to watch; I trotted off in a manner that I hoped wouldn't attract attention from any onlookers.

"Now what?" I asked myself when I felt sufficiently distant from the warehouse. I had a moment of panic at the idea of being alone in a city with no resources or help, but managed to lecture myself into a moderately calm state. "Alan wouldn't have a hissy fit. He'd figure out where he was, and make his way out to where the *Enterprise* parks when it's in town. What Alan can do, I can do."

My words sounded a lot braver than I felt, but by the time two hours had passed, and I'd made it out to a field west of Marseilles, I was feeling a lot more confident. The farm where Octavia parked the airship was isolated, and evidently owned by some people who knew her foster parents.

"That's it." I pointed when the man whose cab I hired told me there was no such farm in the area, and insisted on turning his horse and returning to town. "To the left. See the barn? And beyond it, in those trees, you can just see the glimmer of silver on black. That's the *Enterprise*. Thank god they came early. They weren't supposed to be here until tomorrow. Can you hurry, please? I've had a very long day, a long week, actually, and I really want to see a friendly face. Not that you haven't been kindness personified, but I am paying you after all, and that kind of makes the friendliness de rigueur, you know?"

Since I was speaking the last few sentences in English, the man said nothing, just sucked his teeth, and obligingly stopped at the entrance of the farm. I paid him from the small reserves I had left, thanked him, and, with a sudden lightness of spirit that gave my feet wings, dashed toward the copse of trees that mostly hid the *Enterprise*.

No one came out to greet me as I panted my way to the cargo doors. "I … dude, seriously … hello … have got to get into some exercise regime. Hello?"

I tried to open the door, but it was bolted on the inside. I stood for a minute, my hands on my knees, then walked around to where a side door led into the boiler room. It, also, was locked, and no one answered when I banged on it.

I sat with my back to a tree, resigned to the fact that the fabulous homecoming that I'd imagined for a whole week was now seriously anticlimactic.

And that's where they found me. It was the volatile Mr. Francisco who saw me first, his voice penetrating the sleep into which I'd fallen.

"Huh?" I asked, blinking at the man who stood next to me, his body twisting to call behind himself, "*Mon capitaine* of the glorious flaming hair so sweet! It is the lady Allie! She is dead, here against the tree."

"What?" I heard a male voice shout. "Hallie is here? Dead? I swear I will have that damned Moghul's head on a platter—"

"Hrn? Mr. Francisco, will you stop thrusting your crotch at me?" I asked, leaning over sideways. He was prone to wearing very tight pants, ones that highlighted everything he'd been born with. "Jack, I'm not dead, no matter what this deranged Spaniard says, and stop threatening Akbar. Would you … thank you."

Mr. Francisco helped me to the feet, and almost immediately, I was enveloped in a bear hug, Jack's voice murmuring in my ear. "Holy shit, Hal! How did you get here? Where's Etienne? What happened to you? We saw Etienne's ship come in, but there were too many of them for us to storm it. Are you OK? Did the bastard hurt you? Why aren't you answering me? Dammit, woman, we've been worried sick about you!"

I laughed, looking up into Jack's eyes, one brown, one green, giving him a hard hug before stepping back. "I'm not answering because you won't stop talking. Octavia, you are a sight for sore eyes." I gave her a hug, too, then went on to hug the rest of the crew, who had gathered around me, all of them asking questions and telling me of their plans to rescue me, until it was all a jumble of voices and I started to feel a bit dizzy.

"Are you all right?" Octavia asked when I weaved, quickly taking my arm. "Jack, stop telling her what you are going to do to Prince Akbar, and help her. I think she's about to swoon."

"It's just the residual effect from the poison," I told them, but allowed Jack to sling an arm around me and help me into the ship.

"Poison? Etienne tried to poison you?" Octavia asked, her voice shocked.

"That or they have really bad food, and it was food poisoning," I said, accepting a cup of tea. We were all sitting around the table in the mess, everyone watching me with such looks of avidity that I suddenly wanted to curl up in bed and pull the blankets over my head.

"That's likely." Octavia made a face. "Etienne never was one for caring much about what he ate, and I imagine he subjects his crew to the same standards, or, rather, lack therein. Now, drink that tea, then you can tell us what happened."

It took me the better part of an hour, but at last I told them how the imperator descended upon Alan, of the agreement with Etienne, and ultimately how I'd run into the Black Hand, and been nabbed.

Jack and Octavia exchanged several glances, none of which I could interpret.

"You're safe now—that's all that matters," Jack said when I finished. "Although I reserve the right to beat the tar out of that Akbar. The nerve of him letting you get kidnapped."

I didn't want to talk about Alan to him. I hadn't mentioned anything about our relationship, other than he was teaching me how to use various weapons, but Octavia cast me a couple of glances that, had I a better grasp on reading emotions, were probably quite telling.

We had dinner, and I was happy to at last have something that I wouldn't be throwing up in the next two hours. We sat up late in the mess, long after the rest of the crew had gone to bed, talking about what they had been doing. Jack seemed loath to leave my side until I told him he was making me nervous by lurking over me.

"All right, but don't leave the ship," he said when Octavia pulled him to his feet so they could go to bed.

"Are you kidding? I damned near killed myself getting here," I said wearily, stifling a yawn. "I just want to go to bed and sleep for a good week. I haven't gotten much sleep, what with all the vomiting, despite trying to nap where I could."

"Of course, you must be exhausted," Octavia said at the door, and hesitating for a moment before turning back to me. "Oh, but your cabin is in use."

"It is?" I hadn't noticed any new crew members. "By who?"

"What, not who." Jack grimaced. "I'm building a new autonavigator, one that we'll be able to use punch cards on for more commands and higher accuracy. It's spread out all over your cabin. If I have to move it, it'll set me back weeks."

"I don't honestly care where I sleep," I said, drooping a little for effect.

"I'm sure Mr. Ho won't mind in the least if you use the spare bunk in her room," Octavia said.

"Sounds good to me. Good night." I smiled when Jack, with a waggle of his eyebrows at Octavia, hustled her off to their cabin.

"Ah, young love," I said to myself, and wondered what Alan was doing at that moment. Was he missing me? Was he looking up at the night sky, and wondering what I was doing? Was he still fighting with his father?

I shook my head, and tapped quickly before opening the door of the assistant steward, a very nice—if quiet—woman named Beatrice Ho, who was referred to, for some bizarre holdover of official air corps etiquette, in the male determinative. "Beatrice? I hope you aren't asleep, but I need a spot to crash for the night—"

A lamp was lit in the room, allowing me to see the wide eyes of Beatrice as her head popped up from under the blankets … as well as that of a dark-haired man, who blinked owlishly at me. "Oh. Uh. Good evening, Mr. Llama. I … yeah, OK. I guess I'll go sleep with Jack's automaton. Sorry for disturbing you."

Mr. Ho said nothing, just watched me, while Mr. Llama slowly sank down into the blankets until nothing of him remained to view.

I closed the door softly, bit back the urge to laugh, and, with a sigh, went to my old cabin. I managed to snag a pillow and blanket, and used both to curl up on the window seat that lined one side of the mess.

I threw up twice in the night, forcing me to face a few hard facts. When morning dawned, I was sitting in the window seat, a freshly scrubbed bucket at my feet.

Mr. Ho was one of the first people into the mess, and she stopped at the sight of me, gesturing at nothing before coming over with an apology. "I'm sorry about last night. I didn't know you would be wanting to sleep in my cabin—"

"It's not your fault. I didn't realize Jack was building a computer in my room. You've got first aid training, don't you?"

Her eyebrows rose at the change of conversation. "Yes, some. Captain Pye sent me to a training course that lasted six weeks so that I could learn what is called triage. Is something wrong?" She glanced at the bucket.

"I think so," I said slowly, my mind numb around the edges. It was hard to think. Not when nothing made sense. "If a woman came to you and said she was sick a lot, and very sleepy, and prone to frequent naps, and one of her breasts was a bit sensitive, and not in a good way, what would you say?"

Her eyes widened. "I would ask her when her last courses were."

"Uh-huh." I stared at the table for a few minutes. "My oncologist said it was unlikely. He said that due to the type of chemo, my eggs wouldn't be viable. He said that I could try fertility treatments, but at the time, I didn't want kids, and so it didn't seem worthwhile pursuing. But now … now …"

She put a hand on my arm, giving me a little pat. "Is your stomach unsettled?"

I nodded.

"I will get you some soda water. My mother had fourteen children, and she swore by it."

I murmured a thanks, my mind spinning and swooping like a bird on the wind. How could this be? And more important, if it was so, what did I feel about it? I wanted to talk to Alan about it, but how would he feel? He hadn't expected this any more than I had, and he had so many things that he had to deal with—did I want to dump the responsibility of a child on him? Did *I* want the responsibility? I could barely handle my own life, but the idea of giving up everything I was in order to care for a child ...

A rush of warmth swamped me, a fierce sense of protectiveness that filled me with an odd sort of elation. If my body had managed to pull off a miracle and produce a baby, then by god, I'd just get my shit together, and be the best mother the baby could ever have.

And what about the father? a snarky voice in my head asked.

I didn't need him. Lots of women were single parents, loving, successful single parents who had loving, successful children. I was strong. I had a warrior breast. I could do anything.

That's what I told myself, but my Inner Hallie knew better. I stood up when Mr. Ho stopped in front of me, a glass of bubbly water in her hand. "He's just going to have to get with the program. There's no way in hell I'm doing this by myself! I know it's a shock—hell, I didn't think it could happen even with fertility treatments—but he can just get over that. I did, and I have the right to be more shocked than him. I refuse to let him off the hook just because this wasn't planned! He's as responsible as me. More, because he doesn't have to go through hell for the next eight months."

"Er ... no?" Mr. Ho asked.

"It's only fair," I told her. "Do you mind if I have a little nap on your spare bunk? I didn't sleep very well."

"By all means," she said.

I tossed back the soda water, and marched out of the mess, fetching from my cabin a spare toothbrush, which I used to thoroughly scrub my mouth before curling up on Mr. Ho's spare bunk. "I am strong," I repeated to myself. "I can do this. And by god, Alan just better resolve himself to doing it with me, or I'll have his guts for garters."

Dooley woke me up a few hours later. "Miss, the cap'n and Mr. Fletcher want you in the captain's cabin."

"Huh?" Groggily, I sat up, rubbing my face and yawning. "What do they want?"

"I don't know. They just said to fetch you. The cap'n said it was important."

"All right." I looked down at my stomach. I hadn't seen any sign that a miracle had happened, but something was definitely off with me. "You had better not let me down now that I'm embracing this idea," I told my womb.

I brushed my hair out of my face, and went to see what it was that had Jack and Octavia in such a swivet. "If it's Etienne," I muttered as I went down the gangway to the captain's cabin, "I want the first shot at stabbing him with a dull dagger. Oh, hell, they're back at Alan's camp. Dammit. I'll just have to get Jack to give me something, which won't be easy, because he insists on not killing people, and if that's not the most unreasonable thing ever, then I don't know what is."

I knocked on the cabin door, entering before Octavia could answer.

"Hallie," Jack said, greeting me.

"Look, I know you don't want me to stab him, but it's only fair. Just one dagger, that's all I want," I told him.

Jack stared at me with an open mouth. "Stab who? That fiend Akbar?"

"Of course not. Etienne." I glanced around. Octavia stood near Jack, and next to her was a man in a dark suit. I glanced at him, but figured he must be the local farmer who owned the surrounding area. "Isn't he here? I thought you called me in so I could have my shot at stabbing him."

"No," Octavia said, looking from the man to me. "It's nothing like that—really, you thought Jack, of all people, would give you a dagger? It's … er …"

She looked at the dark-haired man again. He had been smiling, but that smile faded now.

"What?" I asked, feeling that I wasn't up to whatever it was they were doing with all those silent glances. "Look, I've got a lot going on right now, so if you could just come to the point, I'd be really grateful."

"Er …" She seemed to have a problem continuing, staring at me, then turning to look at the other man.

"Tavy wanted you to meet this gentleman. He's a diplomat, the one who tried to get you out of prison last year. Alan Dubain, this is my sister, Hallie Norris," Jack said, shooting a frown at Octavia.

"What is the matter with … Hallie, did you hit your head?" Octavia asked, coming over to stand next to me, giving me a quick once-over. "Is your vision impaired?"

"No to all of those," I said, then waved politely at the man, who stood still, like he was made of rock. "Nice to meet you. Oh, wait, you're a diplomat? You don't by any chance have connections to the Moghuls, do you? Because I really want to get a message to Prince Akbar."

"A message?" the man asked in an odd sort of croaking voice. Then he cleared his throat and looked at Octavia. The two of them stared at each other before both looked back at me.

"Jack, what's wrong with her?" Octavia asked in a whisper that was loud enough for everyone to hear.

"Hmm?"

"Is her vision amiss? She doesn't seem to see …" She stopped, looking confused.

"Her vision is fine, I think. Except, of course, for the thing."

"What thing?" Octavia sounded frustrated.

I rolled my eyes, waving at my brother. "You can tell her if you want."

"Tell me what?" she asked, turning to Jack.

He shot me a grin, then hustled Octavia out of the room, leaving the door open. "It's this weird thing we have. I have a slight touch of it, but not nearly to the extent that Hallie does. …"

I pursed my lips, then sat down at Octavia's desk and started writing a letter. "If you don't mind, Mr. Dubain, I'm going to write a letter that I very badly want to get to Prince Akbar."

"She has *what*?" I heard Octavia shout in the hallway.

"A letter?" The man sounded like he was choking. He moved closer to me, one hand rubbing the back of his head when he said under his breath, "I must still be feeling the effects."

I stopped writing, glancing at him for a moment, but shook my head. I must have imagined it.

Octavia dashed into the room, panting slightly, "Hallie has facial blindness. She doesn't recognize faces. At all. That's why Jack always says her name whenever he approaches her. She doesn't see faces!"

"Actually, I see them just fine," I said, frowning at Octavia. I didn't mind people knowing about my weird quirk, but I didn't think it was anything to get excited about, either. "I just don't process the information the way other people do. Faces don't stick with me."

"She uses cues to recognize people. Isn't that right?" She turned to Jack, who nodded. "She uses people's *hair* and *clothing* to recognize them, and if they change those things, if they look different, then she has a hard time recognizing them."

"Ah," the diplomat said, looking thoughtful. "That would explain a lot. Hallie, stop writing."

Should I tell Alan in the letter? No, that news was probably best kept for an in-person telling. Plus there was the fact that I didn't know for certain. I gave the diplomat short shrift while I was pondering what to say to Alan. "Look, I know I just asked you to do me a favor, but I am writing an important letter—"

"Hallie."

The word was said in a voice that held a deep, rich timbre, one that sent a shiver down my back. I knew that voice. I knew that shiver. I stared at the man standing next to me. He had dark hair cut short, much shorter than Alan's. This man's hair had clumps of it standing on end as if he'd been running his hands through it. He was dressed in the standard sort of suit that other gentlemen wore in this world. There was nothing exciting or dashing about him. He certainly couldn't hold a candle to Alan, and yet …

His eyes glittered at me. I stood slowly, my gaze on his.

Blue eyes. He had beautiful blue eyes, like gemstones in a river.

"Alan?" I asked.

"Why didn't you tell me, little dove?"

An electric charge seemed to skitter down my skin as I realized the truth. It was Alan! My Alan, not some nondescript diplomat. I stared in disbelief for a moment, then shrieked and flung myself on him, kissing every bit of his face. "How did you get here? What … why do you look so different? Why did you sound different? Where is your father?"

He kissed me, his lips warm and soft and so wonderful, I wanted to get on my knees and cry from the joy of it all.

"Hey, now," I heard Jack say. "What's all this? Why is Alan molesting her with his mouth? When did she meet him? I don't remember them meeting. Now he has his hands on her ass! Dubain! Take your hands and your lips off my sister!"

"I believe it's my turn to tell you a few things, my love," Octavia said, and I heard their footsteps retreat as Alan, my delicious, warm, wonderful Alan, proceeded to check out every one of my teeth, his tongue doing a little dance around mine while his hands were on my behind, pulling me closer.

"He's WHO? Bloody hell, Octavia!"

"Jack's mad about something," I said, pulling my mouth reluctantly from Alan's, not because I wanted to tell him that information, but because I needed to come up for air.

"Ah. Yes. About that." He made a face, looking over my shoulder when Jack burst into the room, his face twisted.

"You!" he snarled, pointing at Alan. "You're that bloody prince! The one who tried to kill us!"

"I don't believe I ever tried to kill you," Alan started to say.

I spun around in front of him, my arms wide when Jack stormed over to us. "Now, Jack—"

"You stole my sister! You had your hands on her ass! You've probably had them all over her, defiling her! My *sister*!"

"Jack, calm down," I told him.

"I will not! I have every reason to be angry! Do you know how much trouble that man has caused us? It's not bad enough I have to put up with him hanging around leering at Octavia, clearly trying to sway her back into another relationship with him, but now he has the nerve to seduce my sister!"

The little happy feelings that were swamping me suddenly shriveled into a cold, dried thing. I turned my gaze upon Alan. "Relationship?" I asked him. "With Octavia?"

"It's not like that at all," the woman herself said, hurrying over to us. "We were lovers, yes, but it was several years ago, and as I've told Jack many times—really too many times given that he knows I love him beyond all others, and always will—but as I've told him, Alan and I are simply friends now."

I stared at the man I loved. I didn't even shy away from that realization—I loved him. He had my heart, and my soul, and all the other bits of me that even now were clamoring to be delivered unto him. We were likely going to have a miracle together—and yet, something burned deep in me, a hot, thick emotion that I realized with shock was rampant possessiveness. He was mine! the possessiveness wanted to cry out to the world. *My* man, *my* lover, *my* mate. I allowed that feeling to well up in me, and used it to pierce him with a look that should have melted him on the spot. "You dated Octavia?"

"As she said, it was a long time ago—" He took my hands in his.

I pulled them from him, then fought my way through the insidious need to rail at the idea that he had, for a time, belonged to someone else, and thought for a moment. A few years ago, I was still in my own world. I dated other men. I had lovers. I might not have thought myself in love with them, but perhaps Alan had that same light, easy relationship with Octavia that I had with the men in my past.

It just made what we had, the deep, soul-twining rightness of being, unique. I had never felt for any other man—my ex-husband included—the emotions that bound me to Alan.

"All right," I said, giving him back my hands, my words coming out stilted and formal with the possessiveness that didn't want to give way. "So long as you don't harbor any unresolved feelings for her, I will allow you to have had, in the past, illicit relations with my sister-in-law."

"Great. Now my wife's lover has brainwashed my sister," I heard Jack mutter.

Octavia bit his ear. "Former lover, Jack. The 'former' part is important."

Alan shook his head ruefully, kissing my fingers, sending little curls of need and want deep within me. "As usual, you have unbalanced me. Octavia says you were not harmed by Etienne."

"Not in the least. Did I ask you where your father is?"

"You did. I assume that by now he is on his way to Prussia to marry the duchess."

I gawked at him, a full-fledged, openmouthed gawk. "The one he insisted you marry? Why is he marrying her? Not that I want him trying to throw her on you, because that is so not going to fly. But why?"

He rubbed the back of his head again. "My father and I have parted ways. In effect, Prince Akbar is dead."

There was more to his appearance than he was telling, but now was not the time to delve further into what happened after I'd been kidnapped. "If you're no longer Akbar, then who are you? What will you do?"

"I'm Alan Dubain, diplomat," he said, bowing. "And covert member of the Company of Thieves, if you'll have me."

"You've always been a member, so of course we will welcome you joining us in a more active role," Octavia said, ignoring Jack's glare.

"I don't know about this, Tavy. Look at him. He's still got one hand on her ass."

I ignored my brother's grumblings to examine Alan. "Is that why you look like this? Where are all your pretty clothes? Never mind, you can tell me later. I want to kiss you. And touch you. And maybe lick you, although it's kind of hard seeing you in those clothes—"

"There will be no licking, touching, and kissing until a few things are explained to my satisfaction," Jack said in a bossy voice. "I have issues, many issues with the idea that a man I thought was our friend was really a vicious enemy."

I turned to pin Jack back with a glare. "Well, you'd better get over your issues with him pretty quickly, because in a few months you're going to be demanding he marry me."

"I will never!" Jack said, outraged. "Prince Akbar? You are insane, that's what it is. He's brainwashed you, and made you insane."

Octavia sucked in her breath, indicating she had guessed. I smiled at her, and turned back to Alan. "I'm sorry, this isn't the way I would like to do this, but as they are family, I hope you don't mind."

"You're not going to propose to me, are you?" Alan said, pulling me to him, his eyes making me feel like I'd been out in the sun, the heat of him soaking into me and making me burn for him. *All* of him.

"No. I think … I don't know how this happened. … Well, I know how, but I don't know *how*, if you get my drift. The bottom line is that I refuse to do this on my own, not when you are here and perfectly able to help me. Especially if your father is out of the picture, because he was truly obnoxious, not that I like saying that about a relative of yours, but I kind of think you'd probably agree. And I think that we just need to do this together. OK?"

"I'm not quite sure what you're asking me to do," he answered, his voice so wonderful, it just made me want to kiss the words right off his lips. "But if you need help with something, I will absolutely assist you."

I gave in to my need and leaned forward, kissing him with every bit of love I possessed. "I sure hope so. Alan, I think we're pregnant."

I may not be able to read emotions very well, but even I could see that Alan was stunned. He blinked at me a couple of times. "You're … we're … I'm going to be …"

"Yes." I bit my lip, wishing like hell I knew what he was thinking.

What if he hated the idea? What if he felt trapped, but was too honorable a man to tell me that? What if he never wanted children? I realized with hindsight that although I knew the depth and breadth of my feelings for him, I didn't know what he thought of me beyond his enjoyment of our time together in bed.

"I know it's a shock," I said. "It is to me, too, because I didn't think I could, but Mr. Ho and I think it's so, and … well … I'm actually pretty all right with the idea, but I think now that maybe you aren't going to want to be a part of this with me, and oh, hell. You aren't happy, are you?"

"Happy?" He stared at me for another few seconds; then he scooped me up, spinning me around until I thought I was going to vomit.

Which I did ten seconds after he put me down.

"No, I'm not just happy—I'm damned near ecstatic. I'll just hold your hair back while you're doing that, shall I?"

"Oh my god, she's pregnant," I heard Jack tell Octavia as I retched into her commode. "That bastard has impregnated my sister. He put his hands all over her person, and impregnated her. What are we going to do, Tavy?"

"I don't actually think it's any of our business, my love."

"We have to do something. She's too vulnerable. Well, that's it. He has to marry her. You, Dubain. You're marrying her. I don't care what you want—you're going to marry her and make her happy, or so help me, I will string you up by your balls."

"Jack, please stop threatening Alan," I said, wiping my mouth. "Also, stop being so medieval. No one these days gets married just because a baby is on its way."

"Maybe not in our old world, but in this one they do," he snapped, glaring first at me, then at Alan. "Besides, I don't trust him. This could be a trick. Some sort of cunning Moghul trick."

Alan, who had been kneeling next to me, started laughing, and fell back onto his ass, he was laughing so hard.

"You're not helping matters," I told him.

"I know. It's just been … this last week has been the most hellish of my life. I imagined all sorts of horrible things, and never, not once thought that when I found you, you wouldn't recognize me, followed immediately by the news that you're going to make me a father. How do you feel, little dove?"

"Relieved. Happy. Nauseous as hell," I said, beaming at him. "Ignore my brother, by the way. We're not actually related. He was raised by wolves."

"This is all part of his grand plan," Jack said, stalking around and waving his hands dramatically.

"Of what?" I couldn't help but ask, both annoyed and amused by my brother.

"Well … he probably … the Moghuls …" Jack sputtered to a stop.

"Uh-huh. You can't think of anything because your brain knows that the idea of Alan having nefarious intentions toward us is outrageous, even if your emotions don't get that," I pointed out.

Jack made an annoyed sound. "Fine! I'm willing to admit that he may not have impregnated you deliberately as a plot to irritate me—"

"Any *other* brother would be happy his sister who didn't think she could have children has managed a miracle," I told Alan. "Any *other* brother would be overjoyed his sister had found a man she'd like to spend her life with."

"Ah, but Jack is not just *any* brother," Alan told me with a little curl of his lips.

"You can say that again," I said, just as Jack stopped in front of me, kneeling to take my hands in his.

"Of course I'm happy that you're having a baby, Hal. That is—I didn't know you wanted one, but if you are happy, then I'm happy, too. And as for finding a partner … well, I suppose you've made your choice." His eyes watched me carefully, and I wished for the thousandth time that I had the ability to read expressions.

I gave his hands a little squeeze. "I have," I answered, a wave of happiness filling me with a sense of well-being despite the experience of having just thrown up.

He released my hands and stood up. "Fine, then. We'll have the wedding here. You can marry people, can't you?" Jack asked Octavia. "You're a captain, so you have to be able to marry them. We'll get them married off, and then I won't have to castrate him for putting his hands and balls and dick all over her."

"He was raised by wolves, you say?" Alan grinned and rose, pulling me to my feet. "He does seem to be under the delusion that he can dictate to us. Hallie?"

"I'm going to need a new toothbrush at this rate," I said to myself before looking up, still trying to acclimatize myself to Alan in mundane clothing. "Hmm?"

He took my hand, and kissed it. "Marry me?"

I shook my head. His eyes widened.

"I am not ordained in any religion, my love. I can't marry anyone, but if Alan and Hallie wish to be married—and I can't help but emphasize the words *if they wish* to be married—then I'm sure we can find a church where they can be married quietly," Octavia said.

"You don't want to marry me?" Alan asked. I could hear the hurt in his voice.

"Of course I do. I love you. I think we're going to have a miracle together. But I don't want to marry you just because my brother is being an ass and demanding you do so, or because you think it's the right thing to do."

"It *is* the right thing to do," he insisted.

A little pang of pain pierced me. I realized then that I had made a mistake—I thought I could tell Alan about the possibility of a baby, but that he'd view it as I did, a wondrous thing, an unexpected blessing. But he was a man of honor, one who took his responsibilities to others very seriously, and now I was one more claim on his time.

Dammit, I wanted him to marry me because he loved me.

"We can talk about it later," I said, wanting to push the whole thing to the side.

"I can't make you accept me," he said, clearly not going to let me avoid the issue. "But I don't understand why you don't want me."

I sighed, and looked at Jack and Octavia, who were now arguing about whether an airship captain had the power to marry people regardless of not being sanctioned by a proper authority. "Ahem," I said loudly.

Jack stopped arguing. "Eh?"

I nodded toward Alan. "Trying to have a private talk, here."

"In *our* cabin," Jack pointed out.

"Yeah, but that's because you are building a robot in mine. Skedaddle, please."

"Yes, Jack, let's give them a little privacy." Octavia pulled him after her when she left. "I really don't know where you get this idea about what a captain can and cannot do. ..."

"And close the door," I yelled when Jack left it ajar.

He muttered something, but did as I asked.

I turned back to Alan. "I really want to kiss you, but can't until I brush my teeth. Please imagine I'm kissing you now, just before I tell you that I do indeed want you. I love you, Alan. I want to be with you. I want to talk to you. I want to feel you next to me, being all dashing and daring and wonderful. I want to wake up to you snoring in my hair. I want to fall asleep smooshed up against your side. I want you infuriating me, and teasing me, and letting me tease you in return. I want to know every single thought you have, and what you're feeling and why you are the way you are. I want you to wear things that I recognize, so I can pick you out of a crowd. I want your mustache back."

"Then marry me," he said.

I waited a minute, but he didn't say anything about loving me in return. I shook my head again.

"Why? If you love me, why won't you marry me? Is it because of my father?" I felt him withdraw, not physically, but emotionally, and immediately I wanted to take him in my arms and reassure him. "It's because of who I am?"

"No, of course not. I mean, your father is an ass, but you're not responsible for that. I love *you*, Alan. Exactly who you are." I eyed the suit. "Or at least, who I thought you were. I really liked your other clothes better, though."

He was silent for a moment, then shook his head. "I don't understand what I've done that makes you refuse me."

I was going to remain in silent martyrdom until he figured out that he loved me, too, at which point I would consent to marry him, and we'd live happily ever after, but that just seemed like such a stupid amount of work for nothing in return.

"For the love of the goddess," I yelled, punching him on his chest. "Stay right here."

"What?" he asked when I hurried out of the cabin. "You're leaving me? Now?"

"Stay there!" I said, pointing at him. "I'll be right back. I have to brush my teeth."

He was waiting for me when I returned, his hands clasped behind his back in the gesture I'd seen so often while he looked off into the distance, across the scraggy landscape of Tozeur that I realized I missed so much. It gave me a bit of a jolt to see him standing in such a familiar pose but wearing the clothing of a stranger.

"Right, now we can do this." I took a deep breath when he turned toward me.

"If it's not my father, it's the fact that I kept my identity as Alan Dubain from you," he said, his voice all gravelly around the edges. "You are angry that I did not tell you the truth. I had intended on doing so, but the time never seemed right—"

"I don't care about that," I said, waving away the idea that I was angry about something so trivial. "You're a badass spy. Of course you have different identities."

"Then for the love of the gods, what is it?" he almost shouted, taking my arms in his hands. "Please tell me so I can fix whatever I've done."

"You're supposed to tell me you love me, you boob! Everyone knows that! It's part of the whole proposing thing, not that you had the chance to think about whether or not you wanted to ask me, because my brother was being his usual bossy-pants self and demanding you do so, but still, it's part of the whole package. Do you?"

"Of course I love you," he said matter-of-factly.

I pointed a finger at him. "Oh no. You have to mean it. And don't think you can just say the words and I'll be happy, because I will know you aren't being honest."

"Oh really?" He smiled slowly, pulling me gently against his body, moving my hips against his. "And how are you going to tell, my sweet dove? Will you read the truth in my eyes? Or will you feel it when I touch you? When I kiss you?" His hands slid along my hips, moving upward to cup my breasts. "Will you need the words when I take you again and again until you're exhausted and panting, lying across me in a boneless heap?"

He moved against me, his entire body wooing me with his words.

"Oh, yes, please," I said on a breath, welcoming his mouth when it claimed mine, my body doing a shimmy of need and desire and want against his. I loved how our bodies fit together. Until I met Alan, I had never realized that a woman's body was made of curves and softness and flesh that yielded simply so that it could fit so well against the hard planes of a man. *My* man.

"Do you really think I could be anything but helplessly, hopelessly, madly in love with you?" he asked when I let him have his tongue back, his breath hot on the shivery spot behind my ear. He pulled my hips tighter against him. "Is there any doubt in your mind that I want to spend every second of the rest of my life with you?"

"I changed my mind," I murmured against his lips when he went in for another one of those soul-scorching kisses. "I'll marry you. Like, today. Right now. I'm going to burn into an ashy blob if we don't start the honeymoon in the next ten minutes."

"I believe we can be forgiven if we have the wedding night first," he said, and, with a quick look around the cabin, locked the door before he swept Octavia's desk clear.

"Alan!" I said, scandalized when he divested me of my top before he lifted me onto the desk. His hands and mouth were all over me, tasting me, teasing me, reacquainting us both with what we'd missed the last week. His hands took possession of my breasts, which was exactly what they wanted, taking each nipple into his mouth while I moaned and clutched his shoulders. "This isn't our cabin! I don't think they would like—oh, dear god, yes, right there."

I struggled with the need to let him work his magic on me, and the desire to give him as much pleasure as he was giving me. I tugged on the tie and stiff collar that hid his throat from me, tossing them on the floor while he slid his hands into the waistband of my pants.

"This is the worst outfit ever," I growled, sliding his jacket down over his arms. "There's too much to it. Please tell me you're not going to wear this again."

"If I wish to fit into the Western world—" he started to say, his mouth on my breasts.

"To hell with that. How on earth is this … Alan!" I gave up trying to pull his shirt out and unhook things. Somehow, his pants refused to budge, as if they were connected to his shirt.

He made an annoyed *tsk*, then grinned and yanked his shirt off over his head. Beneath it, he wore what amounted to an undershirt, a pair of braces holding up his pants.

"Off," I said, pointing at them.

"I do not like being dominated, little dove. I've told you this before," he said, trying to sound bossy and domineering, but he shucked his pants and undergarments in record time.

I used the time to get back on my feet and shimmy out of my pants, underwear, and sandals. "Uh-huh. And yet, you love it when it's my turn to be on top."

"That, my love, is entirely a different matter," he said, hoisting me back onto the table, spreading my thighs as he did so. He hesitated for a couple of seconds, glancing down at my belly. "This won't hurt you? Won't hurt the babe?"

"No. I think we have a lot of time before we have to slow down." I wrapped my legs around his body. "Make me feel just how much you love me."

"Such a demanding little dove," he said, his lips burning on mine when he tilted my hips, allowing him to slide into me, all my intimate muscles rippling along his intrusion. My entire body felt like it was going up in flames, the heat from my private parts spreading like wildfire, making my breath catch, and my heart race.

"You make me burn, Hallie," he moaned into my ear, his body moving with a rhythm that I thought was the most beautiful thing in the world. His shoulder was salty when I first licked it, then bit it when he leaned into me, forcing me backward slightly, while pulling my hips up. He hit all the sensitive spots inside me, making me see stars. "Just when I think I can't stand it, you make me want more. Can you … I don't want to hurt you, but I just want to bury myself in you as deep as I can go. …"

I flexed my hips, allowing him in deeper, his words winding the familiar tension in my deepest parts tighter and tighter. His movements become wild, hard thrusts meant to impale, his body answering the call of mine to join in the most elemental way a man and a woman could. This was no mere lovemaking—this was a pure, primal mating, a claiming, and I reveled in every second of it.

And when it became too much for me and I fell into the most glorious orgasm, he was there holding me, finding his own moment of absolute joy when we stopped being two separate people, and made one glorious, sweaty being.

"I'm just glad that desk is bolted to the floor," I said eons later, when I lay on top of Alan. He was flat on his back on the floor.

He cracked an eye open to look at me.

I grinned. "The way you rocked my world, I was afraid you were going to move the table into the next cabin."

TWELVE

"The *Nightwing* is secure, Alan. What are your plans? Should I sent out scouts to see what Etienne is up to? Or do you wish to make an attack?"

Alan looked across the fallow field, the need to find Etienne and punish him uppermost in his mind now that he knew Hallie was safe. Zand stood patiently by his side, waiting for him to speak.

"I can gather the men if you wish to attack. We will be outnumbered, but that hasn't been a problem in the past, and I doubt if it will be now. So long as William's men are out of the fight."

Hallie was with child, his child, a child they had made together. He hadn't thought about having children before, other than in a vague, "sometime in the distant future" sort of way, but now he was going to be a father. His Hallie, who had thought she was barren, was going to give him a child, one who would be the best part of both of them.

He smiled at the thought of his contrary little dove. Trust her to find yet another way to make him feel off-balance.

Zand looked thoughtful. "Although it might be wiser to wait for the *Falcon*, since Captain Pye said the emperor's men were sniffing around the Black Hand base. Captain Pye said Safie should be arriving this evening."

That aside, Alan was a bit annoyed by the high-handed way Jack Fletcher had informed him he would be marrying Hallie. The fact that Jack had thought he was the sort of man who would deliberately seduce his sister just to strike at him was ridiculous, but he supposed he couldn't really blame Jack, since Octavia had kept his secret from her husband. Still, to demand that he marry Hallie just as if he didn't want to do that very thing was outrageous. The man was far overstepping his bounds. It wasn't any of his business, after all.

"Or we could tie little incendiary bombs to pigeons, and let them fly at the Black Hand ship."

Was that the sort of image Jack Fletcher had of him? That he would leave Hallie to raise his child alone? The more he thought about it, the more incensed he became. Octavia should have informed her husband that he, Alan, was a man of honor. *Of course* he would marry Hallie. He would do so even if she wasn't with child. She was his, and no other man would ever have her. Therefore, it was right and proper that she should acknowledge that fact by marrying him.

"Or cats. Maybe we could tie a few helium balloons to cats, and push them toward the Black Hand ship's envelopes. The damage they could do with their claws would be phenomenal, and most likely unrepairable."

What bothered him the most, however, was the fact that Hallie didn't seem to want to marry him, despite telling him just how much she loved him. "It's not like I'm a monster," he said aloud, his eyes on the clouds that gently floated across the sky.

"Some might say that the man who sent cats in to do his dirty work was a monster, you know."

Alan grunted an agreement; then the words his friend spoke drifted through the tangle of his thoughts. He turned to look at Zand. "What are you talking about? What cats?"

"It's not important."

"Hallie didn't think I loved her."

Zand gave him a look of disbelief. "You? You're besotted with her!"

"I know that, but she doesn't seem to."

"You're as moon-eyed as they come!"

Alan frowned. "She's a smart woman. You'd think she'd have worked out how I felt about her. About us. That we are meant to be together."

"It's downright disgusting how smitten you are with her."

"It's as if she didn't know me at all." He felt mildly indignant at the fact that Hallie, his Hallie, the woman who filled his thoughts, claimed she didn't know if he loved her. "A man shouldn't have to say the words every day. A man's actions should speak louder than mere words. Anyone can speak words. It's the actions that matter."

"The looks you get on your face when you stare at her are downright absurd. You are the epitome of bewitched. Many has been the time I have noted it."

Alan glared at the *Enterprise*, where Hallie had been having a nap while he moved the *Nightwing* from where it had been moored a mile down the road. "And she said she wasn't going to wed me."

"She should apologize," Zand said, nodding. "For doubting that you love her. It's downright insulting."

"It is," Alan said, wrapping himself in righteous indignation. Hadn't he done everything he could to make sure she was happy, safe, and contented in every way that mattered? "Gather the men. We're going into town to find someone who will marry us."

He turned on his heel and would have strode into the *Nightwing*, but at that moment a brown-and-gold airship crested the trees, and started a descent. It was the *Falcon*.

"Safie! Thank god she's here safe," Zand said, and ran to help the *Nightwing*'s crew moor the larger airship.

Alan returned to the *Enterprise*, wanting Hallie to meet his sister, and also to inform her that he had thought things over, and she was just going to have to admit that she knew he loved her, and that they would be married that very night.

"I thought we had this settled earlier?" Hallie asked fifteen minutes later when he led her over to where the *Falcon* was now moored. "You proposed; I accepted; you told me in wonderful, wonderful words and some really fine hip action that you loved me. What more is there to discuss?"

When she put it like that, he was at a loss for a reasonable answer. "Your brother was interfering. He had the nerve to tell us what we were going to do. I have thought the matter over and made a decision regardless of his demands," was all he could come up with, even though he knew it didn't make much sense.

"Alan," she said with a knowing smile, and curled her fingers into his. "You are so stinkin' adorable when you go Akbar on me."

"I will be going Akbar all over your fair body tonight, after we are wed," he said, kissing her hand and sending her a look that should leave her in absolutely no doubt as to his feelings, before turning from her when his sister, calling his name, threw herself into his arms.

"Zand says you have broken with Papa? And that you have a woman at last? Is this her? She's very pretty, isn't she? And Zand and I can be married? You look different. You look happy. I'm sorry you had such a hard time with Papa, but oh, Alan, I love Zand so very much, and now we can be together, yes?" She spoke in Kazakh, her words tumbling over one another as she kissed his cheeks and cast shy little glances toward Hallie.

"Yes to all of it," he said in English, and, taking Hallie's hand, pulled her to his side. "Hallie, this impertinent bit of baggage is my oldest sister, Safie. Despite being the smartest of all my father's children, her mother was a less favored concubine, and thus Safie was married off to an ogre who treated her very badly."

Hallie, who had been smiling, suddenly looked horrified. "I'm so sorry," she started to say, shooting him odd looks, obviously questioning why he was smiling over something so horrendous as a brutal marriage.

Safie laughed, then leaned forward and hugged Hallie. "Don't believe a word he says. My late husband lifted his hand to me once, and the following day, he found himself in the garden hanging upside down, with Alan holding a gelding knife to a very sensitive part. He didn't so much as glance my direction after that, and in fact died six months later."

"But …" Hallie glanced at the *Falcon*. "Jack said there was a female captain that I would meet one of these days, but I had no idea you were Alan's sister. Doesn't your father … er … mind that you're doing this?"

Safie put her arm through Alan's. "Papa would have apoplexy if he knew I wasn't at Alan's home in the south of Italy, where I'm supposed to be mourning my husband in seclusion." She gave a roll of her eyes. "Instead, Alan conscripted me to monitor the Mediterranean for the Company. But I had no idea you were the sister of Jack! You are so very pretty, and I can see you love Alan as much as he loves you. But when are you to be married?"

"Tonight," Alan said, nodding when Jack and Octavia hurried over to greet Safie, followed by their crew.

"About time," Jack said, glaring at him, after all the greetings were exchanged. Safie didn't meet up often with Jack and Octavia, since Alan didn't like her going to areas where she might be seen by someone who would pass on reports to the imperator, but he was pleased to have the opportunity to introduce a favorite sister to Hallie.

"You know, I get to have a say in this, too," Hallie said in a mild voice that didn't fool Alan for a minute. Her eyes positively danced with amusement … and love. He basked in the emotion in her eyes, feeling as if he were invincible when she looked at him like that. "And I've changed my mind again."

He frowned at her, his deliriously happy mood turning sour. "What is this? You're not going to make me declare myself again? I have said the words you wanted to hear, and you accepted me. You can't change your mind a third time."

"I'm sorry," she said, shaking her head, her eyes filled with laughter. "I refuse to marry a diplomat. Akbar may be dead, but is there anything to keep you from becoming the dread pirate Alan, who honors the famed prince by wearing his dashing and extremely sexy clothing?"

Alan relaxed, the panic that Hallie would slip away from him evaporating into nothing. He thought about what she asked of him. "I suspect William's court will have a thing or two to say if I was to appear in the dress of a Moghul."

"Fine, I'll let you wear these boring clothes when you absolutely have to," she said, flipping his tie in a disgusted gesture. "But the rest of the time … ?"

"Nothing would please me more. Our armor is an important part of our heritage, so it is not something I cast aside lightly. Plus, it is infinitely more comfortable," he agreed, his heart so full of happiness, he would have given her whatever she asked.

"Well. It sounds like we're going to have a wedding tonight." Octavia glanced at Jack. "I think we should do this properly, don't you?"

"Absolutely," he said, taking Hallie by one arm, and pulling her toward the *Enterprise*.

"Hey!" she said, frowning at him before glancing over her shoulder to where Alan stood. "What are you doing? I don't want to leave Alan. We've been away from each other for an incredibly long week. Besides, I could be a mother-to-be. You can't drag mothers-to-be. It's traumatizing."

"It's bad luck for you to see the groom until the wedding." Jack paused and consulted with Octavia for a moment, before calling back to Alan, "There's a church on the southwest edge of town, near the depot. Do you know it?"

"I can find it," he answered.

"Good. We'll meet you there in an hour."

"Two hours," Octavia corrected him, smiling and taking Hallie's other arm. Their crew cheered, and accompanied them back to their ship, all of them talking at the same time, each of them demanding a role in the ceremony.

"Alan, best of all my brothers—" Safie started to say, her dark eyes laughing almost as much as Hallie's.

"I am your only brother," he interrupted.

"If you do not allow Zand to marry me tonight, I will see to it that your marriage bed is filled with honey and fire ants and all sorts of uncomfortable—"

He clapped a hand over her mouth, and gave a shout that stopped Jack and Octavia. "Go," he said, pushing Safie toward them.

She whooped, kissed him, flashed a gaze that was unmistakable at Zand, and ran off to catch up with the others. Alan's heart was warmed to see Hallie slip her arm through Safie's.

Zand grinned like an idiot. Alan studied him for a moment, then punched him on the arm. "If you make her unhappy—"

"You'll hang me upside down and threaten to geld me, I know, I know," Zand continued, laughing.

"I won't just threaten, my friend," Alan said, but he knew that he had nothing to worry about on that front. Zand and Safie had waited so long for each other, praying that the imperator would one day consent to their marriage, something that he realized now would never have happened. "Let us go and see what finery we can dig out. Hallie won't let me hear the end of it if I dared turn up in this Western suit."

The crew fell in behind them, making ribald jokes, and in general chaffing the two bridegrooms.

For the first time in a very long time, Alan felt like life lay before him as a rich feast, one that held everything he could ever desire.

It just remained for him to reach out and take it.

THIRTEEN

"This is ridiculous. I can't fit into any of that, even if I wanted to. I refuse to wear a corset!"

Octavia frowned at me. "I understand that you do not wish to wear the clothing traditional to ladies in your normal day-to-day life, and I have always been supportive of your desire to march to a different drummer, so to speak. But, Hallie, this is your wedding."

"Pfft," I said, waving away that subject. "I did the big wedding once. It was meaningless. I'd be happy if we just had a registry-office wedding."

"Registry office?" Safie, who was roughly the same size as Octavia, cooed when she pulled out a black-and-white striped skirt and bodice. She was a pretty woman, with big brown eyes, and short-cropped curly hair. I was a bit surprised to see the latter, since most women in this world had long hair, but it suited her elfin looks. "Are you sure you won't mind me borrowing your gown? Unlike Hallie, I have clothing on the *Falcon*, all uniforms, of course, and not anything nearly as elegant as this. Most of my clothing is at Alan's house."

"By all means, help yourself." Octavia returned to considering me. "I see your point of not fitting into the garments, Hallie, but I couldn't be happy knowing you were wed to a dear friend wearing something so … er …"

I looked down at myself. My once pretty blue-and-green tunic and pants were now showing the strain of solid wear for the last week. "Maybe Alan brought my things—oh."

Octavia opened her cabin door at a knock, which turned out to be the two wooden trunks I'd inherited from Alan's sister Leila.

"Talk about timely," I said, diving into the first trunk. Safie and Octavia clustered around me, murmuring approval when I showed them the outfits I'd had created in Tozeur. "The question is which to wear."

"I like the red one," Octavia said. She fingered the scarlet material heavily embroidered in gold. "It must look lovely with your hair."

"I'm quite envious of the blue," Safie said, holding it up in front of her.

"You're more than welcome to wear that if you would prefer," I said, diving back into the chest to pull out the gold tunic and leggings, and leather armor. I ran my fingers across the engraving on the breastplate, my mind filled with memories of Alan teaching me how to fight.

"I wish I could, but you are much taller than me," she said, reluctantly putting the tunic back. "But I am going to have something similar made for me, if you don't mind."

"Not at all." I chewed my lower lip for a moment, wondering if I dared do what I wanted to do.

Octavia and Safie chatted while the latter got out of her Company of Thieves wool coat and skirt, and into Octavia's pretty dress.

Would Alan be offended? My fingers stroked the leather, knowing I shouldn't even think about it. "But dammit, it's my wedding," I said, getting to my feet. "And after all, you only live once."

Octavia glanced over from where she was helping Safie hook up all the buttons on the back of the dress. "Yes, of course it's your wedding. What did you pick out to wear? One of those pretty trouser suits? I'm sure Alan would have no complaint with you wearing something so elegant, even if it's not a gown suitable for such an occasion."

"Something like that. Er ... I think I'll go dress around the scattered parts of Jack's new navigator," I said, hauling one of the trunks to the door.

Octavia looked up, a frown between her brows. "Are you sure? I'm happy to help you dress for the wedding, since you were so kind to me when Jack and I were married."

I smiled and gestured toward Safie, who looked a little worried. "I appreciate that, but I'm happier getting ready on my own. Besides, you know I don't like all the fussy bits that the women here go in for, and Safie appears to enjoy them. I won't feel slighted in the least if you help her get ready."

"Very well," Octavia said, clearly hesitant. I managed to escape, and was almost to my cabin when Jack came down the stairs, frowning when he saw me.

"Hallie, what are you doing?" He took the wooden chest that I was dragging. "You shouldn't be moving things in your condition."

"You sound like something out of a nineteen fifties sitcom," I told him, but opened the door to my old cabin. "Don't worry, I'm not going to touch your project. I just wanted somewhere quiet to get ready."

He set down the trunk and studied me for a good minute before saying, "Are you sure about this, Hallie? Really sure? Akbar ... Alan hasn't manipulated you into thinking you have to do this, has he?"

"No, no, no," I said, giving him a kiss on his cheek. "Really, Jack, you need to give up this ridiculous idea of brainwashing you have. I love Alan. He loves me. We're having a miracle together. I couldn't be happier."

He was silent a moment, then gave a heavy sigh. "You always did do things your own way. I'll admit to being worried that you're happy about this, though."

"The wedding?" I shrugged. "It'll be all right. You know how I feel about that sort of thing."

He grinned. "That weddings are a ceremony wrapped around signing a piece of paper? Yeah, we're alike in that."

"Which is why it was nice you let Octavia have the wedding she wanted last year." I kissed him on the cheek. "But I'm not her, and so long as I get to do this my way, then that's what I'm going to do."

He looked a little confused by the admittedly incomprehensible sentence. "So long as you're happy," he said, patting my arm. "I'm going to go check on that bast—er—the groom, to make sure he's not trying to slip out without anyone noticing."

"Right, it's time for you to get over yourself," I said, shaking a leather gauntlet at him. "Alan isn't a bastard, or a heartless monster, or a violent murderer. He's loving and sweet and funny and patient, and you need to embrace having him as a brother-in-law, because he's all-around awesome, and will help the Company of Thieves immensely."

"Hrmph," my brother said, stomping off. I smiled to myself. I knew Jack, and he liked to grouse about any sort of change, but in the end, he'd learn to see Alan for what he was.

An hour later, I thought the crew were going to choke when I trotted down the stairs to the cargo area where the others were gathered.

"Bleedin' hell," Mr. Piper said, squinting at me with a grizzled face that had seen so much. "Ye look like ye'r goin' in t'battle."

I adjusted the falchion, flipped the tail of the lay over my shoulder, and once again tugged the breastplate down a smidgen. I'd still had to stuff the breast area with a soft pair of leggings in order to fill it out, but all in all, I was pleased with my appearance. "Why, thank you, Mr. Piper. I thought it was only fitting that a man of Alan's reputation be honored thusly."

Mr. Ho, who, like the rest of the crew, had donned civilian clothes, studied the armor, murmuring little comments of approval. "It really is quite unique. And is it comfortable to wear?"

"Very," I told her, feeling proud of the dashing figure I made in my borrowed armor. "It's not hindering at all, and whoever made this for Alan's sister was a master craftsperson."

"Indeed," she said, then stepped back, casting a glance to Mr. Llama.

"I've brought the carriages," Mr. Christian, the red-haired young man who served as navigator, said, bursting into the cargo area carrying with him a sense of excitement. "Where's the captain?"

"I'm here, with Captain Safie," Octavia said, tripping merrily down the spiral stairs with Safie in tow. She caught sight of me, and stumbled to a stop. "Oh. I … er … Hallie …"

"Ooh, is that Leila's armor?" Safie said, coming forward in her elegant black-and-white gown, a sparkly comb pulling her curls back from her face in a way that made her look even more ethereal. "It looks very good on you."

"Do you think she'd mind me wearing it?" I asked, suddenly feeling like I was encroaching on a family heirloom.

"Lord, no. She was with us for a bit, but then she married a Turkish prince and is quite happy in Anatolia. I'm sure she will wish you nothing but the best with the armor. I always did like it, but it was far too big for me."

Octavia had been opening and closing her a mouth a couple of times while Safie cooed over the armor, but eventually she gave a little shake of her head and let it go. "Well, if we are ready, I believe we can continue to the carriages. Mr. Piper, Mr. Mowen, you are both certain you do not wish to accompany us? We can ask some of Captain Dubain's men to watch the *Enterprise* while we are in town."

"So long as I may kiss the bride"—Matt Mowen, ship's engineer extraordinaire, gave me a big smile and kissed me on the cheek, his grizzled mustache tickling my cheek in a way that Alan's never did—"then I'm content to guard the ship."

"Aye, 'tis the same as me," Mr. Piper said, hobbling over in his odd gait, giving me a wet peck on the cheek before doing the same for Safie. "Dooley'll go for us old bachelors. Ye mind yer manners, now, lad."

Dooley rolled his eyes, but grinned and dashed out to the carriage.

"Mon capitaine," Mr. Francisco said, sidling up behind Octavia. "You shall allow me, your most devoted and faithful Francisco of your heartstrings, to accompany you to the weddings of the sister of the evil one?"

"Jack will escort me, thank you, Mr. Francisco," Octavia said firmly, disentangling herself from the hold he had on her hand.

Safie looked startled. I leaned in and said, "He's got a crush on her hair."

"Her … hair?"

"Yes. Evidently he wants to roll around naked on it. Drives Jack nuts, as you can imagine."

She giggled, and put an arm through mine. "I'm so glad you're marrying Alan. You're going to be very good for him."

"I hope so. I have been around Zand long enough to know he's a very nice man, and a devoted friend to Alan, and I hope you both will be very happy. I take it you've been engaged for a while?"

"Many years," she said, sighing. We followed the others to the two waiting carriages. I was a bit surprised to see that they were the fashionable steam carriages that larger towns like Rome and London sported, but evidently technology—of a form—had come to Marseilles since the last time I'd been there.

Mr. Llama, Mr. Ho, Dooley, and Mr. Christian rode in the first carriage, while Octavia and Safie and I climbed into the second, waiting for Jack, who came at a run from Alan's airship.

"Just made sure the groom got off to the church, and wasn't going to do a runner—" Jack stopped when he sat down opposite me, his brow furrowed. "Er. Hal. You're wearing Moghul armor."

"I'm glad to see your eyesight isn't going," I said placidly, scooting over when Mr. Francisco, with a glare toward Jack (who was sitting with his arm around Octavia), pushed in between Safie and me. "Is everything all right with Alan?"

"Yes." Jack returned Mr. Francisco's glare. "He said he sent over your clothes. Was there nothing else you could wear?"

"You wore what you wanted to your wedding," I said complacently, looking out of the window as the steam carriage lurched forward. I'd always been amused by the steam technology that people in this world embraced. "I'm doing the same. Oh, hey, who is that?"

"Who is ... bloody hell," Octavia said, peering out of the window. Overhead, moving with the grace peculiar to airships, a long shape drifted toward the east. "That's an imperial ship."

Jack craned his head to see, whistling softly. "Not transport. It's too small for that."

"There are two others," Safie said, pointing out of the other window.

We all looked, even as the steam carriages bumped from the farmyard onto the main road leading into town. Two other airships, both done in navy blue with a large stylized *W* on the front envelope, flew over our heads.

"Three ships?" I glanced at Jack. "Traveling together? I didn't think they did that."

"They don't normally," Jack said, rubbing his jaw. "Not unless ..."

Octavia sucked in her breath, and took his hand. "Not unless they bear contingents of guards."

"The emperor's guards," Jack said, nodding.

"Which means that's William on the first ship?" I asked, my gaze on my brother. "The same emperor who Octavia—"

"Yes, yes, we all know about her relationship with him," Jack said, then quickly corrected himself. "Her former relationship."

Octavia clicked her tongue and elbowed him.

"What does that mean to us?" I asked, worrying that Alan would have to don the disguise of a diplomat immediately. And just what was I to do while he was dancing attendance on William?

"I don't know yet," Octavia answered, but her gaze was troubled. "I suspect we'll have to wait and see."

"I can tell you one thing," Jack said, his voice hard. "It's going to be lively with the Black Hand, William, and us in town at the same time."

I said nothing during the rest of the ride, being busy with my own thoughts and worries. I had just decided that if Alan had a diplomat's disguise, I'd have to arrange for the same, which meant I'd have to wear the long skirts and corsets favored by ladies of society. I was grimacing over that idea when we arrived at a small church made of dark gray stone, one with a slight air of being abandoned, which suited me just fine. Dusk was falling, and a lamplighter moved slowly lighting the gas lamps that cast warm puddles of light onto the cobblestone street.

"Do you see them?" Octavia asked, looking toward the north.

"There," Jack said from where he had climbed onto the rear driver's seat, pointing to the east. I peered, seeing just the top of a dark, oblong shape over the rooftops of Marseilles. "What's he doing over there? The airstrip is just north of us."

"I wish I knew," she answered, looking decidedly worried.

"Maybe we should put off the wedding—" I suggested, knowing that a visit by the emperor himself meant we might be in danger.

"No," Safie and Jack said at the same time.

"It's not like William is going to start bombing the town," Jack said, taking my arm. "I want you settled before that blaggard—sorry, Safie—that rogue Alan has a change of heart."

"Oh ye of little faith," I told my brother when he led me into the church, blithely ignoring the fact that just earlier that day my own faith in Alan had been on less than solid ground.

We entered the church, Jack's crew and Safie ahead of us, with Jack and me following.

"This is kind of awkward," Jack whispered as we walked down the center aisle of the church. "I feel like I should be talking to you about the glory of womanhood and offering advice, and all I can think of is that bastard touching my baby sister in ways that raise the hairs on the back of my neck."

I couldn't help a little laugh. "If it makes it any better, tell yourself that I receive the same pleasure from Alan's touch as Octavia does when you molest her."

"I don't molest," Jack objected. "I woo. I seduce. I make sweet, sweet love."

"Yeah, you know how you don't like thinking of Alan touching me with his assorted body parts that I really, really enjoy? Well, the same applies to you talking about what you and Octavia get up to together."

He snorted, but by then we'd reached the altar of the dimly lit church, and I paused when I saw Alan standing in his gold tunic and leggings, a brace of disruptors strapped to his hips, and his beautiful leather armor glinting in the candlelight.

I grinned at him. "I see we had the same idea."

He smiled in return, his voice full of promise when he took my hand, kissing it before saying, "This is why we are so perfect together."

"Er …" A small man emerged from the vestry, his eyes first on Alan, then on me. "This is highly irregular. Highly irregular."

"We wish to be married," Alan told the man. "I see nothing irregular in that."

"But you are … and she is wearing … yes. Well. Highly irregular."

"Maybe we should go somewhere else," I said, starting to turn away, but evidently the old priest took umbrage at that, for he shot me a sour look and said quickly, "No, no, I will not have it said that the parish of Saint Dalrymple the Pierced turned away supplicants. You will please stand before me, and we will—"

A distant boom rattled the grungy windows. We all turned to the east.

"Was that—" I asked, but before I could continue, three more booms sounded.

"That's William," Octavia said, her hand on Jack's arm. "He's opening fire on something."

"Or someone," Alan said, turning and snapping an order in Kazakh to his men, who had filled the first three pews.

They all got to their feet.

"Hold on—" Jack yelled, stopping them when they would have filed out. He pointed at the priest. "Continue."

"Jack," Octavia said, tugging at his arm. "William is firing on the town. We need to leave."

"Not until he marries Hallie," Jack said, nodding at Alan.

"For the love of all that's good in this world," I said, exasperated. "If William is beating up Etienne, I want to be there to see it. Come on, Alan."

"Don't you move a single foot from this church!" Jack roared, scowling furiously at the priest. "Get on with it!"

"Oh, for heaven's sake." I made an apologetic gesture at Alan. "I'm so sorry about this. He's incredibly stubborn at times."

"Perhaps the monseigneur will be willing to give us the condensed marriage ceremony?" Alan suggested, gesturing to his men. With the exception of Zand, who stood behind us with Safie, they ran off, no doubt to get the *Nightwing* ready.

Another two booms sounded, followed by several whistles of the police force, and a roaring explosion. The old priest gave a little gulp and hurriedly said, "Yes, of course, it shall be as Monsieur desires. Do you ... er ... Hallelujah Norris take this Moghul?"

"I sure do," I said, smiling at Alan.

"And do you, Akbar Basir Alan dit Aurangzeb take this ... er ... also Moghul?"

"Yes," Alan said, turning around when one of the men appeared at the entrance of the church, yelling something to him. "Yes, I do. Can we hurry, please?"

"You are now married," the old man said, sketching a cross in the air before turning to a small table beside him. "Please sign both copies."

"Hey, don't I even get a kiss?" I asked when Alan hurriedly signed two copies of what I assumed was the marriage certificate.

"Later," he promised. "Wait here."

"Alan!" Zand yelled when Alan started down the aisle at a run.

He paused.

Zand tipped his head toward Safie.

"Marry her," he said, and would have continued, but Zand yelled, "And the *Falcon*?"

"Can Zand be captain, please?" Safie asked. "I'm really tired of the responsibility. I just want to live in a house and raise horses."

"Yes, yes, you're captain now." Alan didn't wait for any other distractions—he just bolted.

I picked up the nib pen he'd dropped, and signed my name on the two forms, sighing to myself as I did so.

"What should we do?" Safie asked, obviously worried.

The priest shoved one of the copies of the certificate into my hands, clearly happy to be done with the whole thing.

"Marry us," Zand told the priest, moving into the spot where, a few seconds before, Alan and I had stood.

"Congratulations," Jack said, kissing me on both cheeks. "I hope you'll be as happy as we are." And then he, too, was off. Octavia would have followed, most of her crew already at the door, but Mr. Ho stopped her, saying in a low voice, "Captain, since we're here ... would you mind if we ..." She nodded toward the priest, who was asking Safie if she would take Zand.

Octavia looked from Beatrice Ho to Mr. Llama, who stood smiling behind her. "Oh! I had no idea that you—well, of course, if you think that's a good—yes, yes, you have my blessings. Just join us when you can." She ran off, calling for Jack to wait for her.

"I guess we can be each other's witnesses," I said, feeling a little lonely while I watched Safie and Zand get married.

Zand kissed Safie, grinned at me, and, taking her by the hand, raced down the aisle with her in tow.

Another boom shook the rafters of the old church, dust and fine particles of debris wafting softly to the ground around us.

Mr. Ho looked at Mr. Llama. He smiled at her. They stepped up to the priest.

"Another one? Very well, but this will have to be quick. I do not intend to stand around waiting for the walls to come down upon me. Do you take him?" he asked Mr. Ho.

"Yes, I do."

"Do you take her?" he asked, pointing the pen that he still held in his hand at Mr. Ho.

Mr. Llama nodded, and said in a soft voice that he most assuredly did.

"I declare you married. Sign both copies."

They signed. The priest grabbed up the three marriage certificates, and ran for it, calling for us to get to safety.

I stood outside the church, looking to the east. Night had fallen while we were inside, but the sky over Marseilles was glowing red, smoke filling the air.

"Come with us," Mr. Ho yelled from where she and Mr. Llama had commandeered a dray driver.

"You go," I said, waving them on. "Alan knows I'm here."

"Are you sure?" she asked, but Mr. Llama was already turning the crank on the steam boiler, sending the dray roaring forward down the road.

I waved and looked around for the likeliest spot, running down toward the water a couple of blocks until the buildings dropped away to the docks. I turned and looked to the west, and waited, hoping I had guessed correctly.

"He's not going to just run off and leave me," I told myself, covering my ears when the three imperial airships to the east of town unloaded another volley of cannon fire. "Jack may not have any faith in him, but I do."

FOURTEEN

Fifteen minutes later, I was starting to wonder if I knew Alan's mind as well as I thought, but just as I was about to go in search of someone to take me out to the farm, a black shape blotted out the smoke, the dull hum of the propellers reaching my ears as the *Nightwing* glided over my head.

I waved the white cloth of my lay, and watched with relief as the ship slowed, then stopped.

A rope and wood ladder was tossed over the side of the observation deck. I didn't wait for Alan to come down to fetch me—I was a third of the way up it before he had started down.

"OK, I really need to take up some sort of cardio work," I panted when I reached the top, grateful for Alan's strong hands pulling me up the last few rungs. "Because I am seriously out of shape. Hello, new husband."

"I was coming down to get you," he said in a disgruntled voice.

I kissed the tip of his nose. "I know, but we don't have any time if we want to see Etienne blown to smithereens, and I very much want to see that."

"Have I mentioned how much I admire the fact that you are more bloodthirsty than I was ever reputed to be?" he said, gently pushing me back into the gondola while one of the men pulled up the rope ladder and rolled it up.

"Where are the others?"

"To the north." He grinned at me. "I had a feeling you'd wait in the open for me."

"I was starting to wonder if I'd mistaken the *wait here* command. Why is the emperor blowing up Marseilles?"

"He's not." Alan pulled me along the gangway to a small forward deck. "Can you see?"

I looked where he was pointing, the smoke in the air making it hard to see. Fires glowed in a five-block radius around one of the low, wide warehouses. The three imperial ships were clustered in a formation best suited to blowing the hell out of an airship that was hiding inside a warehouse. "Someone told him where Etienne was. Wow. I'd like to kiss whoever did that."

"I'm not going to go so far as to offer to kiss them, but I would most certainly shake his hand, and offer him my best wine. Ah, there's the *Enterprise*."

"And here comes the *Falcon*," I said, pointing to the west. A sudden worrisome thought struck me then. "We're not going to fight William, are we? Because I know he's the enemy and all—although he didn't stop Octavia's crew from rescuing us when we were going to be hung—but those ships have a lot of guns on them."

"Worried the *Nightwing* can't take on an imperial warship or two?" he asked, his hand warm on my back.

"Can she?" I asked, not sure whether Alan's ship, fast as she was, would be able to hold her own in a heated battle.

"One or two, yes, but not all three at once." He pulled out the small speaking tube from where it was attached to the wall next to the door. "South forty-one degrees, Abhishek," he told the navigator.

I trusted Alan. I knew he had a lot of experience fighting on the ground as well as in the air, but now there was more at stake than just ... well, us.

"Alan," I said, one hand on my stomach. "You know I'm totally on board with fighting evil, and kicking ass, and having exciting adventures, but—"

"We're too high." He turned from where he was leaning out trying to see beneath us, and pulled open the door, bellowing into the interior. "Az! We need to be lower."

"Too high for what? Alan!" I dashed after him, grabbing the back of his armor. "What are you planning on doing if not fighting?"

He stopped at the top of the stairs that led down to the lower decks, stopping to kiss me quickly. "You don't think I'm going to engage William with you on board in your condition, do you? Octavia and Zand will make sure the emperor's attention is elsewhere while we help ourselves to his resources."

I smiled a slow, admiring smile. "You really are the most amazing man. Can I help steal the things?"

"No," he said, patting my cheek before clattering his way down the stairs.

"Dammit, you're not going to turn into one of those overprotective men who think that just because a woman might have a miracle pregnancy thing going on, she can't help steal stuff, are you? Because I'm not made of glass, nor am I an idiot who won't protect herself at all cost, and if you think I am, well, then, the words 'I am so divorcing you' are going to come up a lot. Don't think I won't do it! I divorced my first husband and I didn't even love him."

It took a good fifteen minutes of maneuvering before we managed to land in a relatively safe spot on the wharf, hidden by a building that, from the smell of it, processed fish.

Alan had left his horses at the farm where the airships parked, so we had to skulk through the streets on foot to get to the storage depot. Guns still sounded to the north, although there was a different timbre to the sounds. "Is that the *Falcon* firing on William?" I asked in a whisper when we paused at the corner of the fish-processing building, while Alan quickly scanned the street for threats.

"The *Falcon* and the *Enterprise*, yes." He gestured, and we all hurried across the street, keeping to the shadows wherever possible.

"Isn't that dangerous? They are outnumbered, too, and you said the *Enterprise* wasn't good for attacks. I wouldn't want them getting involved if we aren't there to help them. But on the other hand, I really don't want to be left behind, and that's what you'd have to do in order to engage with them. Dammit, I hate worrying like this." I did a little teeth gnashing while I fretted about the ships being overwhelmed by superior numbers. I had every confidence in the other two crews, but if all three of William's ships focused on Jack and Octavia, they wouldn't stand a chance.

"They would be in danger if they were close enough for William to fire on them, but they're just doing a bit of chivying, trying to draw William's fire and attention so that he's not aware that his goods are in danger of being stolen. There's a guard up ahead, so no more talking unless it's vital."

We moved as silent as wraiths through the near-empty streets. Luckily for my peace of mind, Alan had made no objection when I insisted on bringing along the bow and quiver, assumedly because he thought I was as inept with the bow as I was with the dagger, sword, and those devilish disruptors that I swore wouldn't work for me because I hadn't been born in this world. My mind shied away from the fact that both Jack and Octavia were quite deadly with them, and focused on what was important—watching Alan's back.

"There," he said, pausing at the corner of a small grocery shop. Az moved up past me, flanking one side of Alan, while Ajay took the other side. I took a certain amount of pride that all of Alan's crew had gone back to their Moghul clothing (with their distinctly different armor, thank the goddess), feeling that we were much wilder, more dangerous, and far more daring than the rest of the Company, who had to conform to societal standards.

"We don't need no stinkin' badges," I quoted softly to myself, making a mental note to ask Jack if he remembered which movie that line came from.

A movement at my shoulder had me glancing over. "What badges?" Yussuf whispered.

"Boy, you have good hearing," I told him. "You got stuck with guard duty, eh?"

He grinned, immediately looking contrite when Alan glared back at us. I blew him a kiss.

Alan spoke quietly to Ajay and Az, then turned and pointed to a small fruit stand outside the grocer's, obviously telling me to park myself there. I nodded and moved over to it with Yussuf, while the rest of the men divided into two groups, half of them following Az, while the rest of the men trailed after Alan and Ajay.

"Help me up," I told Yussuf, pulling over a couple of wooden crates to use as steps.

He eyed the fruit stand. "You want to get on top of it?" he asked, clearly hesitant.

"Yes, I'll have a better line of sight if I'm up high. Come on, it's sturdy enough."

It took a few minutes of convincing him, but at last he helped boost me up onto the flat top of the stand, from which a ragged banner hung announcing the freshest fruit in all of France could be found within. I knelt, testing the bow, making sure it hadn't been damaged in transit, but it seemed just fine.

Ahead of us, two one-story buildings sat with small grimy windows set high on the walls, clearly some sort of storehouses used for cargo from incoming ships and airships. I counted four guards on the side nearest us, and watched with interest as, one by one, the guards disappeared into the dense shadows of the building without so much as a yell.

"He really is good at what he does," I said softly.

"Aye," came the equally soft answer from below. "It's why I wanted to join his company. Everyone knows that Prince Akbar is fearless in battle, and would never ask his men to do anything he wouldn't do himself."

I was about to answer when there was a shout from the building nearest us, and the peculiar splatting noise that meant someone was firing disruptors. I pulled out an arrow, ready to nock it should I see someone to take down, but it was difficult to see in the darkness, angled as we were away from the front of the building. There was a gas lamp on the corner, the dull yellowish light from it making the wet cobblestones glisten, but beyond that pool of light, I had no idea what was going on. "Do you see anything?"

"No," Yussuf answered.

"Maybe you should go help them." I didn't want to think of Alan being overwhelmed and possibly hurt. We'd just found each other again, dammit.

"Do you know what he'd do to me if I left you?" Yussuf's voice was rife with horror.

"Would it involve a gelding knife?" I asked, trying to distract myself from the need to go help Alan.

"That and so much more."

Men spilled out of the building then, at least fifteen of them yelling orders in French and English, followed by Alan's men. Swords flashed in the gaslight, bodies dancing in and out of both my view and the pool of light. I held the bow and arrow, hoping to get a clear shot at one of the imperial guards, but the fighting was too confusing and fluid to pick any one person out for more than a second.

At that moment, a dull sound like distant thunder came from the street to my right, and I watched with horror as a group of men mounted on horses thundered down the slight hill that led up to where the airships were still firing at each other.

The men all wore the scarlet uniform of the emperor, obviously a company of guards that had been sent to help protect the emperor's stores.

"Oh, you are so not going to join the fray," I said, nocking an arrow and sighting the front-most horseman. Luckily, he was a big man, with broad shoulders, and streaming blond hair. Just as he was directly in front of me, I pulled the bowstring back until it was level with my cheek, and let the arrow fly.

The man had lifted a sword high in the air, clearly about to attack Alan's men, but the arrow hit him dead in the shoulder, sending him jerking to the side, toppling off his horse.

I saw a man on the ground—I couldn't tell from this distance who it was other than he wore Moghul clothing—turn toward where I knelt, lifting a hand in what I hoped was thanks. I didn't acknowledge it. There were far too many men still pouring down the street. My bowstring twanged over and over again, each arrow but one striking a target. I went mostly for the torso and arms, since I didn't want to inadvertently strike one of the horses, but one unlucky soul got an arrow through his neck.

I felt sick about that. Although Jack and I had been raised as Quakers to believe in nonlethal force, I had strayed from that path, seeing things differently than my brother. Or at least I thought I had. As I watched the man fall from his horse, his hands on his throat before he slumped into an unmoving blob on the ground, I realized just why Jack refused to kill anyone.

Tears welled over my eyelashes, my heart aching at what I'd done, but I pushed down the guilt and sorrow, knowing I'd have to deal with both emotions later. "But not right now. Not while Alan is out there, at risk of being skewered by one of those bastards."

The last few men had evidently figured out that some-one was responsible for picking off their fellow horsemen, and two had paused, clearly looking for me. I flattened my-self on the roof of the fruit stand, but the movement must have caught their eye, for they both charged toward us. Yus-suf immediately ran out in front of the stand, his sword in hand, but I didn't like his odds.

I grabbed my last arrow and quickly picked the horse-man who made the best target, sending an arrow right into his upper arm, causing him to scream and drop his sword.

The second man tried to decapitate Yussuf, but he had been trained well and dived for the ground, before popping up and dragging the injured horseman from his horse. I yelled encouragement from the top of the stand, hoping to distract the remaining horseman long enough for Yussuf to disable him, but at that moment, a shadow loomed up from the side, and the blond man that I'd shot first grabbed me by the arm, hauling me down over the edge of the roof.

I screamed and kicked at him, but it was no use—he just hauled me down onto the boxes.

"Alan!" I screamed, struggling and trying to hit the man with the bow, since I had no more arrows left.

"Oh, no you don't," he growled in English, his accent all polished syllables and upper-crust. "You've done quite enough damage with that for one night, I think."

"You bastard! Stop that! I'm possibly pregnant!"

The man, who was more or less dragging me, stopped and glared at me. "You're a woman?"

I tugged down my leather breastplate before pulling back the bit of lay I'd wrapped around my face in the style of the men (evidently, they did that as a matter of course when engaging in battle). "Damn straight I am. And I may be a mother soon. I'm not exactly sure, because I haven't found out if there's such a thing as a pregnancy test, but I should know soon. And stop bleeding on me! You're getting my nice gauntlet bloody."

"You're the one who shot me, so you can put up with a bit of blood on your armor," he said in a gritty sort of voice. It wasn't nearly as nice as Alan's, but it held a tone of command that made the hairs on the back of my neck stand on end. "Who are you?"

It was on the tip of my tongue to answer "Your worst nightmare," but by then Yussuf had finished with the two horsemen and loped over to help me, his sword bloody.

"Hold!" the man said, pulling me so that I was in front of him, a hostage shield. "Do not come closer, or this woman will suffer."

I cursed myself as Yussuf backed off, his eyes narrowed on me.

"It's OK," I told him, more to keep him from doing something stupid than to reassure him. "I think Bleedy Mc-

Bleederson here wants to talk to Alan. Unless I'm mistaken about who you are, that is." The last sentence was directed to the man who forced me across the street, toward the front of the storehouse.

"Alan, eh?" The man behind me gave a loud and extremely piercing whistle, one that had me wincing, and to my surprise, the men who were still fighting with Alan's men suddenly stopped and turned toward us.

"Hallie!" A roar came from behind a couple of men, both of whom went flying as a man stalked forward, blood splattered across his armor, obscuring the symbols on it.

"Dammit," I swore, pulling my lay off so I could wipe the blood from his armor, knowing no one else but Alan would sound so furious. "Who messed up your armor? You know I need to be able to see that!"

Alan seemed to stumble when he got close enough to get a good view of the man who held me. "I … William? What—uh … you appear to be bleeding. And also, using my wife as a shield."

"I shot him," I told Alan, unable to keep a bit of pride from my voice.

His eyebrows rose. I smiled.

"Your *wife*?" The man behind me sounded mildly bemused. "I don't believe I was informed of your wedding, let alone received an invitation to the event. Perhaps the fact that you and your lady appear to be wearing garments more suited to the Moghuls than a diplomat in my service might have something to do with the current state of affairs? Also, you appear to bear a startling resemblance to the imperator's son. What's his name? Abdul? Abrahim? Although I do believe he has a mustache the size of a small lapdog."

I was about to argue that Alan's mustache hadn't been *that* big, but decided it was better if I kept that bit of information to myself.

Instead, I wriggled my way out of the grip of William VI, emperor of the British Isles and Prussia, and hurried over to where Alan stood. His men gathered behind him, while William's soldiers, at a gesture from him, regrouped in front of the storehouse.

"Are you in trouble?" I whispered to Alan when he pulled me tight to his side. I used the long tail of my lay to wipe the blood off the decoration of his armor so that I could make out the lion and the birds.

"I suspect I am," he said, but there was a note of humor in his voice that relieved the biggest worry in my mind. He said to William, "I suppose you'd like an explanation of just why I'm looting your storehouse."

"Oh, I think I can guess what's going on," William said politely, then with an irritated click of his tongue, pulled off his scarlet coat and white shirt underneath it, carefully examining his shoulder. The wound was fairly gory, making me avert my eyes. "Just look at what you've done. Now I'm going to have to have stitches. Do you know how much I hate having stitches? It's very unpleasant, and I'm already in a bad mood because a former lover, a woman whom I have gone to great lengths to aid despite the fact that she has pillaged my goods nonstop for the last year, is even now trying to lure my airships away from where I want them."

"Ah," Alan said, his arm tightening around me. "About that—"

The emperor turned back to his men and ordered one of them to come forward, swearing profanely when the man bound up his shoulder.

"I will now go have this sewn shut," William said with flared nostrils, and a very pointed look at me. "As well as having the other men you left alive patched up. When that is done, I will expect to see you, Alan, as well as Octavia and that American she married."

I pursed my lips, hoping Alan wasn't thinking of doing what the emperor ordered. If ever there was a trap being set for him, that was it.

Alan gave a little bow. "When and where would you like to see us?"

William put his good hand on his hip and glared at the groaning men scattered all over the street. "Two hours. At the *Constanza*. And I expect to find anything that was in the storehouse intact."

Then he simply turned on his heel and marched off, calling for his horse, and for the wounded and dead to be cared for.

I looked at Alan. "That was … bizarre."

He scratched his chin where a bit of blood had dried. "But interesting. You weren't hurt?"

"Of course not. But did you see how many men I took down?"

"Yes," he said slowly, giving me an unreadable look. "And I'm going to want to talk to you about that, but right now, I believe we would do better to consult with Octavia and Jack."

I cast a glance at the man who had been covered with a red coat being lifted onto a steam wagon, my heart heavy, but at the same time I knew I would go to extraordinary lengths to save the man I loved.

"You look troubled, little dove," Alan said, glancing at the body, and moving so that he blocked my view of it. "Are you feeling ill? Is it the babe?"

"No," I said, swallowing down my grief and guilt, my gaze skimming him, looking for any signs of injury. Thankfully, the blood on his armor didn't seem to be his. "I'm just a bit … befuddled by the whole thing with William. You aren't going to trust him, are you?"

"That is a very complicated question to answer," he said, his hand warm on my back as he escorted me back through the streets to where the *Nightwing* was hidden. "And not one I'm sure I know the answer to. I believe we are going to have to have a council of … well, not war, but perhaps preparation."

I nodded, saying nothing more.

Adventure, I decided as I looked out into the dark soul of the night, was not for the faint of heart.

FIFTEEN

"Is there such a thing as a pregnancy test here?"

Alan, who was strolling past Octavia's cabin en route to the mess, where he was to discuss William's demand, paused and stepped back to look in.

"There is, but it involves killing a rabbit," Octavia told Hallie.

"Ugh. No thank you."

"I'm afraid women here just have to wait before they are certain." Octavia patted Hallie's arm, her gaze going over her shoulder to where Alan stood. "I wish I could offer you something to ease your stomach, but Mr. Ho says she's given you your mother's best advice. I do hope things settle down in that regard."

"Me too," Hallie said, sounding tired. Alan swore to himself. He should never have allowed Hallie to come with them on the raid of the imperial stores. She was clearly taxing herself, and although he knew she would not put herself in any danger now that she was with child, she was no doubt letting her enthusiasm overestimate her stamina.

He said nothing when Octavia slipped out past him, giving him a rueful smile, but he watched Hallie when she stretched, sighed, and turned, pausing to tip her head to the side at the sight of him. "Damn me, but you are the handsomest man I've ever seen, and I've seen a lot of men."

He laughed, shaking his head. Would he ever guess what her mind was thinking? "I'm filthy, covered in blood and sweat, and my lip itches."

She moved over to him, stroking a finger along his upper lip. "Mmm, but it will be worth it when you have your 'stache back. Stop looking like that."

"Like I want to take you to bed and do numerous things to your delicious, nubile, smooth body?"

"No, like you're about to turn into one of those men who think women who are pregnant don't know their own limits, and need to be protected from themselves."

He started guiltily, wondering just how well she was able to read expressions. "Just out of curiosity, not that it has anything to do with your quite outrageous statement, because I would never in a million years be one of those husbands who think to tell you what you may or may not do, but does your difficulty in recognizing faces extend to expressions?"

"To a certain extent, yes," she said suspiciously, her eyes narrowing. "I mean, I can see your face. I can see what it's doing. Like right now, your eyes are open wide, and your eyebrows are raised a bit, so that means you could either be trying to look innocent or you might be thoughtful, or even scared, but although I can see the expression on your face, it's a bit difficult for me to interpret what it means. Jack is much better at this than me, but then, he only has a slight case of the facial blindness. My mother had it, too, which means we might have a child with it, as well. Just fair warning."

"Actually, I find it all rather fascinating," he said, brushing his thumb over her freckled cheek. "And you will please tell me if I ever do something that confuses you."

"I'm not befuddled," she said, whapping him on the arm. "I just have a hard time with faces. Speaking of that, are you going to grow your hair out, too? It's cute short, but …" She eyed him, her expression making him want to laugh again.

He heaved a faux sigh. "You want me looking just like Akbar, don't you?"

"I kind of do," she said with an apologetic expression. "Do you mind?"

"Not really. It will make things difficult with William, although to be honest, I suspect that isn't going to be an issue much longer. And with that said, let us go speak with the others so that we can determine the best course to take."

"I love it when you talk all proper and British, even though you had the most outrageous accent when I first saw you."

"I didn't know who you were," he admitted. "Prince Akbar speaks … spoke … English with a very heavy accent just in case anyone met me in both guises."

"Holy shit," she said, pausing before they entered the mess, turning to him. "That's right, you're a prince, even if you told your dad that you were done being Akbar. Does that mean I'm a princess? A real one? Like, is there a crown? Can I make Jack call me 'Your Highness'? Please tell me I can do that, because that is going to make up for years of being tormented by an older brother."

The bubble of laughter rose in him again. "Yes, yes, no, but you may have my share of my mother's jewels, and I believe there is a tiara in there, and the correct form of address would be 'Your Imperial Highness.'"

"Holy shit," she repeated, giggling when he pinched her on the behind. "Jack!" she said loudly when entering the mess. "You're never going to guess! I'm an Imperial Highness! So you can stick that in your plebeian pipe and smoke it."

"Oh, god," Jack said, rolling his eyes before he frowned at Alan. "I told you not to mention that to her! Now she's never going to stop lording it over me."

"That's Imperial Highnessing it over you, brother mine."

"She asked," Alan answered Jack, taking a seat next to Hallie at the long table. "You can't expect me to deny her anything she wants, can you?"

"That's right, suck it, nontitled brother," Hallie said, putting her hand on Alan's thigh in a gesture of possessiveness that delighted him.

"Hallie!" Octavia said in an outraged voice.

"Sorry. Got a little carried away. Are we ready to talk about William, and how he's setting an obvious trap for Alan?" She looked around the table, accepting the glass of soda water that Mr. Ho placed before her, while looking wistfully at the ale that Mr. Francisco passed around before he left the room.

"What's this about a trap?" Jack frowned. "I won't say I have forgiven Alan here for not bothering to mention the fact that he was one of our most hated enemies, but Octavia swears he isn't pulling some sort of devious Moghul trick on us, and as he and Hallie are now married, I supposed it's best for him to remain alive."

"Just so you know, Alan says that Octavia knew all along who he was," Hallie pointed out, brushing a bit of nothing off her sleeve. "And she didn't tell you, either."

"That's different," Jack said while Octavia made more outraged noises, glaring at Hallie. "My darling Octavia is an honorable woman who takes seriously a promise to keep a secret, even when it's obvious that she would clearly rather bare her soul to her much-loved husband."

Octavia, who had stopped glaring at Hallie, now cast a startled glance at Jack before adopting an expression of noble regret at not being able to tell all the secrets she held.

Hallie snorted, then surprised Alan by giggling and leaning into him to whisper, "Aren't they adorable together? I love riling Jack up so he gets defensive of Octavia. I think it's good for her to know just how much he loves her."

"You truly are not jealous of her?" he asked, not wanting to stir trouble with regard to his own past relationship with Octavia, but more than a little amazed. Hallie, he imagined, would not have the slightest hesitation in being jealous should he cast more than the most innocent glance toward any other woman, and yet after an initial flare-up over Octavia, she seemed to accept it with an equanimity that both surprised and pleased him. "Of the past that we shared? Jack has issues with that."

"I told you—what we did before we met each other doesn't matter. So long as you aren't pining for her, or any other ex-girlfriend, then no, I don't mind about your past with her any more than you care about all of the men I've been with before I met you."

All of the men ... the phrase reverberated around his head in a distinctly unpleasant manner, and although Jack was asking for information about what William had said to them, Alan suddenly had a desire to know just who were all the men to whom Hallie alluded.

He wasn't being unreasonable or jealous, he told himself; it was simply a matter of him having at hand the information needed should he be, sometime in the foreseeable future, called upon to beat those men to a bloody pulp. "Do you happen to have a list of their names and locations?" he asked Hallie, ignoring the fact that everyone at the table was waiting for his response. "And while we are on this subject, how many men are on that list?"

"Oh, are we getting to numbers now? Are you sure you want to go there, you, a man who had a harem that you had to dismiss when we hooked up?" She took a sip of her soda water, looking as beatifically innocent as a Madonna.

"Alan, perhaps you could tell us what William said to you while we wait for Safie and her new husband," Jack asked again.

"I didn't have a harem," he told her.

"You said you did! You said you were going to dismiss them when I told you that I didn't share," she protested.

"That's because you were so insistent that I had one. I don't. I never have. Unlike my father, I don't hold with the idea of having a group of women in thrall to me. I would hope by now you would realize that about me."

"Alan?" Jack frowned at him.

"I do now, of course," she said with blithe disregard of the fact that she clearly didn't know for certain. "I wouldn't have married a man who was liable to have vast hordes of women thundering around his bedroom at any given moment."

"Hallie," he said in chastisement.

She smiled. "All right, I may have originally believed you had a small harem, but that was only because Akbar was just the type to have one. It seemed prudent to ask you to make sure you were going to disband yours. You wouldn't want me if I was still seeing all my previous boyfriends, would you?"

"Of course not. And you will please provide me with a list of their names and where they live." The words emerged from his lips having been ground through his teeth.

"Alan? Did you not hear Jack's request?" Octavia asked. "As Safie and Zand appear to be … er … delayed … perhaps we could begin without them, since time is limited?"

"Now who's jealous?" Hallie asked him, smiling sweetly at the table in general.

"I am not jealous. It is purely for your protection that I wish to locate and puni—er … *meet* with your former lovers so that I might make sure they are of no threat to our future."

"They appear to be having an argument," Jack told Octavia. "A whispered argument. That can't be good. They were just married a few hours ago."

"Oh, like that's not jealousy pure and simple?" Hallie scoffed at Alan's wholly reasonable and proper determination to ensure her former lovers didn't cause them any strife, not that he could immediately call to mind just how they might do that. She placed her hand on his, her thumb making gentle circles when she said, "Would it make you feel better if I told you that I can absolutely, one hundred percent guarantee that my exes will not cause us any problem whatsoever?"

"If you recall, my love, we had an argument on the way from the church on the day we were wed," Octavia pointed out. "Due to your most improper ideas of activities suitable to riding in a steam carriage."

Jack grinned at her.

"I would feel more comfortable if I was to meet with them myself," Alan said. "I have a few things I wish to say to them."

"I'm afraid that's going to be nigh on impossible," Hallie answered, but before he could ask her why she insisted on protecting her former lovers if they meant nothing at all to her, Octavia spoke.

"Alan, if you are done with your discussion with Hallie, we would all, I believe, appreciate it if you would come to the point of this meeting, which, as I understand it, has something to do with an offer that William made you. We are naturally all attention to hear just what this offer was."

Her voice cut through the thoughts of what he wanted to do with Hallie's previous lovers. "Eh? Ah, yes, that." He shot Hallie a quelling look, but she just raised her eyebrows, her eyes sparkling with an inner joy that warmed him to his toes despite the desire to continue arguing with her. Quickly, he recounted the conversation with William.

"He gave no idea as to why he wished to meet with us?" Jack asked, looking thoughtful.

"No, although I have a suspicion my days as a diplomat in his court are over," Alan replied, and again rubbed his upper lip. His embryonic mustache was at the stage where it annoyed him.

"You think he recognized you?" Octavia asked, glancing from him to Jack.

"William saw him dressed just like Akbar, with Akbar's men, in the act of pillaging his storehouse," Hallie replied calmly, earning her a look of approval from Alan. "You said yourself that the emperor isn't stupid. Of course he recognized him. What I want to know is why he wasn't angry about it."

"That would be because there wasn't that much in the storehouse to steal," Alan said, leaning back in his chair, draping his arm over Hallie's shoulders, his fingers tangled in her hair while he stroked the back of her neck. "In fact, it was almost empty, with the exception of a company of guards who resided in a makeshift barracks at the back. Etienne's tales of William stockpiling goods was either false or he'd been at them before us, and I find that difficult to believe given the time of Hallie's arrival at the *Enterprise*."

"I'm so sorry we're late," Safie said, hurrying into the room, followed by Zand, the latter of whom, Alan was amused to note, wore an expression that was part guilt and part satiation. Clearly, his sister had wasted no time in acquainting herself with the charms of her new husband. "We were held up a bit. Did we miss anything?"

Everyone politely ignored the fact that it was evident just why they were delayed. Alan recounted for a second time the brief meeting with William.

"You shot him?" Safie asked Hallie, clearly admiring her prowess. "But Zand said … erm … he said that you …"

"Suck at other weapons?" Hallie sighed. "He's right, although I don't think I'm nearly as bad as Alan makes out. The accident with the daggers was just a fluke, and I didn't really shoot off the toe of one of Alan's men. I just singed his boot a little when the disruptor malfunctioned. Yes, it did set fire to one of the men's tents, but that wasn't really my fault, because the man I'd only *just barely shot* went running around screaming that I'd blown off his foot, and the flames from his leg caught hold on the tent fabric. It's very dry in Tunisia, you know. I really liked the area, although I suppose that's neither here nor there in the subject of how unreliable those guns are. Honestly, I don't know how you people use them. They're so temperamental."

A silence followed Hallie's statement, one in which everyone present stared at her for a few stunned seconds before their gazes all shifted to Alan.

"She didn't blow off his foot, although he did take my offer to leave my company a few days later," Alan told them. "But as Hallie pointed out, that's not a pertinent point. The decision that faces us is what we are going to do about William's invitation. Do I go meet him by myself in case it is an attempt to trap us?"

"How about hell, no?" Hallie said firmly.

"Or do the captains meet with him to see what it is he wants?" Alan rubbed his upper lip again, his mind turning over all the possible reasons why William might have acted as he did. "It's not beyond the bounds of possibility that he has something up his sleeve with regards to Etienne."

"I believe now would be a good moment to discuss the future of the Company of Thieves," Octavia said with a glance at Jack, who nodded. "With the addition of Alan and Zand to active participation with the Company, we may wish to move in a new direction."

"What sort of new direction?" Alan asked. "You don't intend on fighting William outright, do you?"

"No," Jack said slowly. "Our thought was that since our company has filled out with your arrival, and Zand taking over for Safie—not that we wish her replaced, since she has been an able and dedicated captain—but Tavy and I thought that the Company might start shifting from a purely reactive status to one more proactive."

"Fighting," Hallie said with satisfaction, patting Alan on the leg again. "At last, we'll be able to make some real changes."

"What sort of changes?" he asked, frowning at the puzzle she presented. He knew full well how upset she'd been at the sight of the soldiers that had been killed at the storehouse, and yet now she was advocating for more fighting? Had he misread her character so badly?

"We'll be able to help all those people who have been caught between William and the Black Hand and the Mogh—your father," she said, her eyes bright with excitement. "Real help, not just a few supplies stolen from the baddies to get them through a few days like Jack and Octavia and the others have been doing."

Alan lifted Hallie's hand from his thigh and kissed it, relieved that his sudden doubts were ungrounded. Hadn't she told him the first time they met that she had wanted to learn to fight to help Jack and Octavia? His little dove had a core of steel in her that he was only now learning to appreciate.

"We thought—Tavy and I—that we might be able to help bring about the end of these wars," Jack said, his expression solemn. "I realize that sounds borderline egomaniacal to think we have that sort of power, but it's been our intention all along to work toward the destruction of the holds on Europe by both the Black Hand and the Moghuls."

"And William?" Alan asked.

"William is another matter," Octavia said slowly, meeting his gaze with one that spoke volumes.

He made a little gesture. "I believe now is the time for plain speaking. You mean you will not attempt to dig William's grasp from his empire because of your relationship with him?"

"He did rescue us when we were all about to be executed," Octavia pointed out.

"And he promptly placed a bounty on your head," Alan reminded her.

"One that, oddly, no one has sought to collect on," Jack said, smiling at Octavia.

"No one?" Alan felt himself surprised by that. "There's been no attempt to capture you?"

"Not by William's men, no," Octavia told him. "I don't say I know what his plan is—which is why I will suggest we meet with him, because he might well tell us—but I don't believe he is the enemy we think him."

Alan shook his head. "You have not been a diplomat in his court. William is a devious man, with many plans of an intricate and detailed nature."

"That may be so, but the fact remains that we have never been harmed by him. And just look at your meeting this evening. He did not harm Hallie or you."

"She's got a good point," Hallie said, looking as thoughtful as Alan felt. "I still think it may be a trap, though."

"Possibly," he answered, thinking over the various options. He glanced up as a thought struck him. "Do we know how badly Etienne's ship was destroyed?"

"We do, as a matter of fact," Zand said, giving Safie a googly-eyed look that left Alan both annoyed and amused. "Just before we left the *Falcon*, one of the men we'd sent out earlier to scout the area returned and told us that although William's airships had more or less destroyed the warehouse that we believe held Etienne's ship, it wasn't there. Certainly not by the time William's ships arrived."

"That's very interesting," Octavia said, frowning at the table. "He must have departed almost immediately after we returned to the *Enterprise* and found Hallie. Otherwise, William would have seen him."

"Why would he leave so quickly?" Jack asked. "He just got here."

"Yes, but Hallie wasn't there anymore," she answered.

"What do I have to do with it?" Hallie asked, scooting her chair over so she could lean against Alan.

Instantly, he had to fight down the urge to insist she go rest. He reminded himself that she was an intelligent woman, and she would do nothing to endanger herself or their child. It didn't do much good, but mindful of the saying about bringing a horse to water, he decided he'd just have to gently guide her to the path he preferred. "There are other ways to get a horse to drink," he murmured to himself.

"I'm sure the horses are fine," she told him, patting his hand before turning her attention back to the discussion.

"Your role in Etienne's plans very much depends on just why he kidnapped you in the first place," Jack was saying, looking speculatively at Octavia. "You know him best of all of us, Tavy. Was he just smitten with her, or do you think he had some nefarious plan afoot?"

"He stole her because he knew she was mine," Alan said, well aware of his driving need for action. "A fact that my father also knew, and probably played upon, damn his soul."

"That still doesn't explain why he'd hightail it out of here when he found I'd gotten away," Hallie said.

Alan dragged his mind from the depths of the anger that wrapped around the memory of Hallie being taken from him, and put it onto the problem at hand. "I believe that is a point we may need to set aside for the moment, until we know just what it is William wants of us."

"Does this mean that we're going ahead with being more kick-ass?" Hallie asked the table in general. "More proactive? Doing more than just salvaging goods for the people who need them? We're going on the attack?"

They all looked at one another for a minute.

"Shall we take a vote?" Octavia asked. "Jack and I will be happy to be more aggressive in our dealings with the Black Hand and the Moghuls. We have wanted to refit the *Enterprise* to become more able to take down other airships, and have the funds to do so."

"And my new autonavigator—when I get it finished—should make maneuvering a hundred times easier and more effective," Jack said, nodding.

Zand looked first at Alan, then at Safie. "We will do as the rest of you wish. I've spent my life fighting with Akbar, and I would consider it an honor to fight alongside Alan in the Company."

Alan was silent for a few minutes, well aware that the others were watching him closely. Hallie said nothing, obviously allowing him to make up his mind without pressure. He looked at everyone at the table, then gave a shake of his head. "I reserve judgment about just how impotent you feel William is, but it has only ever been my wish to dismantle the Black Hand, and curb my father's hold on Europe. We will continue to work toward those goals in whatever capacity is needed."

"Then we are decided," Octavia said with a smile at Jack. "We will meet with William, and once we find out what he wants, we will gather to make plans to take the Company in its new direction."

"Despite your belief that the bounty that William placed on your head is not being enforced, perhaps you should remain behind when we meet with William," Alan told her. "Just in case this is a trap to gather all of us in one net."

Octavia didn't like that any more than Jack did. "We're a team," the latter told him, one arm around Octavia. "Where I go, she goes, and vice versa."

Octavia looked pleased, and shot her husband a heated look that he returned.

"I hope you're paying attention," Hallie told Alan, nodding toward them. "Because that's the sort of attitude I expect you to have, too."

"You are with child," he reminded her. "There are some situations where it would not be suitable for you to participate."

"Probably pregnant, but not absolutely certain, although I'm not going to kill a sweet little bunny to find out."

"I don't suppose that if I asked you to stay behind—" Alan started to ask, but as he suspected, he wasn't given the chance to finish the sentence.

"No. Absolutely not. Under no circumstances," she told him.

It was decided, after another fifteen minutes of debate, that they would descend en masse upon William, but would have their respective crews on standby should it turn out that William did not wish to release them from his presence.

"I hasten to point out that if we wish to display a united front of nonaggression to William, the act of you insisting on bringing with you the very same weapon that you used to wound him earlier might give a false impression," Alan told Hallie later, when they were in a horse-drawn carriage with Zand and Safie.

Hallie clutched her bow. "It makes me feel better to have it. You have a sword and those blasted guns, and daggers in your boots, so don't make it seem like I'm the only one here who is armed. I bet Zand has the same, and if it comes to that, Safie looks loaded, as well."

Safie smiled. "I might have a dagger or two hidden upon my person. Alan insisted I learn how to protect myself, and as you must know, he's very proficient in teaching one the art of ... oh."

"I don't want to have to give you and your brother a pointed look," Hallie said with thinned lips, "but I will if you continue that train of thought."

Safie laughed, and Alan, mindful that he wanted to celebrate his wedding night with a wife who didn't make references to the fact that he was unable to teach her the same skills he'd taught his sister, changed the subject. "Zand, I expect you—dammit. No, I can't expect that anymore now that you are no longer my lieutenant."

Zand looked mildly surprised. "I'm not? Did you wish for me to not be a part of your company?"

"I would be happy for you to remain with me, but that isn't the point I was trying to make. You're captain of the *Falcon* now, unless Safie has changed her mind?"

"Absolutely not," she said quickly, leaning into Zand. "I want to live in a house that doesn't move around from place to place. I want to walk in gardens, and enjoy bathing in the sea, and not have to worry every spare minute about my crew, and whether or not Father will find out what I'm doing."

"In which case, as captain of the *Falcon*, Zand will no longer be at my beck and call," Alan said, a pang of regret dimming a little the pleasure he took in his friend and his sister finally finding happiness together.

"Is there some rule I'm unaware of that says I can't be both a captain and remain in your company?" Zand asked, glancing at Safie. She nodded.

"If you have joined the Company of Thieves for good, Alan, then perhaps you could take my place in it, and Zand could captain the *Falcon* when necessary, but other times help you … and also join me in our home."

"That sounds like a smart plan," Hallie agreed, looking at him. "Would that work for you?"

"You'd be willing to do that?" he asked Zand.

"I never wanted to be a captain, you know," his friend answered, smiling. "So long as you let me have enough time with Safie, I'd be happy with captaining just when you need the *Falcon* in action, and doing what you wish the rest of the time."

"As you have my sister to support now, I suppose I could take you back into my company," Alan said with faux regret, which just made Zand grin at him. "Although you do realize that by changing our purpose, our futures just became that much more liable to end quickly."

"We've always lived on the dagger's edge," Zand said with a shrug. "If anything, now that I have Safie, I will be doubly careful to return to her in one piece."

Hallie squeezed Alan's hand. "That goes for you, too, buster."

"Alan," he corrected her absently, wondering if the others understood just what this change in intention would mean for the Company.

The *Constanza* was a midsized warship, done in shades of white and gold, with a heavy complement of guns that Alan was interested to note were the latest type of oil-injected aether cannons. He'd heard that the Prussians were perfecting this new type of weapon, said to be more effective than the standard aether cannons, but he hadn't seen one in person.

"Those look different than what we have," Jack commented when they gathered before the *Constanza*, which was surrounded by armed imperial soldiers. He stood back, squinting in the darkness at the noses of the cannons, which still remained in firing position.

Alan suspected William had left the cannons in place in order to remind his enemies that the imperial ships were more than able to take care of any threats. "If a smaller gauge of cannon is available, I believe I will look into some for the *Nightwing*."

"We need them, as well," Jack told Octavia. "They're better than the ones we wanted to get."

The head of the guard marched down the ramp leading into the cargo bay, informing them that the emperor awaited them inside, his gaze touching first on the two disruptors strapped to Alan's hips, then on the same that Zand bore, finally resting on Hallie's bow. To Alan's surprise, they were not asked to disarm before being escorted up two flights of stairs and into a grand reception room at the rear of the gondola.

"Ah, you come at last," William said, sitting at a massive gilded white desk. He rose at their arrival, moving around to take Octavia's hand before pressing a kiss to it. "Octavia, my dear, how well you look. Wedded life clearly agrees with you. I'm delighted to see that no one has yet claimed the bounty that was placed upon your head."

"A bounty *you* put there," she said somewhat acidly.

Jack took her hand back from the emperor, and put a possessive arm around her, before narrowing his eyes on William. "Speaking of which, you can just bloody well remove that bounty."

"Ah," William said, studying Jack for a moment. "I believe we will come to that in time. And this is?"

He stopped in front of Zand.

"My lieutenant," Alan said, gesturing toward Safie. "Zand has recently wedded my sister Safie, and is the captain of the *Falcon*."

"My felicitations," William said gravely, bowing over Safie's hand before turning to where Alan stood with Hallie at his side.

"And you've met my wife, Hallie. She is Jack's sister."

"Indeed?" He pursed his lips at the bow that Hallie held, his hand straying to his shoulder. "You will no doubt be relieved to know that my physician has decreed the wound you inflicted upon me was of a minor nature, and should heal nicely with care."

Alan half expected her to make a comment that would stir William's ire, but once again, she surprised him. "I wish to say how very sorry I am that I was responsible for the death of one of your men, and I hope you will allow me to make a reparation. I don't have a lot of money, but I would like very much for what I do have to be given to the poor man's family."

William's eyes widened for a moment; then calculation entered his blue eyes. "Have the Moghuls adopted a new policy toward those they fight? Can I expect a payment for all the men who have fallen under their onslaught?"

Alan smiled to himself. "As you appear to be under no delusion as to who I am, I believe I can say that such reparation would need to go both ways, and since you've slaughtered far more Moghuls than we have imperial forces, I doubt if you'd be willing to enter into any such agreement."

"Ever the diplomat," William said, bowing, then gestured to one of the three guards who remained in the room to leave. "Sit, please. We have much to discuss." He paused in the act of retaking his own chair, asking Alan, "I had no idea, you know. Not until I saw you today, and I might say that I wish I had known the truth about you, since it has created a good deal of trouble for me. You were a very good diplomat. I regret your loss to my service. I assume, that is, that you will no longer wish to remain in service to me?"

Alan was amused despite himself. "I think it would probably be for the best, since I have devoted myself and my men to the Company of Thieves. I might be accused of having some sort of bias against your best interests, otherwise."

"Ah, yes, the Company of Thieves. Unusual name, that," William said, sitting at last. "One that I might take issue with, considering ships bearing the emblem of it have reportedly raided my stores in a number of locations across Europe."

"Only a few," Octavia said with complacence. "And only when there were no Black Hand resources available."

"I am grateful for such mercy," William said, his gaze moving amongst them all before settling on Alan. "So grateful that I have a proposition to make you, one that I feel you will find beneficial to your interests."

"Oh?" Alan asked, slipping into the negotiation mode so familiar to William's diplomats. "In what way?"

"My original proposal was to ask Octavia for her company to join the Imperial Aerocorps in order to better fight the Moghuls and Black Hand, but I gather the rumors that Prince Akbar has been killed are true." He gazed mildly at Alan. "That means that rather than having three goals, we have only two: to eliminate the imperator's hold on the

Hungarian empire, and to destroy the Black Hand once and for all."

Alan was silent. He'd known the time would come when he had to commit himself to a path that would be difficult for many reasons, but he had thought he might have a bit of time before he actually had to walk it. "The imperator will not relinquish the Hungarian empire easily," he answered. "His intentions are to hold as much of Europe as is possible and, toward that end, has joined forces with the Black Hand. Etienne made an agreement with my … with the imperator that gave the latter Bohemia, while Etienne would rule Prussia, and assumedly points west."

"So those rumors were true, as well," William said, his expression thoughtful. "I had heard that the duchess had agreed to a marriage contract with the prince, but obviously, that is no longer valid."

"It never was," Alan said evenly, reaching over to take Hallie's hand. "The imperator signed the contract, not the intended bridegroom."

"Interesting."

Alan glanced at the others, but they had all evidently ceded the floor to him, allowing him to deal with William as best he could. "I have heard that the imperator intends on wedding the duchess himself."

A flash of anger flared in William's mild blue eyes, but it was so quickly gone that Alan wasn't absolutely sure he'd seen it at all. "I believe the phrase that comes to mind with regards to the duchess marrying such a man is that she has made her bed and now must lie upon it."

"I will admit to being shocked at hearing you speak so harshly of her," Octavia said, drawing the emperor's attention. She glanced at Alan before continuing. "As I was shocked to hear that your wedding to her was canceled."

Alan raised his eyebrows, and studied the paintings that hung on the wall.

"Yes, well, the Moghuls made certain that the wedding did not happen," William said drily. "And then Constanza insisted on arguing about some trivial matter or other, and one thing led to another, and we agreed to part. But that is past history, and not important other than to reflect on the capriciousness of women."

"Hey, now," Hallie said, frowning at him. "Let's not tar everyone with that sin."

He bowed, and murmured something about present company being excluded.

"If you think we're going to join up with you when you have put a bounty on Tavy's head, you're flat-out insane," Jack told William. "Even if that was lifted—as I assume you intend to do—then I fail to see what reason we would have to join your force."

"Naturally, I will make sure that the bounty is removed off the fair Octavia's head," William said with an air of graciousness. "As members of my Imperial Aerocorps, you would command the best crews to be found in all of Europe. In addition to which, you would have access to my airships. My not-inconsiderable force of airships."

Alan looked to Octavia and Jack, then Zand and Safie. They all looked back at him, once again leaving him to speak for them all. Alan shook his head. "Tempting as that offer is, I believe I can safely say that we're all happy with our ships, our crew, and our own company."

William made an annoyed gesture. "Do not force me into a position where I must act to defend myself from you. I don't believe any of us would enjoy that, although I hasten to point out that I am infinitely better suited than you to survive such a situation."

"Dude," Hallie said, twanging her bowstring. "Did you just threaten us?"

"Yes," William said calmly, and added, addressing Alan, "Your wife appears to be quite antagonistic."

"She is in an interesting state," Alan said just as calmly, his fingers on Hallie's in warning, which thankfully she took. "I believe that allows her a little leeway with regards to strong emotions. Despite that, I second her sentiment, if not the manner in which she expressed it. We none of us will stand for being threatened. If there is another element to your proposal, we would all like to hear it. Otherwise, I believe we will take our leave."

William didn't like that, but then, he never did like having his plans changed. However, he clearly wanted their help, so after a few moments of inner struggle, he sat back in his chair and said, "Iago, the king of Italy, has decided to throw his lot in with the imperator. He has informed me that I must commence moving imperial troops out of Italy immediately."

Alan frowned. "Why would the king take such a dramatic step against you? I may be mistaken, but I was under the impression that he was a friend."

"He was." William grimaced. "He has decided that he values the Mediterranean more than a friendship that dates back to our school days, and thus has come to an agreement with your … with the imperator."

Alan glanced at Zand. "He's carving up Europe."

"Or trying to," Zand agreed, looking as worried as Alan felt.

"Would you be agreeable to working for me in a non-official capacity?" William asked with bald frankness. "The Black Hand I can handle. The imperator, I may be able to keep at bay at least until such time as I have the revolutionaries eliminated. But without a base in southern Europe, and with my one remaining ally no longer reliable …" He let the words trail off.

Jack cleared his throat. "Octavia and I are not unaware of what we owe to you, despite the damned bounty that you put on her head."

A fleeting smile crossed William's lips.

"For that reason, we would be willing to put the *Enterprise* and our crew at your disposal, but we will not speak for the entire company. What you ask poses great danger, and with my sister pregnant, Alan may not wish to risk his life. And Zand may very well wish to spend some time with his new wife before he is called upon to take such perilous actions."

"I can speak for my father, Robert Anstruther," Octavia said quickly. "He is in Ireland, but I know he will do all he can to aid to curb Etienne's plans."

"Robert Anstruther," William said slowly, looking curiously at her. "That is a name I have not heard for some time, and unless I'm mistaken, it belonged to a man who died many years ago."

"Yes, well, sometimes people appear to die, but don't really," Octavia said with a gesture toward Alan. "As we have proof."

"Just so," William said, then pinned Alan back with a steely look. "You understand what I am asking, no doubt. While the others will be of immense use to me in tackling Etienne, your knowledge of the Moghuls and the imperator places you of vital importance in my attack on Turkey."

"Not Turkey," Alan said slowly, thinking over his father's plans. Even after the "death" of Akbar, he knew his father would not change his plans. He never did, not once he had decided upon a path. It was one of the things that they had argued about the most. "Bohemia."

"Really?" William thought about that for a few seconds; then his eyebrows rose. "Constanza."

"Yes," Alan said, meeting his searching gaze. "The imperator wants Bohemia above all else."

"It would serve as a very handy gateway to the rest of Europe," William said, nodding. "Very well, then I will modify my statement to ask you to face your father in Bohemia. I will understand if your wife's delicate condition gives you pause—"

"We'll do it," Hallie said, squeezing Alan's fingers, then saying under her breath, "Sorry, I didn't mean to steal your thunder, but you were going to say that, right?"

He gave her a wry smile. "Yes, but in the future, I would prefer for you to consult with me before making any such promises."

"Sorry," she repeated. "I just couldn't help myself, but yes, in the future, we'll make the decision together."

"Excellent," William said, looking at Zand.

Alan watched his friend, seeing the slightly panicked look in Zand's eyes. Although he trusted his faithful lieutenant with his life, it was clear that Zand felt more than a little out of his depth with the idea of going into battle as the captain of his own airship. Alan thought he would do quite well at the job, but mindful of Safie's soft, pleading eyes upon him, he said slowly, "Zand has, until recently, been a member of my personal company, and unless he wishes otherwise, I would welcome him at my side while we dealt with the imperator."

Zand's shoulders slumped in relief. Safie mouthed a thank-you to Alan, before leaning back against her husband.

"I care little how you arrange your forces, so long as you are able to do what I need you to do."

"Then we are agreed," Octavia said, nodding. "The Company of Thieves will undertake to assist the empire for the purpose of dismantling the Black Hand, and stopping the imperator from breaching Bohemia."

"I think it's going to take rather more than simply stopping the breach," William said, his gaze touching lightly on Alan. "I believe that the imperator's son will need to rise from the dead and take his place."

Alan looked in horror at the emperor.

Next to him, Hallie gasped. "Is he serious?" she asked him in a whisper. "He wants you to kill your own father?"

"Not kill, depose," Alan said softly, then continued in a louder voice. "I do not seek the position of imperator. I neither want nor need power. I am content with my life as it is."

"And you get bonus brownie points for that," Hallie told him softly.

"You do not seek it, no, but it is the only solution," William insisted. "The imperator must be removed from the throne, else he will continue to be a thorn in my side. How you do it is your own business, but you are the likeliest person to not only remove him, but to rally the Moghuls to your side and lead them to a future less fraught with destruction."

They went round and around for a half hour before Alan reluctantly agreed that he would attempt to remove his father from the throne, although he refused to promise that he would claim it once that had been done. "I have seven other sisters, any of which would be perfectly fine to rule in the imperator's place."

William waved that away, too. "We will leave that discussion for another date. Have we come to terms? I wish to be away before the sun rises, since this news about Bohemia means I must stop my fleet from flying to the Hungarian empire."

After the delicate question regarding financial remuneration had been settled to everyone's satisfaction, maps were shared, and Alan was given a specific set of instructions, while the others made plans on how best to tackle Etienne.

"My spies tell me he's headed to Prague," William said as they were about to part. "That is where you should focus your attention. Cut off the head of the organization, and the rest will crumple."

Alan said nothing as they made their good-byes, and received a list of codes used to communicate with imperial ships, before they all returned to their respective airships.

Octavia and Jack departed almost immediately. Alan hurried his crew into readying the *Nightwing*, after which he joined Zand in getting the *Falcon* ready to fly.

"Leave the *Falcon* outside of Prague, where it will be safe," he told Zand. "Safie and you will join us on the *Nightwing*, and then we'll tackle my father."

"One ship, even the *Nightwing*, isn't going to be able to bring your father to his knees," Zand pointed out.

"Which is why we're going to find an alternate method to seeing to his downfall," Alan said.

Safie appeared in the double doors of the *Falcon*, looking pointedly at her husband.

"You'd better go before she decides to ensure I am unable to enjoy my own wedding night," Alan said with a nod toward his sister.

Zand laughed, punched him on the shoulder, and hurried off to get the airship on its way.

"It's almost midnight," Hallie said when he arrived at the *Nightwing*. "And you look exhausted. Please tell me you don't have to stay up all night."

Hallie bore black smudges beneath her eyes, but her face glowed with love for him that made him feel nigh on invincible. "Just long enough to make sure we're under way without problems. Go to bed, dove. I'll join you as soon as I can."

"Just so you know," she said, heading for their cabin, her hips swaying in a deliberate attempt to lure him, "I have a long list of things I want to do to you. With my tongue. And for every minute you make me wait, I'm crossing off one of them."

They were aloft and headed off through the moonlit night in record time.

SIXTEEN

"Eleven minutes," I said, glancing at the clock when Alan entered the captain's cabin.

"It would have been sooner, but one of the boilers had a sticky valve. What have you struck off the list? Is it something I'm going to regret greatly, or was it more moderate pleasures, like you staring at me while I stand naked?" Alan asked, stopping in the middle of the cabin, slowly removing his weapons before pulling off his clothes and laying them neatly folded on top of a chest that sat at the foot of the bed.

I'd been reclined against the headboard, holding his pillow and enjoying the scent of Alan that clung to it, but now I sat up, the better to watch him perform what was an amazing striptease.

"A couple of them involved looking at you, but there was one erotic massage, and two uses of my knuckles on your sensitive spots."

He looked thoughtful. "Damn. I do like your two-knuckle move."

"Evidently there's another way to stimulate the same area, but I've never been able to bring myself—"

"No," he said quickly, giving me what I was coming to think of as the Akbar Scowl. "I would not care for that."

"Good, because it's not really something I'm interested in, either. I'm fine with just molesting those bits of you that are handy. Speaking of which, I have several other items on my list that didn't get scratched off. Ones involving much application of my flesh to your flesh. Oh, yes, please turn around. Hoochiwawa, Alan. Your behind has gotten even more fabulous in the week we were parted." Alan flexed his butt muscles, sending a ripple of pure heat from my chest upward. "I just want to make sure you're OK before we dive fully into wedding-night fun."

He paused in the act of splashing some water on his face and chest, looking over his shoulder to me. "You wish to make sure I'm all right? In what sense? In that I want you with a passion that makes it difficult to walk? Or that I want to touch and taste you, plunging into your depths until you writhe beneath me with my name on your lips?"

"Yes, please, to all of that," I said, watching his ass flex as he moved. "I meant I wanted to make sure that you're OK with William forcing you to go after your dad. That has to be a hard idea to swallow."

"It's not what I would have chosen to do with my time," he said, giving himself a quick wash at the basin, no doubt to rid himself of the residue of the fight with William's men.

I toyed with the suggestion that we have a bath together, but baths in this world take time to set up and fill, and the desire that prickled along my flesh wasn't going to wait for any of that.

Alan continued despite my smutty thoughts. "I can see that it's inevitable. My father's plans have gone well beyond what they once were, to the point of threatening all the citizens of Europe. He will not balk at killing anyone who stands in his way, and since I am loath to have my inactivity responsible for genocide, I must do what I can to stop him before he can do more damage."

"I'm just sad it's come to this. I want you to know that I will help you however I can. And also, that I will be here when you want to vent about your dad, and being the only one who can make him stop, and when you just need to be held because the world can be a big pain in the butt sometimes."

"Your help, and support, and particularly you holding me, is much appreciated," he said.

"While I'm on the subject of butts, can I add that I really want to take your behind in my hands again, Alan. I want to touch the thick muscles of it that curve so delightfully. I even want to bite it, and I've never wanted to bite a man's behind before."

He froze for a few seconds, then flung down the towel he had been using to wipe his face and chest, and was suddenly there on the bed, flipping me over onto my belly, his hands hot on my back and thighs as he bent over me. "You may say that, but I will go first."

"Hey! No fair! I'm the one who came up with the idea … oh, lord, Alan! You're biting me!"

His tongue made a warm swirl on the spot on my left butt cheek that he'd bitten, taking the sting from it, and sending streaks of heat pooling deep into my hidden depths. "It was just too much for me to resist. Are you up to a wedding night, my dove? I don't wish to tire you if you would rather—"

I bucked and twisted until I got to my knees, and pushed him over backward, his head narrowly missing hitting the chest at the end of the bed. "Don't you even think about denying me a wedding night, new husband. I said I had a list, and I fully intend to work through at least a half dozen of the items on it."

"I might have my own list," he said, his hands warm on my breasts, his fingers working their usual magic in making my flesh feel hot and heavy and so very needy. I let my breasts have a little time with his hands, but moved back when he tried to pull me over his mouth.

"Oh, no you don't. I've decided that I get to do all the things I want to do to you before you make me go mindless with pleasure. It's only fair. I'm a bride. Brides get to do things to their new husbands, and I decree that you can't touch me until I say you can."

"That doesn't sound very fun," he said, his hands sliding down the curve of my hip before he pulled me forward, his mouth capturing one nipple for a second, making me moan with pleasure.

"No!" I said sternly, and with an effort pulled myself back from the delightful heat of his mouth. "I am the master of my breasts, buster! They do not get to dictate to me when they want to be in your mouth and hands, and pressed up against your body, rubbing their little hussy selves against your chest hair in that way that makes me feel like my whole front is on fire, smooshing themselves against all the hard muscle you have there. …" I stopped, my brain overflowing with need for a few minutes.

"Each and every item you just listed sounds like a most excellent suggestion to me. I suggest we start with your breasts in my mouth, and then we can proceed to the others," Alan said, reaching for me again.

"Bad husband!" I scolded, sliding off the bed. My breasts were unhappy with me, but I promised them much joy to come.

"I am not! I am the very best of husbands, and will prove it to you if you just bring your breasts and hips and that delicious ass back over here so that I may defy such obvious slander. What are you doing, wife?"

He had rolled onto his side to see what I was doing in one of the small chests that had been his sister's. "You're getting dressed? Now? Now is the time for bare flesh, Hallie. Now is the time when you allow me to fulfill all those fantasies I have about you."

"I'm not getting clothes, but I am getting these," I said, holding up the long scarves I'd had made for me in Tozeur. "I had planned to make a lay of my own with them, because they're prettier than just the white cloth in the ones I've been borrowing, but I think I have a better use for them." I knelt on the edge of the bed, first eyeing the solid headboard, then the trunk at the end of the bed. The trunk top had two brass rings where leather straps could be attached, keeping it closed while it was being transported.

Alan frowned at the scarves. "I have a feeling that you intend on using those in a manner that I will not at all like."

"Oh, you'll like it," I promised, tying one of the scarves around his wrist, making sure it wasn't too tight, but sturdy enough for my purposes. I quickly repeated the process with the other one before threading the scarves through the rings on the trunk. "You may not think you will, but I'm confident you will, and I promise that if you don't like it, I will stop."

"I've told you that I don't care to be dominated in bed," he told me, his frown deepening when he tested first one arm, than the other. I didn't pull his arms straight up, but gave him enough slack so that his hands were around his ears. "If you continue, I'm afraid you will discover that this has the opposite effect you hope for."

"I'll take that chance. Now." I sat back on my heels, rubbing in my hands the little bottle of orange oil that I had found in the bottom of the chest. Before me, Alan lay splayed, every gorgeous masculine inch of him. His eyes watched me carefully as I allowed my gaze to caress him. "You really are fabulous, everything from your nice feet on up your calves, which aren't scrawny like so many men's are, upwards to your thighs. Alan, your thighs—I feel like I should sing songs of praise to them. Just look at them."

Obligingly, he lifted his head and looked down at himself. "I spend a lot of time in the saddle."

"And for that, I'm thankful, although if you could maintain those thighs without horses, I'd be even happier. And then there's your belly. We've addressed it, I believe, as well as your chest, which brings new meaning to the word 'magnificent.' And your arms are so nice without being too bulky. Your arms make me feel very feminine. It's the strong forearms and the biceps, I believe."

"Just so you know," Alan warned, giving the scarves an experimental pull. They held his hands in place. "When you are finished, I will be taking my turn to catalog and torment and tease you within an inch of your sanity, just as you are doing me."

"Deal," I said, smiling. "Now, let's see where this orange oil should be applied. Just here, do you think?"

"Oh, lord, yes, right there." His hips bucked upward when I poured a little oil into my palms before sweeping up the long length of his very erect penis, making sure to include his balls. The lid on the trunk creaked when he tried to reach me, but I simply moved over so that I was straddling one of his thighs, my hands full of private parts.

"You are so very warm, Alan. Hot, even, and hard as steel, yet soft as velvet. Are you ready for a little tongue action?"

He moaned something in Kazakh, his biceps straining when he tried to pull his hands free.

"Good. Let's start here." I touched my tongue to the very base of his penis, tasting the orange oil. It wasn't sweet, but wasn't bitter, either. I decided I didn't mind it and, with a wicked smile that had Alan's eyes widening, made one long sweeping lick from the base to the very tip of him, making the muscles in his belly contract, his hips move, and his thighs tighten. "That was a pretty impressive reaction, but I think we can do better," I told him, eyeing the scarves when he tried again to get free. They held, so I dipped my head, and took him into my mouth, trying to remember what sorts of things men enjoyed. I swirled my tongue, I applied light suction, and I rubbed sensitive spots, enjoying the nonstop moans that Alan made, along with the hip thrusts that he seemed unable to keep from making.

"Oh, what the hell," I said, giving the sensitive underside a swipe of my tongue. "I can't punish you when you were just doing your job. Let's try the two knuckles again, shall we?"

"If you have any mercy in your soul, and at this point I doubt that you do, because your torment is almost more than a mere mortal man can survive, you'll stop torturing me and impale yourself on me," Alan demanded, his voice rough with passion, and his eyes blazing a blue light at me.

I smiled. "Two knuckles?" I asked, not wanting to push him past what was pleasurable.

He panted at me, his big chest heaving. I had planned on teasing his nipples, but I figured they could wait until I was done at his groin. "You are the cruelest woman I know! You delight in this torture, don't you? Well, I will not stand for it! Release my hands, woman. You must be punished for these acts of heinous sexual suffering!"

I waggled my knuckles at him in question.

"Yes, fine, after the two knuckles," he snarled, looking aroused and disgruntled at the same time.

"I'm not sure I'm ready to release your hands," I said, rubbing the backs of my fingers along his testicles, making sure they were slippery with the orange oil. "I'm enjoying being able to touch you in all the ways I want without being distracted by your hands and mouth and chest and arms and, oh dear lord, your ass. I get to oil up your ass next, but first, it's knuckle time! Let's see, where was that magic spot … here?"

I pressed gently along the part of him that I knew could bring him pleasure, while at the same time sliding my hand along his well-oiled length, my thumb making an extra swirl at the tip of him. "Not there," he gasped, his hands clutching the scarves, which were stretched taut.

"No? Here?" I slid my knuckles a tiny bit, gently pressing and making small circles.

"No. Dear lord, no. That's very good, but it's not the exact spot." His breath was ragged and every bit as rough as his voice.

"Right. This must be it. …" I shifted my hand a half inch, leaning down to take the tip of him into my mouth again as I applied a little pressure with my knuckles.

He shot up off the bed. Just shot straight up until he was standing up staring down at me wildly for a moment, the scarves dangling from his wrists. "That, madame wife, was the spot. And now, it's time to pay for your torment!"

"Oh, shit," I said, startled for a moment, then giggled when Alan dived onto me, the orange-oil bottle upended on my belly, his hands rubbing it all over me, into my breasts, down into my girl parts, and along my hips. He was soon just as covered with it as he rubbed himself on me, his hands and mouth everywhere, lighting my soul on fire with his caresses. I writhed and squirmed and moaned, my entire body an erogenous zone, and when he finally felt he'd paid me back for my fun with his body, he plunged into me, his movements hard and fast, the intrusion of him making not just my body hum, but every iota of my being sing.

What seemed like hours later, I attempted to put into words the feelings that he stirred in me. "You are … you are …" I couldn't seem to catch my breath enough to actually speak. I looked over to where he lay on his back, so wonderfully male, and yet with a caring and gentle heart.

"Magnificent at lovemaking?" he asked, his eyes closed, and his chest heaving. "The master of all sexual pleasures?"

"All that, and so much more." I rolled over until I was propped up on him, leaning down to kiss his orange-flavored lips. "I love you, prince of sexual pleasure. Promise me that you won't do anything foolish."

He opened his eyes at that, his hands moving around to pull me up tighter to him. "It's not my intention to leave you a widow, little dove."

"I know it isn't, but I just want you to remember that when your father does something to enrage you, which I know he will. So long as I have to stay in this world, I don't intend on doing so without you."

His eyes narrowed. "In this world?"

"If I told you that Jack and I came from another world, different from this one, would you think I was crazy?"

"No," he said slowly, sounding thoughtful. "I'd say it wasn't very likely, but …"

"But?" I prodded, not wanting to go into a detailed explanation of how we got there.

"But it does explain why you have such a difficult time accepting certain aspects of society." He studied me for a minute. "Do you want to tell me about it?"

I thought about that, then shook my head, gently biting his shoulder. "No. It honestly doesn't matter how we got here. Once, I had wanted to go home so badly that I was ready to die for it, but now I can't think of anywhere else I want to be than sharing my life with you, and our possible miracle. Does that make you feel weird?"

"It makes me feel blessed on many levels," he said, sliding a hand between us to caress my belly. "Do not fear for me, Hallie. I'm not about to do anything foolish when I know I have you and your knuckles to return to."

I smiled into his collarbone, and relaxed into him, sated, loved and in love, and so happy I felt like bursting into a Disney song.

Four days later, I learned why Alan was famed as one of the most respected warlords in Europe: it wasn't because he was brutal like his father, but because he was just the opposite—although he defended himself and his company when needed, he seldom used lethal force when attacking a target, preferring instead to find alternate ways to achieve his goals.

Which was why, instead of using brute force to try to beat the crap out of his father, we walked into a church in Pest, Hungary, and met with the last person on earth I ever thought Alan would agree to see: Etienne Briel.

"Etienne," he said, his voice diplomatically neutral even though I had previously sat through an approximately half-hour-long lecture of how I was not, under any circumstances, to leave his side even for the direst of situations.

Etienne's eyes narrowed at Alan, who was in his pretty armor, gold Moghul wear, and dashing turban, the tail of which hung down over his shoulder. I could see the moment when Etienne correlated Alan's elegant voice with the body of Akbar. His eyebrows shot up, and he swore under his breath before giving me a swift glare and Alan a curt nod. "I see there is more depth to you than I previously imagined. I will not underestimate you again, Akbar. Or do you prefer Alan Dubain?"

"The latter is fine," Alan said mildly. To my right, Zand stood silent, one hand on the hilt of his sword, while on Alan's left, Az lurked in a generally menacing manner. "We would like to discuss with you the arrangement you have with the imperator."

Etienne smiled an unpleasant smile, the four men behind him smirking along with him. I wished I had convinced Alan to allow me to bring my bow, but he insisted that it would not leave Etienne in a mood conducive to negotiation.

"You wish to make your own agreement with the Black Hand?" he asked, much to my surprise. I'd figured Alan would have to do a lot of fast talking to get him to agree to work with us. He made a gesture that was part bow. "By all means, let me hear it."

"You seek to take control of Prussia from William," Alan said, his voice now smooth as silk. I realized that was the tone he used when stretching his diplomatic muscles.

Etienne rolled his eyes. "I would have thought that was fairly obvious to you when you and that treacherous Octavia were members of the Black Hand."

Alan inclined his head in acknowledgment. "What I don't understand is why you look to the imperator to make that happen."

"What is the point of this?" Etienne asked, suddenly suspicious. "Do you seek to make me question your father's intentions? We have an agreement."

"An agreement that he will disregard as soon as he gains what he wants, just as he's disregarded every other agreement that did not fit in with his plans. You look skeptical, Etienne, but surely you, with your network of spies, must know that the imperator has had many treaties in place that he has ignored once he had what he wanted. Do you think he claimed control of Turkey, Greece, and Italy because their rulers were weak? Iago could have called William—and did when he finally wanted the Moghuls out of Italy—while the king of Greece spent thirty years in exile before he finally ousted my father. Turkey is still under the imperator's control, while the former king and his family are buried under the palace floors."

I looked at Alan in surprise. His voice was now flinty.

Etienne looked skeptical, but Alan was at his most persuasive, and it would have taken a stronger man than him to resist. "How does this matter to me?"

"The imperator intends on marrying Constanza. You realize what that will mean, don't you?"

"He wishes to replace the son he says abandoned him," Etienne snapped, but I heard a thread of concern in his voice.

Alan's eyebrow rose. "And the coincidence that marriage to the duchess will give him a claim to Prussia, easing his way into Western Europe, means nothing?"

"Our agreement is for me to take Prussia once we have William's forces out of the country—"

"And just how do you expect to claim Prussia when the imperator allows William to defeat you and the Black Hand?"

Etienne smirked. "That won't happen. Not with the imperator's forces behind us. This is my chance to remove the empire once and for all."

"Oh?" Alan cocked an eyebrow. "And are there Moghuls in Prussia now, ready to help you? William is on his way to clear out the Black Hand, and given that you've fought against him for more than ten years without defeating him, I don't see that you will do so with only your mad bunch of revolutionaries at hand."

"You don't know what you're talking about," Etienne sneered.

"No? During much of the past ten years, I supported you, doing my part to bring down an empire that I no more think should hold Prussia than you do, and yet now you believe that you can simply take it from William?"

"Your father's forces—" he started to say, his brow furrowed.

"Are in Buda, where they will stay."

"*We have an agreement!*" Etienne shouted, his face red. "Your father signed it."

"And it's worth only the paper it's on," Alan said, waving a dismissive hand. "I'm sure the imperator will have some sort of an excuse why he cannot send troops to aid you with the coming battle in Posen, but if you are willing to believe that, then we have little to discuss. William is on his way; once he has wiped out the Black Hand in Prussia, he will turn his attention to Hungary. I will not see my men caught in the middle of what is sure to be a bloodbath. Come, Hallie."

He put his hand on my back, turning me and taking three steps before Etienne stopped us. "How do I know you are speaking the truth? You could be trying to sow dissent between your father and me. Or are you working for William?"

Alan looked back at Etienne. "Do you honestly think that's likely? He has a bounty on Octavia's head. My loyalties lie with her Company of Thieves, not with the empire that I have worked so hard to break."

Etienne made an annoyed gesture. "What do you gain by turning me against your fath—" He stopped, his eyes widening. "Ah, I begin to see. You wish to be imperator in his place."

Alan said nothing, just looked at him.

"I have to give it to Alan," I whispered to Zand, who was now slightly behind where Alan stood facing Etienne. "He's a damned good bluffer. Remind me never to play poker with him."

"He'll take you for everything you're worth," Zand said with a wry twist to his lips. "I'm lucky that in the past he's felt guilty of bankrupting me and returned my property."

Etienne eyed Alan for a few minutes before saying, "Very well, I will hear your proposal."

"It is quite simple. Marry Constanza yourself," Alan said, taking me by surprise.

I had a moment of appreciation for just how devious his mind was. If Etienne married the duchess, that took her out of his father's grasp, and eliminated his potential claim on

Prussia. It left Etienne to be dealt with later, but William himself said the revolutionaries were of secondary importance.

Etienne was silent for a moment, clearly thinking about that. "And if I do so, what will you ask of me?"

"Withdraw your forces in the Hungarian empire," Alan answered. "The people are not pleased with the imperator, and he does not have the strength of numbers to keep Turkey under his domain and deal with insurrection in Hungary and Austria. If the Black Hand is removed from those regions, the people will revolt and overthrow the scant forces the imperator left."

"Ah, that is how you are thinking," Etienne said slowly, his voice filled with pleasure. "It is true that without my members, control would slip through your father's fingers. If I do as you ask, and you claim your father's throne, you must cede to me the Hungarian empire."

Alan inclined his head. "I have no desire to rule it."

"Oh? You are not very like your father." Suspicion was once again evident in Etienne's voice.

"No, I am not. I am newly wed, and my wife is in a delicate condition. I have fought for the Moghul empire my entire life. I am not getting younger, and wish to enjoy the time that remains me in the company of my wife and what children we are blessed with. The days of Akbar are in the past."

Etienne's gaze slipped toward me. "I will need a guarantee that I can trust you. Your woman—"

"*My wife* is not an object to be passed around," Alan snapped, his voice now filled with anger. "Nor do I offer a guarantee for my behavior. I am *not* my father. When I give my word, I keep it. Either you will recognize that, or we are through here."

I expected the volatile Etienne to get his knickers in a twist over that, but to my surprise, he shrugged. "Your reputation is not tarnished with betrayal, as is your father's. Very well. I will wed Constanza, and you will remove your father from power, following which you will recall Moghul troops, what remain of them, from the Hungarian empire. Do we have an accord?"

"We do," Alan said, and the two men shook hands.

Without another word, he put his hand on my back and escorted me from the church, Zand and Az falling in behind us.

"Hoo," I said on a long breath when we trotted down the stairs to the street, feeling the strain of having not wanted to speak lest I mess up Alan's delicate maneuvering. It was worth it to watch a master in action. "That was intense. Do you think he'll do what he said he'll do?"

"Remove his men from Hungary and Austria? Absolutely not. His hunger for power has increased just as the imperator's has, but he will instruct his people to no longer act as a police force for the Moghuls, which is what will save them in the end."

"I don't quite see how," I said, taking his hand, relishing the feeling of his fingers as they twined around mine.

"The Black Hand is not as feared as the imperator. It is that fear that keeps them in check. Once the threat of the imperator's destruction of the populace is removed, the people will fight for their freedom, and Etienne will find himself facing a war on two fronts. He is obsessed with Prussia. He'll choose it over the Hungarian empire."

"That is some pretty devious thinking right there," I said, proud of him. "So what's our next move?"

"We will have to find a way to remove the imperator from the throne. I will admit that I'm at a loss as to how to do that without killing him outright. If I could find some way to spirit him out of the palace …" He shook his head. "But I don't see how without using force. I would prefer to do this without bloodshed. Enough lives have been given in my father's name; I don't want any more added to that."

We got into a carriage drawn by two horses, heading toward the outer edges of the city where we had left the *Nightwing*. Across the Danube River, the town of Buda sat, and in the middle of it, like a great spider, the imperator lurked, spinning his web of deceit.

He was no match for Alan, though, and remembering something Jack had told me, I smiled, taking Alan's hand and rubbing his knuckles against my cheek.

He glanced toward me, his eyes a brilliant deep blue, like the deepest pool of water, so pure I felt like I could dive into them.

"I think, my dashing no-longer-Moghul-prince, I have a solution to your problem. We're going to have to talk to Jack and Octavia, but I think … yes, I think it's exactly what you need."

He gave me another one of his unreadable looks, but I sat back, pleased with the fact that, at last, I had a place in this world. I had a reason for getting up in the morning, and a part in bettering the world. Life was pretty damned awesome.

Assuming we could work a miracle or two.

I patted my stomach, and explained to Alan my plan.

SEVENTEEN

Alan paused at a seldom-used annex to St. Stephen the Eunuch's Chapel, glancing around for signs of guards. Down the length of the great, sprawling reddish-tan and gray stone building that dominated the Buda side of the Danube, he knew guards would be posted at entrances that led directly into the castle, but this …

"This is a side way into the castle, if you will," he told Hallie in a voice low enough for just her to hear. "It connects to the Emperor's Staircase, which leads to the imperator's private apartments."

"Ooh, a secret passage?" Hallie's breath tickled his ear, making him wish he were back in bed, having his turn of tying her down and driving her insane with touches and nibbles, and long, long licks of his tongue. "I've always wanted to see one."

"It's not secret, just never used." Alan carefully opened the door, wincing when it squeaked a bit, pausing to see if the guards located at the bottom of the stairs heard it.

No sound of alarm reached him. He eased the door open a bit more and stuck his head out. The silhouettes of two guards standing at the outside entrance could be seen reflected on the etched glass door, but the staircase itself was empty.

Alan glanced back. Hallie stood bright-eyed with excitement, a cloth satchel slung across her chest. Being the bearer of the satchel was the only way he could dissuade her from bringing along that damned bow that she was so fond of, and he made a mental note to find a good archer to give her advanced training, since she seemed to be a natural at it. Beyond her, Zand, Az, and three other members of his company stood, all watchful, waiting on his command.

"We'll try this Hallie's way first," he said softly, gesturing toward the satchel. "But if it doesn't work—"

"It will, Jack swears by it," Hallie interrupted in a whisper, giving him a poke on the chest armor to emphasize just how annoyed she was by his lack of faith.

"If it, for some reason, fails, then do what you must to keep yourselves safe. Are you ready, my stabby little dove?"

Hallie whipped out a handful of glass syringes, fanning them in a manner that made Alan nervous. "Jack's patented superfast knockout drugs at your service, Your Imperial Husbandness."

They were silent as the proverbial church mouse when they ascended the stairs into the imperator's apartments.

"The royal entrance hall," Alan murmured in Hallie's ear when she gawked at the long, rectangular room. The room was lit only by two gas jets on either side of an ornate stone fireplace bearing the bust of the imperator. A dull glow came from the moonlight that gleamed in through three massive windows that opened to the courtyard.

"Antechamber," he whispered, dodging the chairs and occasional tables that littered the room.

"So pretty," she answered, eyeing the gold-and-white floral wallpaper and stucco decorations. "But if you're going to want to live here after we take care of your dad, I'm going to have a few things to say to you."

"I have no intention of residing here," he answered, and opened the doors to the adjacent room. This, too, was silent as the grave, just the faint sputtering of gas jets left on should the imperator need attendants during the night. "And this is the audience room."

"OK, this is beyond gorgeous," she said, looking at the windows on two sides of the corner room. "That crystal chandelier is bigger than your whole cabin on the *Nightwing*."

"Not quite, but it's close. Quiet, now. This next room may be occupied."

Alan opened the door to the writing room slowly, peering in. Sitting at a large golden console table were four men in guard uniforms, cards, glasses, and two decanters laid out on the table before them.

Hallie peered around him, and silently handed out syringes to their men, nodding when Alan gestured for her to stand back. He threw open the door, and with his shoulders back—and donning Akbar's arrogant strut—entered the room, scattering orders.

"I want the windows checked, and a guard at all the doors. The imperator's life is at risk." He stopped and glared at the men who had scrambled to their feet, two of them whisking the decanters behind them. "What is this? Why are you not at your posts?"

The men all exchanged looks. Then one of them made a smart bow and said, "We are, Your Imperial Highness. We guard the imperator's bedchamber."

"Faugh," Alan said, gesturing to his men. "Relieve these guards of their duty. I will speak to the captain in the morning."

"But, Your Imperial Highness—" The ringleader stared in surprise when Alan whisked out a syringe and jabbed it into the man's arm, quickly depressing the plunger. The guard looked first at his arm, then at Alan; then, just when Alan was about to swear under his breath that he knew Jack's concoction wasn't as effective as Hallie had sworn it would be, the guard's eyes rolled back in his head and he toppled forward.

Alan looked toward the doorway to where Hallie stood with one raised eyebrow. He made her a little bow, saying softly, "Yes, yes, you were right. You won the bet. You get to be in charge two times consecutively."

"And I get to use the scarves both times," she reminded him, moving over to stand at his side, glancing down at the guards who now littered the floor. "Jack says they should be out for about twenty minutes, so we should probably get cracking. I assume your dad's bedroom is through there?" She nodded to the door set between two massive urns.

"Yes. Stay back." He accepted two syringes and, after a glance at Zand, opened the door to the imperator's bedchamber.

No gas jets fluttered in here. The room was close and humid, filled with a rumbling sound that came from the center of the massive canopied bed that dominated the room. Thankfully, the bed had only one occupant, Alan noted when he peeled back a bit of the blanket to expose the imperator's arm.

"Hrmm? What is it?" The imperator grunted and snorted when Alan plunged the needle into the arm that lay on the bed, clamping his hand down on it when it jerked. "Who is that? What are you doing?"

Alan signaled to Zand, who lit a lamp next to the bed.

The imperator looked up at Alan with confused eyes. "What the devil do you think … Akbar? What are you … doing … heee …"

"I owe Jack a barrel of the imperator's finest rum," Alan said when his father fell back against his silk pillows, his mouth open and slack.

"Two barrels. And one for us, too. Well"—Hallie came forward and rubbed her belly—"we can save ours for after the miracle is born. I assume he's out cold?"

"Yes."

"I have to say, that's kind of anticlimactic," she said in a disappointed tone, watching when Alan quickly peeled off the blankets and, with his men, used the sheet beneath the imperator to lift him, wrapping him in it just as if he were a cocooned moth. "I expected us to have to shoot our way in, fight with your dad before you handily jabbed him with the knockout stuff, and then fight our dashing way out. This is just … easy."

"I much prefer easy to your dire imaginings, although to be honest, I fear the escape is going to be much more difficult."

"Oh! That's my cue," Hallie said, and rushed to the window. She threw it open and leaned out to look to the north. "He's there! At least, I think it's William. There's an airship where you said he would be."

"Excellent." Alan made a quick search of the drawers of small tables that sat on either side of the bed, pulling from one the imperial seal, which he pocketed before asking Hallie, "Would you go to the dressing room and collect some clothing for the imperator? Nothing too ornate. He is larger than William, and will need something to wear."

"Sure. I assume it's this way?" She pointed to a door on the far side of the room.

"Yes, that should lead to the dressing room, bathroom, and the body servant's room. Do not enter the last one, as it will be occupied. Zand, do you see the strongbox anywhere?"

"No. Are you sure it is here, and not in the treasury?"

"The treasury is full of things he didn't care about," Alan said, peering into cupboards and drawers. "He always kept the most valuable items close by. Ah. Does this look different to you?"

He squatted to examine a square of wood in the parquet floor that looked a bit darker than the other pieces.

"It does indeed," Zand said, pulling out a dagger while Alan did the same, the pair sliding their blades along the seam of the square, loosening it so that it could be lifted. "And that looks very much like an emperor's hoard."

"Which I will take great pleasure disbursing to those who have suffered the most from his atrocities." Alan hauled up a small metal chest that was much heavier than it looked. "Az, you and Yussuf take the imperator. Zand, I leave the strongbox in your charge."

Zand hefted the chest, grimacing at its weight.

"The emperor is waiting in the courtyard. Take the imperator to him, and tell him I'm right behind you."

He waited until the men were through the writing room, the guards still crumpled blobs on the floor, before returning to the bedchamber. He glanced around it, mentally going through a checklist of items he needed to ensure the imperator's supporters would have no ability to carry on in his name, then frowned at the door to the dressing room, opening it while he said, "Dove, you do not need to clean out his wardrobes—" He stopped when the room was empty of his wife.

A wave of cold fear hit him, followed immediately by heat, red-hot fury that sent him charging across the room, flinging open the door to the bathroom and, through it, the door to the body servant.

The vizier stood in a gold-embroidered nightdress, his bald head glistening in the gaslight, but it was the woman he held protectively in front of him, a dagger at her throat, that held Alan's attention.

"I knew you would come, you murdering scum," the vizier said, his high-pitched voice cracking with emotion. "I told His Imperial Majesty that you would come for him one day, but he did not believe me. Did you kill him? Did you slit his throat, and then send your whore in to steal his clothing?"

"No, I did not kill him, and do not speak of my wife in such a manner."

"Wife?" the vizier snapped, then sneered down at Hallie's head. "You wed the whore? Your father will have much to say about that."

"I have no doubt about that," Alan said mildly, his eyes on the dagger at Hallie's throat. She was, to his infinite relief, looking more annoyed than frightened.

In fact, she sounded downright put-upon when, sighing, she said, "I told you I should have brought my bow. He grabbed me before I could jab him."

Jab him. The words resonated in Alan's head, pushing around the mental images of the sorts of torture he would enact upon the vizier. He leashed his anger, and forced himself to think coolly, one hand brushing against a hard glass syringe that was hidden in his pocket. If he could get close enough to the vizier, he could pull Hallie from the old man's foul grasp and sedate him. ...

"You know," she said with obvious meaning. "The jab-by thing. Of which someone not a million miles away from here might have had two."

"Be quiet, whore," the vizier growled, tightening his grip on Hallie, yelling suddenly, "Guards!"

To Alan's horror, the vizier jerked open a door to the hall and hauled Hallie backward out of it just as two guards, looking startled and hesitant, entered.

Alan snarled an oath and leaped forward, slamming the first guard into the doorframe, the man slumping to the ground just as Alan turned to the second. He had a disruptor out, firing at the moment that Alan lunged, the searing pain that bit deep into the left side of his chest warning him he'd been hit.

The thought of Hallie in the vizier's grip was all that mattered, not the burning pain of flesh that had melted un-der the aether, nor the weakness that made his left arm feel like it was made of lead.

He could bear pain. He could bear losing the use of an arm. He couldn't lose Hallie, not his bright, irreverent, en-ticing dove.

He couldn't live without her love. He couldn't live with-out her, period.

His dagger flashed in the gaslight, a spray of blood fol-lowing. Alan didn't wait to see how badly the guard was in-jured before he raced down the passage after the vizier. The man had dragged Hallie down a flight of stairs, spinning around at the bottom when Alan leaped down the stairs, his heart pounding in his ears, his soul calling for vengeance.

One of the vizier's hands was in Hallie's hair, her lovely amber hair, pulling her head back so that her throat was ex-posed, the curved dagger having evidently pricked her throat a few times, since several narrow lines of blood dripped down into her armor.

She squawked, her eyes widening at the sight of Alan stalking forward.

"Stay back," the vizier called, shifting and glancing nervously around him. "Guards! Guards!"

"There is no one here," Alan said, his fingers twitching with the need to throttle the man. "No one but me. Release my wife, and I will let you live."

"You do not frighten me—" the vizier started to say.

"You have three seconds, and then you die."

Hallie stared at him in surprise, but he kept his eyes on those of the old man, allowing him to see the depth of his fury, and the inevitability of his intentions.

The second the man wavered, he'd be on him.

To his amazement, the vizier must have read just as accurately as Hallie what his fate would be, because he dropped the dagger and shoved her forward at him, spitting out an oath that Alan ignored.

"Are you hurt badly?" he asked her, his eyes still on the vizier.

"No, but please tell me you're going to knock that bastard out so I can administer a few kicks in his kidneys. Oh! Well, that was fast."

Alan moved while she was speaking, spinning the vizier around and jamming his face into the wall while he stabbed the syringe into the man's upper arm. The vizier screamed and moved feebly for a few seconds before slumping to the ground.

"I totally rescind that comment about taking down your dad as being anticlimactic—hey. What's wrong with your sleeve? Why is it black … oh my god, that's your arm! Alan!"

He grabbed her with his good arm and gently pushed her from him. "Do not touch it, sweet. I will have it attended to later."

"But you've been hurt! Oh my god, the whole left side of your armor—Alan! What happened?"

"One of the guards had better aim than I supposed." He grunted painfully when he tried to heft the vizier one-handed, but it was impossible to get the man onto his shoulder. "Can you help lift this bastard without harming yourself or the babe?"

"What? Oh, yes, but you shouldn't carry him, not with you being shot to hell and back again—"

"I can't leave him here." Alan took a couple of bracing breaths. "I don't think he has the support of the courtiers to challenge me, but I would prefer him being out of the way regardless. On three."

A very painful five minutes followed during which Hallie helped him hoist the vizier's deadweight onto his good shoulder, after which they mounted the stairs and retraced their steps.

As they left the royal apartments and reached the staircase, a dark figure emerged from the opposite direction.

For a moment, Alan and Etienne considered each other. Like him, Etienne bore the limp form of a person over his shoulder, this one a woman in gauzy nightwear whose long golden hair brushed the floor.

"Etienne," Alan said, with a nod at the other man.

"Alan." Etienne nodded back, his gaze on the vizier's unconscious form for a second. Then without another word, he strode off.

"Was that—" Hallie started to ask, staring after Etienne.

"The duchess? Yes."

"Ah." She turned and yelled after Etienne's disappearing figure, "I hope you treat her a damned sight better than you treated me."

They made it out to William's airship just as the pain that Alan had tried so hard to ignore started to overwhelm him, the weakness growing across his chest and spreading down to his legs. He staggered the last few steps when Zand and Az burst from the hold, the latter holding him up while Zand pulled the vizier's limp body from him.

"He's been shot," he heard Hallie say from a long distance away. "I hope to god you guys have a doctor on board, because I am not losing him. Do you understand? I refuse to let him die! Alan! Alan, my love, don't you dare die on me! I will make your life a living hell if you do!"

He smiled to himself even as he slid slowly into the red haze of pain that had crawled across his mind. She wasn't being a dove now. She was a fierce little falcon, fighting for him, fighting for them both. And for that, he would be eternally grateful.

EPILOGUE

"I told you that stuff was good. Didn't I tell you?" Jack sounded very pleased with himself. I decided that since he had helped us, he deserved to be praised.

"It was everything you said, and we couldn't have done it without your help," I told him, giving him a kiss before moving over to the chaise lounge where Alan rested. I eyed him carefully, noting that the lines of pain that had been evident around his mouth since he'd been shot had smoothed away at last.

"Stop looking at me like you're going to demand to check my bandages again," he said, holding his hand up for me.

"I can't help it. I don't like you being hurt. I want you back in action so I can—oh lord."

I dashed off, racing for the bucket that I'd had set behind a couple of round shrubs, and heaved up the bit of toast I'd managed to eat an hour earlier. Since I'd ordered the servants that milled around the palace to also place a ceramic ewer filled with water, a bowl, toothpaste, and one of the ten toothbrushes I now owned near the bucket, I was able to brush my mouth three times before going back to the main section of the little garden that sat off one end of the massive palace.

"Sorry," I said, waving a wan hand. "I'm really going to be glad when this passes. What were we talking about?"

Alan pulled me down onto his lap with his good hand, positioning me so that I leaned against the unhurt side of his chest, his left arm and ribs bandaged. "You were going to tell me how you wished for me to be well so that I can do all of the many and varied things you'd like me to do to your delicious, enticing body."

"This is really uncomfortable," Jack said, grimacing at us. "I mean, I'm happy that you two clearly are almost, but not quite as much, in love as Tavy and I are, but at the same time, that's my sister you're fondling and thinking sexual thoughts about."

"You're going to have to just get over yourself, nonroyal brother," I told him, pressing a kiss to Alan's ear. "I like it when Alan fondles me. I like it more when he works through his own list of things that he wants to do, although that one with the honey and yogurt just sounds sticky."

"Oh, you'll be very sticky by the time I'm done," Alan said in a near growl, his good hand sliding around to give one butt cheek a quick grope.

"There, see? That is exactly what I'm talking about," Jack protested.

"My love, about this I am in agreement with Alan and Hallie. They are perfectly within their right to enjoy each other just as you and I do." Octavia's eyes sparkled at Jack in a way that had him sitting up straight and waggling his eyebrows at her. "I think we should just be thankful that Alan was not harmed seriously, and discuss instead what is to be done now."

Alan sighed. "With the imperator—"

"Former imperator, you imperial sexy thing, you," I interrupted.

Jack made a face, which, to my amusement, Alan duplicated before he said, "With my father, and that bastard vizier who almost slit your throat, safely en route to one of William's holdings in England, the empire will crumble."

"Unless you take charge of it," I said, waiting to see what he would say to that idea. Although he'd said previously that he didn't want his father's position, I worried there was a chance he might change his mind, feeling he could do much to restore the damage his father had done.

His gaze met mine, the blue in them fathomless, and so gorgeous it sent little shivers of anticipation down my arms. I reminded myself he was recovering from having his arm and side scorched, and that although he expressed the idea that he would be fine to indulge in all the things I badly wanted to do, he needed some time to heal.

"I have never sought the position of imperator," he said slowly, his good hand stroking little circles on my hip.

"But if you don't lead the Moghuls, what will happen?"

It took him a minute before he admitted, with what sounded like regret in his voice, "Moghuls are a warring people. It's why they followed my father's wishes even when it meant decimating our own ranks. Without a leader, they will break into clans and fight each other for supremacy rather than living in peace."

"That sounds undesirable on all accounts," Octavia said, leaning into Jack.

"And like it might cause trouble to others outside the Moghul empire," Jack added, looking pointedly at Alan.

I looked at him, as well, noting that the love of my life appeared tired. I wanted badly to protect him and keep the sorrows of the world from him, but knew that, with this, I could only offer support, not do the job for him. "I know. They need someone to lead them." His gaze met mine again. "What would you think of living here?"

I looked behind him, at the glorious spread of the palace. I'd seen enough of the inside of it to know it was filled with the most amazing art, room after room of pictures, vases, statues, and assorted *objets d'art* from all eras and locations. I'd seen Greek statues, Roman mosaics, rococo figurines, and even what looked like a couple of bucolic depictions of the English countryside. The furniture was just as awe-inspiring, most of it gilt and a bit too fussy for my taste, but still impressive. The palace itself was worthy of a Hollywood costume drama, leaving my brain boggling during the half hour I'd spent walking from one end to the other while Alan was resting.

It was the most over-the-top experience I'd ever lived.

"Hallie?"

I stopped looking at the palace, down to the face of the man who filled me with such happiness. "I think I'd much rather live in a big tent outside of Tozeur where we could watch the sun rise over the desert, and set over the mountains. Although if we could have running water and a toilet, I'd be even happier."

He laughed and kissed me quickly, so as not to ruffle Jack's feathers. "The tent was just a temporary lodging. If you like the area so much, I'm happy to build you a house complete with running water, a nursery, and as many toilets as you'd like."

"But you have a house in Italy, near Venice," Octavia protested. "Why don't you live there?"

He shrugged. "Safie loves that house. She and Zand can have it. I won't always need him with me, and he likes Italy, so they might as well benefit from it."

"Can you run the Moghul empire from Tozeur?" I asked, worrying about what that sort of stress would do to him. I didn't want him worried and concerned about the Moghul empire. ... I wanted him happy and carefree, teasing me and making me pet those damned horses he loved so much, and teaching me how to fight and shoot things, and making wild, sweaty, unbridled love to me at night. And occasionally, flying off to have dashing adventures together, doing good, and relieving the world of its villains.

He looked thoughtful for a moment; then a slow smile curled up the edges of his mouth. "Have I told you about my sisters, little dove?"

"Other than Safie? I know nothing about them other than the fact that Leila has bigger boobs than me."

"Ah. Well, I have eight sisters in total, three of whom are married. Four, now with Safie. The other four are in Constantinople, at the imperator's palace there. Sia is the most adventurous of them next to Safie. Kiana is the studious one—she writes copious amounts of poetry, which she insists on reading to anyone who is nearby. Ashti is a little devil, with a sense of humor that you will much enjoy. And Bita is the bossy one, Safie's younger twin. She was also widowed, and has no intention of finding another husband."

"I look forward to meeting them all," I said politely, wondering what he was driving at.

"That's four sisters who are currently at the palace doing nothing but costing a fortune to keep them happy. I think it's time for that to change." The smile on the corners of his mouth grew. I touched the short little mustache that was filling in over his lip. It was still at the spiky stage, but I could tell it would soon go as soft as the one he'd shaved off.

"Oh, what a smart idea," Octavia said, obviously understanding what I didn't.

"Yes," Jack said, nodding. "If they will do it, I think that would answer well to our problem."

"Right, what am I missing? What is it you expect your sisters to do?" I asked, poking Alan on his good shoulder.

He pushed me off his lap, then stood, wrapping his unhurt arm around my waist. "The Moghul empire consists of four main regions, excepting Hungary and Austria, and those I discount because I have agreed to withdraw our troops from them. Anatolia is the biggest region in the empire. Bita will be the perfect vizier for it. Sia would do best with the wild Balkans, while Ashti should shine at governing the Byzantine regions since she has a fondness for all things Greek. That leaves Kiana with Varna, but I'm sure she will find much there about which to write endlessly long poems."

"You're planning on putting your sisters in charge of your empire?" I asked, wanting to shout with laughter.

"Why not?" he asked, his mustache-stubble smiling at me. "They can act in my name with my full blessings. I'd hand over the title of imperator to them if I could, but the Moghuls are not as enlightened as we are as to the worth of women. I, on the other hand, have a very fine appreciation of the full value of them, which I would like to discuss with you. Right now, in depth. *Privately*."

"Alan," I said, unable to keep from smiling at the heat he put into the last word. "You are recovering from a grievous injury. And Jack and Octavia came to talk to us about the future. It's rude to run off when they are here to help us."

"Don't mind us," Jack said, scooping up Octavia in his arms. "Alan, do you mind if we use one of the bedrooms? Making love in an actual palace is suddenly on the top of my bucket list."

"Jack!" Octavia said, clearly scandalized, but at the same time, she twined her fingers through his hair, and bit his ear.

"My old rooms are at your disposal," Alan said. "Left at the top of the stairs, two rights, then go in through the double doors with the falcon mantel."

"You didn't tell me you had rooms here," I said when he hustled me toward where the *Nightwing* was moored in the courtyard alongside the *Enterprise*.

"I seldom stay here. I don't particularly like the palace."

"Oh, thank god," I said, smiling when, as I mounted the two flights of circular stairs to the upper decks, he put a hand on my rear. "I mean, it's gorgeous, but so not me. Alan." I stopped in front of his cabin and said his name with the full weight of my wifely concern.

"Hallelujah," he answered gravely, reaching beyond me to open the door.

"If you think you're going to tackle your own bucket list with me, you can just think again. You were wounded twelve hours ago. You are not up to lovemaking. I will check your bandages, give you another dose of that fever draught that William's doctor left for you, and then you, sir, are going to bed."

"I am," he agreed, locking the door before tumbling me onto the bed. "But you're going to join me. Call it a protective measure if you like, but you, my sweet, tempting wife, are going to be right here with me in this lovely soft bed."

"Well," I drawled, pushing on his good shoulder until he obliged me and lay down on his back. I pulled off his boots and unbuttoned his leggings, taking my time to touch his flesh as much as possible while I removed them. I peeled off my own clothing in record time while he carefully removed the wraparound tunic that we'd gotten him into after the doctor had attended to his wounds. I knelt with my knees on either side of his hips, gently touching the flesh beyond the bandages. It was warm, but not unduly so, and there was no redness or sign of blood poisoning. "Well, if you promise me you won't do anything to hurt your owies, I suppose it is my wifely duty to attend to any aches you might have."

"Yes! Yes, it is your duty, very much so. Do your duty, my sweet dove. Do it long and hard," he said, his words coming out a moan when I wrapped my fingers around a particularly needy part of his anatomy. "I hurt so very bad right there. No, slightly the left. Yes, right there! Hallie! With your warrior breasts? Oh, lord, woman, not the orange oil! I won't last. ..." His words trailed off into an earthy groan, his eyes closing in rapture.

I smiled the special wicked smile I kept just for him, and bent myself to taking care of his every need. By the time he'd taken care of a few of my aches and needs, I lay next to him, my legs twined through his, my hand on his belly.

And for the first time in what seemed like a lifetime, I realized I was home. At long last, I'd found the man who brought me home.

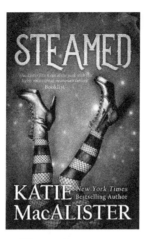

Don't miss
Steamed,
the hilarious first first book
in the Steampunk Romance series!

Jack Fletcher's heart is about to get punked.

Computer technician Jack Fletcher is no hero, despite his unwelcome reputation as one. In fact, he's just been the victim of bizarre circumstances. Like now. His sister happens to disturb one of his nanoelectromechanical system experiments, and now they aren't where they're supposed to be. In fact, they're not sure where they are when…

…they wake up to see a woman with the reddest hair Jack has ever seen—and a gun. Octavia Pye is an Aerocorps captain with a whole lot of secrets, and she's not about to see her maiden voyage ruined by stowaways. But the sparks flying between her and Jack just may cause her airship to combust and ignite a passion that will forever change the world as she knows it…

Available in e-book, print, and audio formats.

CPSIA information can be obtained
at www.ICGtesting.com
Printed in the USA
LVHW091600110321
681234LV00005B/902